One Night Scandal

Katelyn Taylor

Copyright

Trigger Warning

Dedication

To anyone who loves the cheating trope, same bestie. This shit is hotter than it should be.

Chapter One

Nico

My phone rings for the tenth time since I walked away from her at the airport. I don't think she believed me when I told her I was going to check into a hotel. She told me I better start walking then before she slid her spoiled ass into the back of our scheduled ride as she took off to her parents' house.

The plan was to have a nice weekend to get to know her parents out here in Seattle. We live in Boston which is where I first met Carly. She was interning at my company, and we were the stereotypical boss falls for intern story. Carly was a junior at Boston University when we met. She was twenty one and I was thirty. Not exactly a large age gap but enough that we were in very different places in our lives, hence what led to our first two break ups over the last three years.

I was handed the proverbial keys to the kingdom when I was nineteen. My father had created one of the largest financial investment firms in the nation and with him so suddenly passing away, there was only one thing I could do. So, I took the reins of a multibillion dollar company and did my best to keep it and myself afloat.

Surprisingly enough, we've been thriving, all thanks to my hard working staff and very little to do with me, if I'm honest.

My mom was an unofficial liaison up until two years ago when she also passed away, though it wasn't peacefully in her sleep like my father. A car accident took the most important person in my life away. She went into sudden cardiac arrest at the wheel when she was leaving my house one morning after brunch, drove head on into another car and...that was it.

I had just started seeing Carly off and on when my mom passed and though the two of them never really saw eye to eye, she was unwaveringly there for me through the most shocking tragedy I'd experienced. Maybe that's why I've put up with her shit for these last two years. Maybe I feel some weird fucked up loyalty owed.

She's a nice girl, gorgeous obviously, and she wants a big family one day. I want that more than any amount of money or land or anything really. But fuck, I'm starting to think that I need to let go of that dream, with Carly specifically, that is.

She's now twenty four years old and yet she still acts like a self-centered teenager. It's like she can turn it on and off with a flick of her wrist. In the beginning, she was always so poised and 'yes, Mr. Sanders' while simultaneously delivering me lusty eyes that had me bending her over my desk two weeks into her summer internship. As soon as she got used to being on my arm, the high end restaurants, the penthouse apartment, the lavish galas...she changed. Or maybe she was always like this, and her façade finally dropped.

Every single time we've broken up, it's been over something ridiculous like me not remembering our eighteen month anniversary, because honestly, who fucking keeps track of that? The other time it was because she had stormed into a board meeting, whining that the jeweler didn't have the earrings she wanted in store. I was so fucking humiliated I thought I was going to stroke out then and there.

The one we are on the verge of right now, though? This feels like the final fucking straw. She can be a brat to me, I've learned to handle it, but the way she spoke to our stewardess...I lost it.

We took the company plane out here which is fine, that's what it's there for, but do you think she bothered to say thank you or acknowledge that it's a luxury that doesn't come to everyone? Of course not. Fine, whatever. I didn't think much of it, but as we hit a patch of turbulence and the stewardess fell, spilling black coffee on Carly's white shirt, all hell broke loose.

Carly absolutely lost it, reducing that poor stewardess to nothing but a puddle of tears and I fucking snapped. I told her how I couldn't stand her selfishness, her entitlement or her disrespect. The plane had to head down to LA to pick up my CFO for a conference which meant I was stuck in Seattle for at least the night. Didn't mean I was going to fucking spend it with her.

Now it's an hour later and I'm pulling up to X, one of Seattle's finest hotels. Or at least that's what their website said. Whatever, it's just one night. I could really care less where I sleep, as long as I'm fucking away from her. Speak of the devil, as soon as I step inside the lobby, my carry on in tow, my phone rings.

I nod my head in thanks to the doorman before I finally answer it.

"What?" I snap.

"What? Seriously? That's how you're going to speak to me? God, Nicholas. You need a serious attitude adjustment.

A humorless laugh escapes me as I shake my head. Does she even hear herself? My mother was so insanely right about her. She begged me to leave her, told me again and again she was only with me for the money and the status. I didn't want to believe it, I didn't listen. Now here I am, years later wishing I would have walked away from the beginning.

"Seriously, how long until you'll be here? My parents are asking questions."

My eyes widen in disbelief at her words. This woman has balls the size of cannons, I swear.

"Carly, I'm not coming. Tell them I spoiled you fucking rotten and you're no longer someone I want to be around."

The phone goes silent for several seconds before she speaks.

"What are you saying?"

"I'm saying I'm done. We're done. I can't fucking do this with you. I don't *want* to."

Another few moments go by before she explodes.

"ARE YOU FUCKING KIDDING ME? You choose this weekend of all weekends? I thought we got past the hard stuff. This is so typical Nicholas! You're so hell bent to self-sabotage you can't let yourself be happy! Well, fine. You want to let go of the best thing that ever happened to you? Be my fucking guest!"

With that, the line goes dead. I lower my phone from my ear, clenching my teeth as I make eye contact with a man behind the check in counter. He gives me a sympathetic look as I step up to him, sliding him my black card and ID.

"Do you have any rooms available? One night," I ask.

He nods. "Of course. Preferences?"

I shake my head. "Just a bed."

His fingers fly across the keyboard as he nods, his eyes flicking up to me as he does.

"Rough night?"

I scoff, giving him a terse nod.

The rest of the paperwork is completed in silence before he slides the room key to me.

"You're on the twenty seventh floor. Check out is at eleven and if you need anything, please don't hesitate to let us know."

"Thanks," I say as I grab my key when he slides another card across the counter. His eyes flick around as he lowers his voice.

"Just in case you're looking to turn your night around."

My eyes flick down to the black card with silver writing as I pick it up. All it has on it is an address and a password underneath. *Gratify.* I look up to him in confusion as he nods.

"Trust me."

Staring at him for a moment, I slowly nod before heading off to my room. When I step into the elevator, I hit the twenty seven button before glancing down at the card in my hand. No logo or branding. Nothing discernible as to what it is.

The elevator doors open and I wheel my suitcase through the hallway before coming to my room. I wave the key over the reader and push my way inside, shutting the door behind me before flopping down onto the bed. I stare up at the ceiling for several seconds, wanting to think about anything except my spoiled as fuck girlfriend, or I guess, ex-girlfriend.

The card is still in my hand, and curiosity gets the best of me. I pull out my phone, googling the address before being lead to a very discreet and simple website.

One Night you will never forget.

Below their slogan is their business hours, the statement that it is a twenty one and older establishment and masks are required to preserve privacy. I furrow my brows as I try to dig up more information on it. I'm not sure exactly what sways my decision. I really just want to go to sleep and get back to Boston. Despite my first instinct, though, I get up and head for the shower, getting ready for the night because honestly, how could it get much worse?

Chapter Two
Cassi

Excitement runs through me. I feel like I've been waiting for this birthday my entire life. First as a kid you look forward to double digits, then it's sixteen so you can drive, eighteen so you're an adult. We all know that the real prize is that golden twenty one. You can drink, legally, get in anywhere you want. The world is your oyster and being a minor is a thing of the past.

My two best friends and I rented a hotel room downtown for the night and the original plan was to go bar hopping. Until I heard about this club last week. A sex club.

There is no name for it, publicly, that is. Just an address, a few words on an otherwise blank website and a plain brick building on Pine avenue.

When I brought up the idea, Arianna and Naomi both seemed hesitant. Eventually, though, they came around. Now we're standing in front of the address, and my heart is racing. Wild fantasies of what is inside have been dancing in my head all week. I'm just hoping it doesn't disappoint. I mean, how could it? We are three single women who haven't been laid in a hot minute, apart from Naomi who has never been laid period. If all we find behind these doors are a couple of good orgasms and some free drinks, then it'll be more than worth it.

Twisting the strings of my gold masquerade mask in my hand, I knock against the door. A large bouncer steps out as he looks us over. Smiling to him, I speak what I've gathered is the password for entrance.

"Gratify."

He gives me an approving nod before taking our ID's, glancing at them before handing them back.

"Masks on, ladies, and welcome to paradise."

My entire body is practically buzzing as I turn my head to look at my two best friends. Arianna is wearing a little black dress that matches her jet black hair with a matching black mask, my god it's like she doesn't own a single piece of color in her wardrobe. Naomi finishes fastening her red mask, a good color against her blonde hair and grey eyes.

Flipping my red hair over my shoulder, I lead us down the hallway as we follow the bouncer. It feels like the hall goes on forever and I'm only mildly beginning to panic that I've gotten us into a bad situation until we turn a corner and a whole new world explodes right before our eyes.

Lights flash in every direction, drapery is gorgeously arranged all around, sexy music thumps all around us reverberating through the space as the entire room overloads my senses in the best way. My eyes bounce around wildly as I attempt to take it all in. Gorgeous men and women are sprawled out across every corner. Some are flirting at the bar top, a few are walking one another with collars and leashes. Some are getting blow jobs right there in the middle of the room. The place immediately oozes sex, passion and power. I swear to god I'm getting a contact high off it already.

Arianna and Naomi look to see a very beautiful woman bouncing on a man's cock.

"Fuck," Naomi huffs.

"I told you guys, right?!" I squeal. "I wonder where the bondage demonstrations are."

Honestly, that's the main reason I wanted to come here. I came across some Shabari porn last year and I've kinda become obsessed. I've tried to teach myself some basic knots and ties but honestly, it doesn't do the same thing for me as someone else doing it. Not like I've ever found anyone willing to do so.

Chicken shits.

Naomi rushes up the stairs behind me, a level of excitement to her steps that I didn't expect from her as we leave Arianna to fend for herself.

Love you babe.

We all knew we'd split off as soon as we got here. Which is why we agreed to text each other if any of us were leaving and we'd all meet up at the hotel room later. Hopefully not too soon.

When we get to the top of the stairs, a man is standing there with a kind smile on his face and an iPad in his hand.

"Welcome. What desires can we fulfill for you today?"

"Are you on the menu?" I flirt because god he's gorgeous. He's giving businessman meets model.

He gives me a gracious smile but shakes his head.

"Unfortunately not, but two beauties like you should have no trouble finding company for the night. Do you have any rooms, kinks or demonstrations you're interested in? We have sense depravation rooms, exhibitionism/voyeurism displays, group play, bondage—"

"Bondage! Definitely bondage," I say a little too enthusiastically.

He smiles politely as he gestures towards a set of elevators.

"Next floor up, second door on your right."

"Thank you!" I smile as I go to step away when I hear Naomi shyly speak.

"What kind of sense depravation rooms do you have? Or, like, what are they?"

The guy gives her an understanding nod as he speaks.

"We have a dark room where anyone can step inside and be immersed in the moment. We also have an array of toys to take away senses as well as a glory hole room and—"

"Glory holes? That's a thing?" Naomi asks, not near the amount of disgust in her tone as I think she'd hope to convey.

"Oh, very much so. They are pleasurable for both parties, a certain anonymity where you can just...be," the man says.

Naomi's eyes come to me, and I try to hide my surprise. Look at this kinky little virgin go.

"The glory hole room is just down this hall to your left," he says as he gestures behind himself."

"Meet you back at the hotel?" I ask her.

She looks to me, a tint of embarrassment splashing across her cheeks as she nods before scurrying off down the hall.

Smiling to myself, I step into the elevator, hitting the next floor as the doors close. When they open once more, I follow the guy's directions and find myself stepping into an already crowded room. Everyone is circled around a woman in leather lingerie, walking around a chair with a large bundle of rope in her hands.

"Bondage isn't just about the kink of it. It's about power. The power you're relinquishing by being tied up and the power you're receiving by your partner gifting that to you. It's a complicated and balanced push and pull that comes with an act like this. Above all else, safety is always the underlying theme. Safe words are key in order to fully drop your guard and thrust yourself into ecstasy."

Her words are practically speaking to my soul, I feel myself nodding along, agreeing with every word she says as my eyes stop on a man across the circle from me. His eyes are already on me, a fine three piece suit on, with his jacket unbuttoned. It looks incredible on him, paired by his black hair and dark eyes. He's holding a glass of something brown, which could attribute to the almost dazed look in his eyes. Well, dazed isn't quite the right word, relaxed maybe? Dazed means you're out of it and with the way this man's laser focus is on me, he has to be the most alert person in the room.

Forcing myself to break eye contact with the man, I focus back on the demonstrator because if there is one thing I know about men, it's that they want what they can't have. Or at least what they perceive that they can't have.

"Now I'm going to walk you through how to do a basic interrogation chair. Once you master a few of these knots, you can come up with dozens of variations to keep playtime interesting," the woman says. "Do I have any volunteers?"

My hand shoots up despite my racing heart. I don't exactly mind being the center of attention, but I also don't exactly know what I'm signing myself up for, either. Oh well. Here we go.

She smiles nodding and gesturing for me to come forward. I do my best to push my insecurities to the side, smiling as I sway my hips to the chair.

"Sit," she says.

I do so instantly, staring up at her when she turns to the crowd again.

"Can I get another volunteer?"

My stomach dips at her words. For some reason I thought she'd be doing the tying. My eyes drift around the room to see several hands shoot up when the man with the nice suit and dark eyes follows suit, his gaze still heavily trained on me. I swallow at the intensity of it and the demonstrator seems to notice, smirking to herself as she points to him.

"You."

He moves through the crowd easily, setting his now empty glass down onto a cocktail table before standing before me. His eyes are hooded, a deep hazel color now clearly visible. We are locked in each other's stare as the demonstrator continues speaking, though if I'm honest, I barely hear her.

"Good. Before beginning any kind of bondage play, it's important to establish a connection, a trust. You have to be willing to give yourself completely to your partner and you have to be worthy of that gift. Some magnificent eye contact, a few soft touches and even a kiss can go a long way towards establishing that physical connection."

As if her words were controlling him, he lifts a large hand up, cupping the side of my face as his thumb brushes against my bottom lip. Almost instinctually, he pulls it down further and further before letting it bounce free. In the next moment, he leans forward, stealing a kiss before I can even attempt to protest. Not like I would, have you seen him? He's fucking gorgeous.

The softness of his lips steals my breath away as they demand entry that I so willingly give him. Our tongues wrap around one another, the sharp taste of his scotch now dancing across my tongue. His hold on me tightens, deepening the kiss as a sound akin to a growl tears through his chest. Butterflies are racing inside me as I lift a hand up to touch his face. He stops me in an instant, snatching my wrist with his free hand as he grips it tightly. The act of power and dominance has a rush of excitement running through me.

"Well, I don't know about you all, but I'm wet just watching these two. Are we in a bondage demonstration or the voyeur room because, phew," the demonstrator laughs.

A round of chuckles echoes around us and we break apart in the next moment.

When we do, I stare up at him in a daze and he seems to be just as lost as I am. Like we both went somewhere else for a moment. He blinks a few times before swallowing roughly when the demonstrator begins.

"What we are going to do is tie each arm to a chair leg and each leg. Cotton is best when we are just starting out," she says as she hands him several strands of rope.

He releases his hold on me before moving behind me, taking my left hand and pressing it against the chair leg as the demonstrator explains in detail how to tie me up before moving to the next. I don't miss the way he feels my left hand, like he's checking for a ring before moving on. Something about it makes me smile as he moves around to the front of me, both of my hands completely pinned in place.

The man crouches down in front of me, his large hand grabbing my calf as he slowly pulls it to the front of one of the chair legs. He repeats the same tie he did on my hands but being able to see him do it is different. I'm not just feeling it. I'm fully experiencing it. The soft yet firm hold of the rope, his strong hands keeping my limbs in place. It has a dizzying effect on me and the little monster inside me craves more.

When he grabs my other leg, he pulls it slowly, my heel dragging against the hard floors with a scraping sound before he pauses. His eyes flick up to me before moving down between my legs. My dress has ridden up and all you can see now are my black lace panties that leave little to the imagination. He seems almost entranced for a moment, unable to look away before he snaps himself out of it, quickly tying my other leg until I'm fully subdued.

"Beautiful. Now, love, please try to pull on the restraints," the demonstrator asks.

I do as she says, the man still crouched between my thighs, his eyes on my own as I pull.

"Do you see how they don't self-tighten? The knots stay perfectly in place. This is exactly what you want to see. It can get very dangerous very quickly if you don't get this part right."

She goes on to give a few more tips and tricks before she faces me, smiling.

"How do you feel?"

"Good," I whisper hoarsely, my eyes flicking between her and the man in front of me.

She smirks and looks to him. "How do you feel?"

He slowly pushes himself to stand, his hand tracing over my face before his hand digs into the back of my hair, tugging sternly.

"Good," he rasps.

God that voice. It's like butter melting against a hot pan. It's smooth and rich and soaks my barely there panties in an instant.

"This position is great for oral or even interrogation play," she continues on, facing the group.

I can't stop my eyes from flicking at his slacks, a noticeable bulge straining against the fabric. A huge bulge at that. Holy shit.

Slowly, my gaze comes back to find him still staring down at me, his fist tightening and if I'm not mistaken, his hips come towards me, just an inch or so. His arms are shaking like it's taking everything in him to hold back. I know the feeling because I'm practically vibrating in my chair.

A manicured hand lands on his shoulder, snapping us both out of our trance or whatever that just was.

"Great work, you two. Love the chemistry. Do you need some help untying her?" she asks.

We both look around to find the crowd disappearing, several of them carrying rope with them as they move down the hallway.

"I've got her," he says, bending down once more to free me.

Something about his words stirs a feeling inside me. I couldn't name the feeling or even begin to describe it. It's something raw, intense and carnal, though.

One by one, my limbs are freed until there is nothing left holding me to the chair. So, why am I still sitting here, staring up at this man like he is a God amongst us mere mortals.

His hand reaches out in offering, and I slip my palm into his. He wraps his fingers around me, pulling me to stand as he looks down at me. My head tilts up to maintain eye contact with him.

From far away he didn't seem too tall but up close, I understand how wrong that assumption was. I'm 5'9 wearing five inch heels and he is easily four inches taller than me. I've always been the tallest woman in my family, tallest in my friend group. I'm never the short one. The way he's making me feel, though, it's something I've never gotten to really experience, not in heels that is. Like I'm small, dainty. Like I'm something precious to take care of.

"For volunteering, we'd like to offer you two the VIP room for the night, if you're interested," the demonstrator offers, dangling a gold key card in front of us.

The man takes it easily, pocketing it before lacing our fingers together, tugging me down the hall.

"VIP is straight ahead. Golden doors. Enjoy!" she calls out, a smirk in her voice.

Anxiety fills my body from my head to my toes, but so does an equally powerful level of excitement.

Oh, I have no doubt I'm about to more than enjoy this.

Chapter Three
Nico

For a moment, I wonder what the fuck I'm doing. I just broke up with my girlfriend and my first move is to run to a sex club? Kind of sleazy. Then again, I never planned on any of this. I didn't even know it was a sex club until I was inside. Then, I told myself I'd grab one drink and leave. Curiosity is what led me upstairs and when the guy mentioned a bondage demonstration happening, well, I can't exactly tell you what led me towards it.

I definitely didn't come upstairs with the intent of hooking up with anyone. That was the last thing on my mind. A few scotches later and one hypnotic red head making eyes at me from behind her mask and...this is a bad idea, right? Rebounding like this, within hours of a breakup is not only frowned upon, its gross.

That's not stopping me for cupping the soft hand attached to the beautiful red head as I guide us down the hall. I can practically feel her excitement running through her, or maybe it's my own. I haven't felt anything so...connective, ever, I think. That display was in front of dozens of strangers and it still felt like we were the only two in the room. Every wrap of the rope around her creamy skin, every brush of my finger against her only had the anticipation building and building. Who the fuck am I kidding? Us going into this room isn't a choice, it's not a decision either of us are making. It's a need.

When we get to the golden door, I wave the card the demonstrator handed me over it, and the lock whirrs to life, clicking open as I push inside. I hear a soft gasp escape the woman beside me as she looks around the room. Gilded walls, cream white carpet, a golden bedspread and a large chandelier fill the space. It's nothing too extravagant from what I've seen but I can't help but admire the way this beautiful woman's eyes sparkle behind her mask as she takes it all in. Fuck, I've missed that. In a partner but also in myself. I miss appreciating the little things, seeing the beauty in something others could take for granted.

When those bright green gem colored eyes land on me, I push the door shut behind her, closing the distance as I once against cup the back of her neck. She turns to putty in my hands, melting into my touch in a way that is so goddamn responsive it has my cock hardening in an instant.

Her red full lips, almost the color of her hair, tug into a soft smile as I lean over her, ghosting my mouth just over hers as I speak.

"I'm giving you an out. This is your only chance to walk away. If you don't, for tonight, you're mine."

Her eyes attempt to search for mine but we're too close to truly make eye contact.

"I'm not going anywhere," she whispers.

My lips press to hers in the next moment, that same euphoric rush from before thrumming through me, more so now that we don't have an audience. I prefer my encounters to be intimate, not putting on a show.

Her silky tongue runs along mine and I quickly wrap it up with my own, nipping at her lip as I back her up to the bed. She falls backwards and I chase after her, crawling on top of her as I begin peppering kisses up and down her neck. She sighs into me, arching her back as I slip my hand under her, taking every opportunity to press her soft body against my own.

God fucking damn.

Tearing my mouth away from hers, I push off the bed as I turn to move across the room. Slowly, I begin undoing my jacket and waistcoat as I speak.

"Get undressed, quickly. I'm not a patient man."

Once I'm down to only my boxers and my mask, I turn to face her and almost freeze in place. Fuck. She's perfect, flawless. Soft curves, lush tits and a dusting of freckles across her body that are just begging to be licked, sucked and kissed. Every last one of them. If I had all the time in the world that's all I'd spend my life doing, tracking down every single freckle and giving it the attention it deserves. Unfortunately for both of us, we don't have all the time in the world. We have tonight, one night, and I don't intend on wasting it.

Glancing over to the 'wall of treasures' I suppose you could call it, I reach for the black rope. It's soft to the touch and there are several sets of it so I can do what I plan to. Of course when I discovered years ago that I may have a bondage kink, I did an extensive amount of research into it. I taught myself several ties and practiced until I had it perfected. Then when I brought the idea up to Carly, she flipped. She couldn't get away from me fast enough, told me she didn't want a part of my rape fantasies. When I tried to explain to her that bondage has absolutely nothing to do with rape she ran out of the room and wouldn't talk to me for an entire day. That effectively squashed my desire to ever bring it up with a partner again.

Maybe that's why this woman is so appealing. There is no discussion or persuasion. She knows what she's signing up for and she looks more than ready. Eager, even. That's what I fucking want to see. What I crave.

Closing the distance between us, I snatch her two wrists up

before placing them above her head. I begin with a simple double column tie, fashioning a sort of rope handcuffs that have a single tethering point down the middle that I fasten to the headboard above her.

Her arms being pushed into the air force her tits to lift and I can't help but bend down, capturing a nipple into my mouth as my tongue begins swirling around it, my teeth nipping against it in a way that has her bucking.

"Fuck!" she whines, rubbing her thighs together.

I glance down to see her continuing to move her thighs together, desperate for the friction as I release her nipple from my mouth. She moans in what sounds like protest before I climb onto the bed, crawling between her legs as I push them apart.

"Open yourself for me," I command.

She parts her legs further, showcasing her perfect pussy. Goddamn. I've never seen a prettier pussy in all my life. Even from several inches away, I can smell her arousal, and it does something to me. Has the beast inside me beating its chest as I rest my face against her inner thigh, taking a deep inhale as I groan.

"You smell like heaven. Let's see if you taste like it."

Flattening my tongue, I run a long line through her before coming up to her clit, running a soft circle around it before pulling away. Her flavor rests on my tongue and a growl rips through me.

Yep, fucking heaven.

A soft little moan escapes her, and it has me wanting more. Again and again I lick and suck her, earning sweet mewl after mewl from her before I push a finger inside. She squirms at the intrusion, her hands tugging on the rope as I tut against her clit, purposefully letting my lips drag against it as I do.

"You need me to stop?" I check in.

She looks down at me in outrage. "Fuck no! Don't stop."

I smirk at that, chuckling before I go back to finger fucking her and feasting. Shit, I could eat this cunt for breakfast, lunch and dinner and never have enough. She's so delicious, so tight, so perfect.

My cock begins to leak pre-cum as I feel her begin to spasm around my finger, her movements becoming jerky as she squirms.

"Oh fuck, oh fuck, oh fuck!" the red headed beauty cries out as she begins coming.

My tongue moves down, eagerly lapping up every drop she's willing to give me as her orgasm slowly fades. I suck on her clit once more for good measure before releasing it with a wet pop.

She cries out, a mixture of pain and pleasure as I push up from the bed. Staring at me in a daze, her head lulls between her arms as I grab more rope, pulling each leg towards each bed post before tying those securely as well.

I'm torn between shoving my cock down her throat like this and sinking inside her. I then quickly decide that I can get my cocked sucked by anyone, but I won't always get to experience a pussy like this.

I'm assuming she's from the area. How insane do you think she'd paint me if I set up an arrangement for her to come visit me in Boston sometime? Even for a weekend. I haven't been inside her yet and I can already tell that I'll need more.

Pushing down my boxers, I climb in between her legs, pushing the tip of my cock to her when I pause. Fuck. One of the club rules, the only rules they have is suiting up, always. I haven't worn a condom in years, and I'm half tempted to say fuck it. But I don't know this woman, she doesn't know me. For both of our sakes, it's better if I do.

My eyes move around the room before pausing on the side table with a bowl of condoms at the ready. Shit, it's like they know everyone goes through this internal warring. Leaning over her, I grab a condom, tearing the packet open with my teeth and quickly rolling it on before tossing the wrapper to the side.

Once again resuming my position where my tip is just barely

pushing against her, my eyes come to hers. We don't say anything, we don't need to. Just having her eyes on me, so willingly, so obeying, it has me pushing inside her in the next moment.

All of the air in my lungs is stolen, snatched straight from my chest when I press into her fully. Fuck.

A soft whimper echoes through her as her fingers curl into themselves and her toes begin to wiggle. I love this effect I have on her, what just my touch does to her, what being inside her makes her do.

Pulling my hips back, I push inside her once more, again and again, repeating my motions until I find a perfect rhythm. She tries to match me, but she can't do much but take everything I give her. And fuck, does she take me so goddamn well.

I feel her begin to tremble around me already. Shit, she's so fucking easy to get off.

Definitely don't hate that.

"Fuck!" she moans as she begins spasming around me, her sweet moans shaking the walls as she bucks and thrashes against the bed.

I fuck her through her orgasm and when she finally can catch her breath, she shakes her head.

"I don't think I can do much more. I don't think I can take much—"

"You will take what I give you. Relax and just feel," I say as I roll my hips.

A small sound escapes her, but she shakes her head as she pulls at the restraints uselessly.

"I can't I don't think I'm able."

Something about her words feels like a challenge as my hand comes down to her clit, rubbing tight small circles against it.

"C'mon," I say through clenched teeth. "Give me one more."

She moans but still shakes her head as I pull my hand back and smack her clit. Her eyes fly open in surprise as I rub quick circles against her clit again, spanking it once more.

"Oh god!" she cries out.

"Give me one more, baby. I know you have it for me. C'mon, be my good girl," I say, my thrusts becoming more violent, my words becoming more demanding until I'm spanking the fucking shit out of her clit.

She screams and bucks against me like she wants to get closer and away from me all at once before my last smack comes. I can practically see her vision go black as she lets out a moan like nothing I've ever heard before. It goes right down to my cock and has my balls emptying inside her.

My cock twitches and jerks as her pussy literally milks every fucking drop out of me. Our bodies move together in a perfect symphony. Euphoria like I've only ever wished for slams into me as I slump over on top of her, our sweaty skin sticking together as we gasp in heavy breaths.

I don't know how long we lay there for before I slowly crawl off her, disposing of the condom before freeing her from the bed. She rubs her wrists gently as she is freed and I take her hands from her, replacing her fingers with my own as I slowly begin massaging the sensitive skin to help restore blood flow. May have gone a little too tight this time. Oh well, there is always next time. Because with her, I have to have a next.

She wiggles herself into my lap, our bodies wrapped around one another as I continue rubbing her wrists. A sweet sigh escapes her as she seems to nuzzle against my chest and I don't hate it, not like I should. Not at all.

"I'm heading home in the morning. I'd like you to come visit me some time," I say in the quiet room.

She turns her head to look up at me.

"Where is home?"

"Boston," I answer.

Her eyebrows raise. "So, what you're saying is that you want me to fly all the way across the country just so we can hook up again?"

I don't say anything because she knows that's exactly what I'm asking. She gives me a dubious look before it melts into a teasing smirk.

"How could I say no to that?"

Chapter Four
Cassi

The next day after a much needed lunch since we slept through breakfast, I'm driving back to my house, well, my parents' house. I know, I know. I'm twenty one years old and still living with my parents. In my defense, Seattle is one of the most expensive areas to live in the country and free housing is free housing. My parents are also very relaxed and we all kind of keep out of each other's way. It's a win, win.

Ari was the first one back to the hotel last night. She sent us a text letting us know she was back in the room and I was right behind her within an hour or so. The only one that went radio silent until the early hours was Naomi who came strolling in at the crack of dawn.

My man from last night left soon after we were finished and honestly, I didn't feel a need to stick around and find a new partner for the night because I'd already found the perfect one. How could anyone compare?

We exchanged phone numbers, him just leaving his contact name as N and mine as C. We could have exchanged names but what would be the fun in that? This whole anonymity thing is kind of hot, it's freeing. I'm sure I'll find out his name when I come out to Boston because make no mistake, that will be happening.

I'm embarrassed to admit I texted him first. I was waiting for him to text me but when it was approaching one o'clock west coast time and he was already back in Boston, I figured it was enough time. Or maybe I was just eager. Either way, it's now almost four o'clock my time and still nothing. Maybe he only said he wanted to see me again just so he could get past the whole awkward post sex conversation.

I tried and honestly failed to hide my jealousy when Ari told us that she got asked back to the club by the man she spent the night with. They planned to meet up the following weekend and I don't know. Something about it seemed so sure, that he wanted to be with her again more than anything and I was definitely a shit friend for it. I'll call her and apologize tomorrow. Right now I just want to go home, eat some dinner and pass out.

When I pull into the driveway, I check my phone one last time. No new messages. Fuck.

I try not to let disappointment take over me but it's hard not to. Last night wasn't just some great sex it was...something else, that's for sure. The connection we had even before the sex, the way his eyes watched me steadily, the way his hands felt on me. I've never experienced anything like it in my life.

Oh well. I'm quickly coming to the realization that it will have to remain tucked away as the most perfect night ever. The most perfect birthday ever. I guess I can live with that. Better than having the memory tainted when I find out he's actually a sleaze-ball who is married with a bunch of kids or something.

Shrugging it off, I step out of my car, throwing my overnight bag over my shoulder as I head inside. I slipped on some leggings and an oversized sweatshirt before piling my hair on top of my head. I'm not actually a red head. I have the same mousy brown hair as the rest of my family. I dyed it for the first time in eighth grade and never looked back. It's become practically my whole personality, and I don't think that I could ever go to a 'normal' color. Besides, it fits the scattering of freckles my mom blessed me with well. A trait my sister was lucky enough to avoid.

"I'm home," I call out as I push inside, dropping my keys into the bowl by the door as I move into the living room.

My parents have a nice house just outside Seattle. It's been in my dad's family for three generations, hence why we are able to afford it. My mom is a substitute elementary school teacher, and my dad owns a few grocery stores. I am currently enrolled in college, though I don't know what the hell to major in if I'm being honest. My best friends were going to the local college and when I applied and got in, I thought, what the hell.

I've been a receptionist at a dental office for the last two years and it's fine for what it is. I mainly work on weekends or pick up a few hours after classes to help the full time receptionist out. It's not exactly a lucrative position but it gives me enough to pay my bills, help my parents out and have some money for extra expenses. Like getting a hotel room and going to a sex club for my birthday.

We're a very healthy middle class family but in Seattle, middle class is basically on the poverty line with the cost of living out here. Okay, that might be a little dramatic but still.

"In here, sweetie," my mom calls out.

"How was your birthday?" my dad asks as I walk up to him, pressing a kiss to his cheek.

"It was great," I smile.

My parents definitely believe me and the girls rented a hotel room and went bar hopping on capitol hill last night. And that's exactly how I intend to keep it.

"What, not gonna say hi to me?" Carly, my older sister snarks as she plops down onto the couch.

I raise an unimpressed eyebrow. I forgot she was coming to town this week. Could have gone without. My sister and I have always had a strained relationship. She always strives to be the center of attention and god forbid she doesn't get it. She's exhausting and I truly haven't thought about her much since she went to college at Boston University. If she's here I guess that means she finally brought home her on-again and off-again boyfriend. Three years together and she's just now bringing him home. Curious as to what she's hiding with him.

"Hi, Carly," I say with a fake as fuck smile that she reciprocates before flipping me off.

"Nicholas, get in here and meet my bitchy little sister."

I scoff at her as a figure moves from the kitchen into the living room. I do my best to wipe my irritated look from my face because it's not this guy's fault that he's dating my terror of a sister. Wait, I guess he volunteered for the position, so maybe it is.

The polite smile I try to screw into place quickly falls away, as my eyes widen in horror. A mirroring look is displayed across 'Nicholas's' face as he sets his eyes on me, freezing in place. Oh my god. That face, those eyes, that mouth.

The man that I spent last night with. The man that made me see fucking stars after tying me up in a sex club. That man is...my sister's boyfriend.

What the fuck.

I seem to recover faster than he does. Honestly, he looks like he's having a stroke at this moment. I know the feeling. Attempting to conceal my absolute horror, I give a half hearted wave to him as I clear my throat.

"Nicholas," I say, allowing the name to sound as sharp and venomous as I intend. "So nice to finally meet you."

He continues staring at me for a moment before blinking.

"Cassi, right?" he asks.

I nod before his brows furrow, his own head nodding.

"I swear he's usually more eloquent," Carly laughs, once again drawing the spotlight back to her.

Good, because I'm freaking the fuck out right now. Those hazel eyes never leave me, even for a second. They look puzzled and frazzled, I imagine mirroring my own reaction because what the actual FUCK. So, he cheated on my sister. He cheated on her with ME. Oh my god, I think I'm going to be sick.

"Excuse me," I say as I step out of the room, dropping my bag to the floor as I rush for the first floor bathroom.

I almost make it into the bathroom, throwing the door shut behind me when a hand catches it, pushing it open before the owner of said hand steps inside, shutting the door behind him.

"Last night never happened," he says sternly.

I let out a humorless laugh as I stare at him because is he actually fucking kidding?

"What part? When you cheated on my sister or when you cheated on her with *me*?" I hiss.

His jaw clenches as he shakes his head.

"I didn't cheat on her. We broke up."

I scoff at that, crossing my arms over my chest.

"So, you landed in Seattle together, broke up, fucked me and then magically got back together twelve hours later? Yeah, real believable."

"It's the truth," he practically snarls.

"Whatever helps you sleep at night. It doesn't matter. You've been with my sister for three years, you know her as well as I do. You think I'd honestly risk my life telling her that I fucked her boyfriend? Even if it was an accident? She'd destroy me and I hope you take all of the offense when I say this, my life is worth more than a mediocre fuck," I lie straight through my fucking teeth.

What looks like disbelief passes across his face and I attempt to slip past him and escape this suddenly claustrophobic bathroom. In a move that I can only compare to superhuman speed, his hand snatches my own, spinning me around to face him before caging me in against the wall.

My breath is stolen from my chest as I look up at him, frozen in place as he lowers his face to my own.

"Mediocre? Sweetheart, don't even try to pretend last night wasn't the best night of your goddamn life," he says, his words are teasing and playful, but his tone and expression aren't. They are harsh, accusatory with just enough bite to have a chill running down my spine.

I swallow roughly and notice how his eyes flick down to my mouth, a hazy look to his gaze as if he too were reminiscing about our night together. He can try to act unaffected, just as I am, but I think it's obvious last night...and our newfound revelation, has left us both more than a little rattled.

Instead of responding to him, I choose the safer option.

"I think you should let me go before my sister...your girlfriend, walks in and sees you pinning me against the wall like a starved animal."

His hazel eyes bore into me for a second longer before he blinks roughly, tearing himself away from me as he turns his back to me. I don't hesitate to take my escape, scurrying out of the bathroom before running straight into my mom.

She catches me easily, giving me a soft smile.

"Careful, Cass. You okay?"

"Yeah, fine. Kinda hungover," I lie with a short laugh.

My mom rolls her eyes and smiles. "You don't know hangovers until you hit thirty, trust me."

I smile, nodding along with whatever she says right now so that I can just retreat to the safety of my bedroom. Unfortunately, I only make it three steps before my mom continues.

"Why don't you go get ready, we are all going out for dinner. Leave here in an hour?" she asks.

I pause, turning to her with a feigned look of disappointment.

"I'd love to but I'm kinda tired. Rain check?"

She purses her lips as her brows furrow. "Cass, your sister

rarely comes to visit anymore. I know you guys don't always get along but it's just one weekend. Please, for me?"

Well how the fuck am I supposed to say no to that? My mom is literally the best human I know. She does everything for everyone, and she is really the only person that I can't stand letting down.

Releasing a heavy sigh, I resign myself to the idea of going to dinner with them. Mom is right, it's one weekend. It's already Saturday so really, it's just tomorrow and then boom. They are gone. Nodding to my mom, she smiles and presses a kiss to my cheek before heading back into the living room while I make my way upstairs to my room. I honestly couldn't tell you who I'm looking forward to spending time with less, my evil bitch of a sister or her slimy cheating boyfriend. What a match made in hell they are.

Chapter Five
Nico

I find myself ordering a drink at the bar as soon as we arrive at the restaurant. Then, promptly knocking it back and ordering a second before the waiter even has time to ask if anyone else would like anything. I feel judgmental gazes come from Carly's parents as I do so. I'll admit, it's not exactly the move you bust out when you're meeting the parents, but I'm losing my goddamn mind over here.

My eyes move to Carly's litter sister who unfortunately ended up in the seat across from me.

Cassi.

I've heard about Cassi off and on for years. Carly has had more than enough to say about her. Saying they don't see eye to eye puts it mildly, from my takeaway, they hate each other to the core. There is no familial bond, no sisterly love. Just jealousy and spite, at least that's the way Carly has always told it.

Would have been nice if Carly showed me just one picture of Cassi, though. Would have prevented the huge fucking mistake that was last night.

Maybe. Maybe not. Technically speaking, there is no guarantee. The low lighting, the masks and the overall lowered inhibitions and encouragement to live in the moment could have just as easily dulled my mind enough to not recognize her even if I did know her. So, it's not my fault. I did nothing wrong here. Maybe I made an error in going upstairs once I figured out the front deskman sent me to a secret sex club. Chalk it up to curiosity, I suppose.

Everything was supposed to be easy, a release of sorts. Carly and I had broken up, it wasn't cheating and I was...ready to feel something other than numb with another human. Even if it was only for an hour inside a sex club.

And feel I did. A little too much.

My eyes locked on the gorgeous red head from the moment she stepped up to the demonstration area. I figured it was a good of area as any to find a suitable partner for the night, One that, for once, shared my proclivity for things such as that. The instant her bright eyes, smooth skin and wicked mouth curved up into a smile, it was decided. The demonstration we put on in front of a room full of people only confirmed it further. The energy between us was practically magnetic. Like a tangible buzzing pull that drew us together. I'd half convinced myself it was just the drinks that went to my head, the next morning I convinced myself that it was in my head altogether.

Except for some odd reason, I felt it again in the bathroom at her house. Carly's house. Her parents. Christ this is a fucking mess.

When I went to that club, I had the full intention of never seeing Carly again. I was done with her, with us. Then, I woke up the next morning, my head throbbing and body satiated in a way I didn't know was possible. I also had about fifty seven missed calls, thirty nine text messages and even a few voice messages of her begging for forgiveness.

I'm not sure what made me call her back. I certainly didn't owe her anything. Maybe it was something out of habit or maybe it was just what I felt was the 'right' thing to do. Either way. I called, she came to my hotel room, we talked and we had sex.

In the moment, I didn't feel guilty. Sure, we agreed to come together for this weekend, a trial run of sorts to put on a good front for her family and then we would work our shit out properly in Boston. I didn't feel guilty for picturing the redheaded goddess that I had spent last night with while I fucked my girlfriend of three years. I didn't feel guilty for hearing her moans over my girlfriends, imaging it was her soft curves riding me, not Carly's lean, albeit bony body.

I truly didn't feel guilty until I realized that the woman I was lusting after, fantasizing about while I was inside my girlfriend was none other than her little sister.

What are the fucking odds of that shit?

Blinking myself out of my thoughts, I look up just in time to catch the tail end of Henry, Carly's dad, question me about my career. Turning on the charm as high as I can manage given the current state of things, I dive into how my company was built with the three foundations of integrity, diligence and hard work. I spieled him about how important the work we do is, how it's so much bigger than any one person. And he ate it up.

You don't get ahead in life because you have a great idea or business model. You get ahead in life by figuring out what someone needs, what they crave, a delivering it to them. In this case, Henry Fischer is looking to ensure that his first born is in well and capable hands. Though it's not an act, I can't promise how long it'll stay this way if his spoiled rotten daughter doesn't get her attitude under control.

As if she can hear my thoughts, her hand rests on my thigh, perfectly manicured french nails digging into the material of my slacks as she smiles at me. I attempt to smile back at her and based on her pleased look, I think I do a decent job.

Carly and her mother dive into conversation about shopping

and I effectively tune out, my eyes landing on the disinterested woman across from me. Slowly, I lift the bourbon to my lips, taking slow sips as I watch her. Honestly, I'm not even trying to. I'd give anything to never set eyes on this woman again. Something in me can't look away, like a car wreck, or something equally horrific. Maybe that is a touch dramatic but the feeling remains the same.

I expect her to shirk under my gaze. Look away or continue to ignore me altogether. It's what Carly does when she's uncomfortable. I shouldn't feel surprise, though, when those bright green eyes land on me, a fire to them as she rests her elbows onto the table as she speaks.

"Can I help you?"

This gains the attention of her father, as her mother and sister remain in conversation. I lift an unimpressed eyebrow as I set my glass down.

"I'm certain not in the slightest."

Her eyes flash with something akin to dangerous, or at least she believes it to be.

"Do we have a problem, *Nicholas?*" she asks, the sound of my name on her tongue sharp, threatening almost.

The threat is just on the tip of her tongue. She could expose us both here and now, though I'm certain she hasn't thought this through. Her parents may look at me as the one in the wrong but we both know Carly will not see it that way. I can even pinpoint the exact moment Cassi's mind lands on the exact thought. Her fight dims slightly as she removes her elbows from the table and looks at the menu.

I do the same, alluding to absolutely nothing as I peruse the menu. When I've decided on my meal, I set my menu back down and begin staring once more. I'd like to say that I want to, that I crave to. That I desire her in such a way I can't help it. At least that would explain why I feel so goddamn out of control. Unfortunately, none of the above is true. Instead, I'm irritated, intrigued, and overall bothered by her presence. We had a wonderful memory, one that was intent to remain perfectly preserved. Now, whenever I think of that enchanting redhead from that night, all I'll see is this side of her. Carly's bratty little sister who may even rival her own attitude. I didn't think that would be possible.

A new waiter comes over this time to take our meal orders, and he smiles politely to me before his eyes pause on Cassi. A recognition passes in his gaze as he takes her in.

"Cassi?"

Her head moves up from her menu before those green eyes round with shock.

"Alec?"

"Oh my goodness, what a small world!" Mary, Carly's mother smiles. "How are you dear?"

"Doing wonderful, Mrs. Fischer, and yourself?"

"Just lovely."

Henry stands up, offering a handshake to the guy.

"Good to see you."

"Sir," Alec nods, shaking my Henry's hand as his gaze skates over myself and Carly before settling on Cassi once more.

She hesitates for a moment before pushing out of her seat and standing. Alec takes the opportunity and wraps his arms around her. It's an appropriate one, like two long lost friends. Though, I don't miss the way his head nuzzles into her neck just so. Is he smelling her hair? Who the fuck is this creep?

When they pull apart, she smiles up at him and shakes her head.

"How long have you been back in town?"

"A few months. I graduated early and needed to come back home and look after my grandma."

Carly squeezes my thigh before she sits a little higher.

"Alex, this is my boyfriend, Nicholas. Nicholas, this is Cassi's high school boyfriend, Alex."

"Alec," Cassi corrects with a roll of her eyes.

He nods towards me and Carly, though he doesn't offer any pleasantries to us as he continues practically fawning all over Cassi. Talk about a lack of professionalism.

"What are you up to now? How is life? It's so good to see you... so good," he says, his words carrying a heaviness to them that I don't know what to make of.

Cassi smiles at him, a smile I had been gifted not twenty four hours ago. Looks like she hands them out to any sucker that is foolish enough to look her way. Poor guy.

"Sorry," Alec says as he clears his throat. "Are you all ready to order?"

"Yes, I think I'll do the chicken parmesan," Henry answers first.

Alec begins jotting down everyone's order one by one until he finishes with Cassi. A smile curves his face, emphasizing how young he is. The kid can't be older than twenty one, twenty two at the most. Then again, I believe Carly had told me Cassi was some-where around that age so makes sense, I suppose.

"Five cheese ziti but with alfredo instead of marinera?" he guesses.

Her eyes widen in surprise as she sets her hands down onto the menu.

"How did you know?"

"How could I forget? The first time you ordered it here the waiter about looked at you like you were insane."

Her hands wave out energetically as she laughs. "Right?! Like what is so wrong with preferring alfredo sauce?"

"And being allergic to tomatoes," he says with a point of his pen in her direction.

A soft look passes across her face as she smiles and nods, handing him the menu.

"Thank you."

"My pleasure. I'll get all this in and be back shortly," he says to us all before giving Cassi a quick wink.

Mary snickers, pushing on Cassi's arm as she begins whispering, though not very quietly.

"How long has it been since you've seen him?"

Cassi shakes her head. "The day that him and his family moved away. We've chatted a few times throughout the years but I didn't know he had any plans on coming back."

"You'll have to forgive us, Nicholas. Cassi and Alec dated for, gosh, pretty much all of high school. He was essentially part of the family. She was devastated when he moved away, we all were."

"Okay, mom. I think he could infer all that," Cassi says, cutting me a sharp look that I can't help but narrow my eyes to.

I relax my features, turning to Mary with a soft smile as I nod.

"What a wonderful coincidence."

She returns my smile with one of her own. "Isn't it?"

Carly audibly scoffs, shaking her head as she pulls out her phone and begins scrolling on social media. Lowering my voice so she is the only one that can hear me, I speak into her ear.

"Put the phone away. You're not going to sit at the table like a petulant teenager because the topic of discussion is not on you."

She looks up at me in outrage but when I lift an eyebrow in warning, she begrudgingly puts her phone back into her purse, sitting up a little straighter as she does. She's on thin ice, right now, and she knows it too. If she wants me to keep up the appearance that everything is fine and thriving between us, she knows how to behave. Instead, she's like a toddler, pushing the boundaries to determine her limitations. I swear to Christ, we can't get on the plane home tomorrow fast enough.

"So, sweetheart. How was your birthday last night?" Henry asks Cassi.

That grabs my attention, my head turning to tune into the

conversation as I speak without even contemplating considering my words.

"Last night was your birthday?"

Cassi's eyes cut to me, her words careful and guarded.

"Yes."

"Not just any birthday, her twenty first. My baby," Mary says, emotion choking her words.

An eyeroll escapes Cassi but it's accompanied by a soft smile.

"Mom, stop."

"What did you do to celebrate?" I ask, unable to help myself.

Her green eyes cut to me, carefully assessing my intent as she speaks.

"My best friends and I rented a hotel room and bar hopped on Capitol Hill."

A bald fucking face lie.

I nod my head in faux interest.

"What was your favorite bar?"

Her eyes widen in irritation with me, and I can't help but release a small smile. I'm having entirely too much fun riling her up.

The look of frustration muddled with a dash of panic slowly eases as she gives me a perfectly composed smile.

"I'm not sure, it didn't have a name. The place was certainly memorable, the people, not as much."

My teasing smile falls in an instant as Carly butts in with a sneer.

"Well, yeah. Capitol Hill is filled with newly twenty one frat kids. If you wanted to have a good night, you should have searched for somewhere with a little more...class," she says with a wrinkle of her nose, her eyes raking over Cassi like hot coals.

I wait for the meltdown, the sneered insults or something. That's what Carly would do if someone basically said to her face that she has no class or taste. To my surprise, she doesn't react outwardly. She keeps her face poised, her posture unyielding before delivering a sickly sweet smile.

"You are an expert on class, Carly. You were even the head of your econ class in college, or did you just give head in class to your professor, I forget."

Henry practically chokes on the breadstick before him, Mary mutters under her breath to take a sip of her wine and smoke is practically billowing out of Carly's ears as she glares at her sister. She looks ready to throttle her from across the table, but she doesn't, instead panickily turning to me.

"It was before you and I got together, I swear."

Little does she know, I don't give a fuck. I'm not an oblivious man. I wasn't even the only executive she was flirting with during her internship, I was just the one that took her back for rounds two and three. I'd be a moron to be surprised by the fact that Carly used her body to get ahead in school, she certainly used it to get ahead in the start of her 'career'.

I place a placating hand upon her thigh, squeezing it once before facing ahead. Cassi is still staring at her sister, as if she were daring her to challenge her. In the battle of wits, or maybe wills, Carly absolutely lost this round. A fact I'm sure she will not be letting go of easily.

Chapter Six

Cassi

Dinner was tense after Carly and my verbal smackdown. Well, it wasn't really a smackdown, but I like calling it that in my head because the outrage followed by panic that took over her was fucking priceless. To be fair, I was only airing it out for Nicholas' benefit. My parents were already aware. They received a phone call from the dean when she was placed on probation, and her professor was fired. As my sister predictably would, she turned on the waterworks when confronted and claimed that she felt she had no choice. The professor lost everything. His job, his house, his family. Gone.

Do you think my sister has lost even a second of sleep since then?

Absolutely the fuck not.

A few minutes past that, Alec brought over everyone's meals and we ate in relative silence while my parents would intermittently ask questions about Nicholas's family and overall life. Though, their efforts were effectively wasted. He is as closed book as they come. All of his answers were short and clipped, never letting on too much about...anything. Honestly, I'm not entirely convinced that he's even human. He could be some alien or weird AI powered robot impersonating a human. That's how he conveys himself at least. Dry. Rigid. Cold.

Nothing at all like the man I met last night.

Fuck. No. None of that.

I chastise myself internally, shaking my head. I've been doing everything I can to erase that night from my mind completely. Him being two feet away from me isn't fucking helping, though. Despite his personality being more bland than a soggy piece of bread, his body is definitely something I'm having a harder time forgetting. His hands, his eyes, his mouth, his...

Fuck. There I go again. Goddamnit. Tomorrow can't come fast enough. The sooner they are out of here, the sooner I can forget about the time that I was a big ole slut and slept with my wicked bitch sister's boyfriend.

No matter how much I can't stand her, that guilt is going to eat me alive for approximately the rest of my fucking life. So, that's cool.

After my dad and Nicholas fought over the bill, and Nicholas ended up winning, we all gather our things and stand to leave when a soft hand touches the crook of my elbow. I look up to see Alec smiling at me tentatively.

"It was really good to see you, Cassi."

"It was good to see you," I smile before pulling him in for a hug.

His arms wrap around me instantly, a comforting familiarity that grips me as he does. When we pull away, he looks down like he's bashful before his blue eyes land on me.

"Do you think I could get your number? I got a new phone about a year ago and lost all of my contacts. Yours was one I definitely kicked myself for."

A soft stirring of butterflies flutter through me at that. I'd texted him on his birthday at the beginning of this year, but I never got a response. We never had bad blood so I was confused, and maybe a little hurt. Hearing that he didn't ignore me, that it wasn't intentional eases something inside me. Nodding, I smile and steal his notepad and pen, jotting down my number and name, like he doesn't fucking know my name. I'm so stupid.

He looks down at it like he just pulled the winning lottery ticket numbers before pocketing the notepad into his apron.

"I'll text you."

I smile at him as I look to see my family has already left, clearly to give us some semblance of privacy which I appreciate. As I weave through the restaurant, my eyes pause on one individual who is standing at the door, looking down at his phone.

"You shouldn't have waited for me," I say as I walk straight past him.

"Believe me, wasn't my idea," he scoffs.

"Whose was it?" I ask as I reach for the exterior door, though a large hand grabs it first, pulling it open.

I look to see Nicholas standing over me, holding the door open as he impatiently gestures for me to keep walking. God, this guy is such a fucking asshole.

My parents and Carly are already in the car and when I open the back door, I see that Carly is sitting on the passengers side, as opposed to in the middle like when we drove down here. I guess they didn't see a point in renting a car when they were only in town for two days but that means that we are pushing my mom's Camry to the max when it comes to space.

"Move," I say to my sister.

She looks up from her phone, scoffing as she shakes her head. "You move."

Looking up at Nicholas and his six foot plus giant frame and the tiny little middle seat, I know I have no choice. Doesn't mean I enjoy it.

Begrudgingly, I slide into the car, scooting into the middle before buckling in. Nicholas follows suit, shutting the door behind him as his thigh brushes against mine. I'm quick to jerk my leg away, a move that does not go unnoticed by him. He pushes himself further against the car door as he buckles into his seat and the car takes off.

If dinner was eaten in silence, then this car ride is similar to a ride in a hearse. The tension around us is physically palpable and honestly, it's fucking suffocating.

Once we are finally home, Nicholas can't open the door fast enough. He's practically throwing it open and stumbling out before my dad can even put the car into park. My dad laughs as he steps out of the car and shuts the door behind him.

"Sorry about the snug fit there. You could do worse than be in a backseat with two beautiful women, though, am I right?" he teases in a lighthearted way.

A smile touches Nicholas's face that doesn't quite reach his eyes as he nods.

"Men have certainly undergone far more perilous conditions for sure."

I roll my eyes, having absolutely enough of all of this bullshit as I slide out of the car and make my way into the house. I don't say goodnight to anyone. I don't sit around and chit chat like I hear them do. Instead, I head straight for my room and take a much needed breath.

Pulling out my phone, I click on Naomi's contact and type out a text that I've been aching to send to her. It's not like I don't tell Arianna things too. Nay is just...so easy to vent to. She's the nonjudgmental friend, the one who sides with you no matter what. Though I probably deserve all the judgment in the world and Arianna would never come at me from a place of love and respect... I can't fess this up to her. Not yet.

Me: I fucked up...

After I literally vented my life away to Nay, I felt relief that I didn't expect. I mean, I'm still a shit person for sleeping with my sister's boyfriend, but to Naomi's point, I had no idea who he was. I walked into that club single and looking for a consensual partner for the night. He walked into it knowingly in a relationship, seeking to find a partner to cheat with. It's unfortunate that person had to be me, but I'm sure he would have settled for anyone with a heartbeat.

He's the scum. Not me.

Okay, I know how that sounds but honestly, I'm not sorry. On top of being a cheating bastard, he's also just a grade A asshole.

I heard the chatter from downstairs quiet an hour or so ago so I know that means that everyone has turned in for the night. Which is perfect because I have a hard time going to bed without a late night snack.

Tip toeing out of my room, I make my way down the stairs and head into the kitchen. I don't know when the need for late night snacking started. Honestly, from birth if I had to guess. My dad is also a late night snacker and most of my life, we'd meet down here every night. Whether it was a bowl of ice cream, a thing of popcorn or even spoons full of peanut butter, we'd sit at the kitchen island, snack and talk about our day.

When I turn the corner, I find someone already rifling through the fridge, but it's not my usual snacking partner in crime. When the identity of this late night snacker is apparent, my appetite sours and I contemplate heading back to bed. Unfortunately for me, he has already spotted me, and Cassi Fischer is anything but a coward, especially to a man? Ew, no. My pride simply won't allow retreat at this point.

He looks at me and curses under his breath.

"Jesus, do you have to be everywhere I fucking turn? Is there anywhere I can go that you're not right fucking there?" Nicholas snaps at me.

I'm stunned for a moment, physically taken aback.

"Are you seriously yelling at me for being in my own house?" I ask in disbelief.

His eyes bore into my own for several seconds, before he closes them roughly and looks away. When it seems like he composes himself, he opens them once more and looks to me.

"Sorry. You're right. I just...you..." he breaks off, shaking his head before his gaze meets mine once more. "Sorry."

I nod at his apology before slipping past him for the cabinet. I rifle around until I find some of the ingredients I'm in search for. Sliding over to the fridge, I grab the remaining items and begin assembling my late night treat.

"What are you making?" he asks.

I look up at him while spreading the jam against the bread.

"A sandwich."

His brows furrow. "A jelly and...cream cheese sandwich?" he asks, as if the concept was so completely foreign.

"Jam, not jelly. There is a difference," I correct as I spread the cream cheese on the other piece of bread before putting them together.

"You're not seriously going to eat it like that," Nicholas deadpans.

"Of course not," I say with a shake of my head.

Reaching down beneath the stove, I pull out a small pan and set it on top, turning the burner on before dabbing a little butter into the pan. Once the butter has melted I plop my sandwich down and savor the sound of my bread being grilled to perfection.

I do my best to ignore Nicholas' outraged expression but it's hard to do so when he's gaping like a fish out of water. Pretending he's not there, I slip a spatula beneath the sandwich and flip it over, allowing it to become crispy golden deliciousness before I remove it from the heat.

Busying myself with setting up my plate and napkin, I pull my sandwich out of the pan and onto my plate before cutting it in half with a butter knife. When I turn, I find Nicholas practically frozen in place, still staring at me as one stares on at a train accident.

"That's disgusting," he comments.

I give him my best 'I don't give a fuck' expression before taking a huge bite out of it. I chew it very exaggeratingly, moaning my pleasure in the delicious combination. Though, I may have taken one moan a little too far and we are both acutely aware of that moment.

My jaw stops checking immediately and our eyes lock as we both stand like statues. I'm the first to resume, slowly swallowing my bite before clearing my throat.

"So what time do you and my sister get the hell out of dodge?" I ask.

He stares at me for half a beat longer than probably appropriate before he clears his throat as well.

"Wheels up at two o'clock in the afternoon."

I nod at that. "Have a nice flight," I say as I grab my plate and head to my room because whatever this weird tense moment is, I'm not loving it.

"It was your birthday last night?" he asks, his voice surprisingly soft, uncertain almost.

My feet stop on their own accord, no matter how badly I beg them to keep moving. Turning to look over my shoulder, my eyes meet his.

"Yeah."

He frowns like he doesn't like that, though I don't understand what my birthday has to do with him in the slightest.

"You didn't tell me."

My face screws up in confusion as I turn to face him fully, taking a few steps closer so I can lower my voice.

"Why would I? When you and I met the significance of our

presence in the club was not discussed...clearly. Things would have been very different otherwise, Nicholas," I scoff.

His gaze is unyielding, not allowing an ounce of emotion to show. Though, I do see his fists tighten by his sides.

"Nico," he says stiffly.

"What?"

"My name. I hate being called Nicholas. Everyone calls me Nico."

I tilt my head to the side in confusion. "Then why does Carly call you Nicholas?"

He shrugs his shoulders, and I think that's all he has left to say until he purses his lips as if he is deep in thought.

"Was it a good birthday? Last night?" he asks.

My eyes roam across his face, carefully inspecting for some kind of clue as to what the fuck kind of angle he's playing at. When I come up short, I decide enough is enough. Turning on my heel, I make my way to my room once more when he speaks yet again, as if he were intent on not allowing my escape.

"We weren't together, Carly and me. Last night. We broke up... I broke up with her. We got back together the morning after, kind of. She convinced me to at least come meet you parents and we'd figure it out from there."

I turn to look at him once more with a shake of my head.

"So the first thing you decide to do when you break up with your girlfriend of three years is go to a sex club?"

He has the decency to look ashamed as he looks down at the floor while he continues.

"I wasn't sure what kind of place it was until I was there then I..." his words trail off as his jaw tightens.

The air is heavy between us for several moments before a word escapes me before I think better of it.

"Yes."

He frowns in confusion. "Yes?"

"Yes...it was a good birthday."

Chapter Seven

Nico

I didn't sleep worth fucking shit last night. Put aside the fact that Carly and I slept on a full, a bed that I could barely fit on by myself. Also disregard the fact that her parents' bedroom which was right across the hall from us had a reverberating snoring that was so loud, I was convinced the whole goddamn place was coming down.

No, neither of those things are the reason I didn't sleep well. My main issue was simple and absolutely fucking infuriating. A pair of bright green eyes practically haunted me all night. Each time that I'd drift off to sleep, there they were. Over and over. New places, new dreams. Yet, the smart mouthed redhead was ever present. Ever enraging.

I don't know why I told her Carly, and I had broken up. What did it matter? We were back together now, or at least in our own way. Maybe I didn't like that my side of the story wasn't considered in her version of...whatever she thinks of when she thinks to that night. I didn't like that I was painted as a cheater in her mind, a player. I thought that maybe if she knew the truth, that sour judgmental look that pinches her face when she even glances in my direction would fade and maybe I'd see the smallest glimpse of the woman I'd met Friday night. Which believe me, I'm still trying to understand why the fuck I care in the first place.

Running a hand through my hair, I decide to give up on sleep at six thirty in the morning and go for a run. Jogging always helps clear my head. Big breath in, big breath out. You push forward, you fight, and you gain distance with every move you make. It's poetic if you think about it, but really I just see it as a much needed outlet so I don't lose my shit on someone or something underserving.

I change into a pair of shorts and slip on a t-shirt and some running shoes before I head out the door. As my legs begin to stretch out, and my pace quickens, instead of peace overcoming me, I feel chaos. A million thoughts and moments play in my mind. All revolving around that same fucking redhead. Goddamnit. What the hell is happening to me?

Pushing myself to run faster and harder, I attempt to outrun her. She's consuming my head and no matter how desperately I want her out, it's as if she's making herself nice and comfy. Like last night, Carly and I started to get into it once again and I wasn't in the mood. I told her I needed some air and escaped to the kitchen. I wasn't even in search of anything except space.

Carly was laying into me, saying that I've been a grumpy ass this whole trip. She wanted to know what was wrong, why I was so quiet at dinner. I couldn't tell her the real reason, though. I couldn't tell her that I handled our twelve hour breakup by sinking myself inside her little sister. So, I fled, only to run into Cassi fucking Fischer. It's like my mind can conjure that woman and she appears at the flick of a wrist.

As I circle back the way I came and approach the Fischer household, I feel relief. After a shower and some coffee we will get all packed up and head to the airport. We will go back to Boston and Carly and I will...I don't really know from there. I'm not sure what to do with her at this point. I'm tired, I know that. I'm sick and fucking tired of her entitlement and attitude. I'm sick of being seen as a meal ticket and not a goddamn human being. Is that really how I feel, though, or am I just trying to justify my actions of the other night? Because somehow it doesn't feel as bad if I slept with my ex's sister as it does if I slept with my girlfriend's sister. Semantics and all but sometimes they really fucking matter.

Wiping the sweat off my brow, I blow out a heavy breath and make my way up the front driveway of the house. Pushing inside, I kick off my shoes and set them to the side before walking into the kitchen. There I find the coffee machine and fire it up before pouring a glass of water. Mary told me to help myself to anything around the house and normally, I wouldn't take anyone up on such things. Hell, the very concept of depending on anyone or taking anything that is anyone else's feels...wrong.

I know that's how families operate and they are just being kind but the idea is so foreign from me I'm more than uncomfortable in how to take it. I struggled releasing enough control to ride in a car while someone else drove. That's why there was no way in hell I was letting Henry pay for dinner last night. Regardless if Carly and I work out or not, I don't like the idea of my name being marred with negativity like not paying my way...or being a sleazeball in sex club. Fuck, why can't I let that go? I'm starting to fucking annoy myself.

A knock comes from the front door that has me curious. The house is overall quiet, it seems the whole family is the type to sleep in, which means they are definitely not expecting company. You'd think a delivery or something would know that it's too early to knock and would just leave whatever they have at the front door.

Walking through the hall, I come to the foyer before opening the front door. I recognize the face on the other side of the threshold immediately and for some unknown reason, I'm not pleased in the slightest to see him again.

"Can I help you?" I ask stiffly.

He gives me a friendly smile as he holds out his hand for me.

"Hey, Nicholas, right? I don't know if you remember me from last night. I'm—"

"I remember," I cut in. "What do you want?"

Alec looks taken back by my directness but shakes it off easily as he holds up the flowers that have been dangling by his side.

"I'm here to pick up Cassi."

"Cassi?" I question with furrowed brows. "She's not—"

"I'm here, I'm here! Sorry, I couldn't find the right shoes," she says as she steps into the foyer, effectively shoving me out of the way.

I can't stop my gaze from taking her in. From her white canvas shoes to her light blue jeans and cropped white tank top accompanied with a leather jacket. She looks...different. Different than I've seen her. She's not dolled up in an expensive red gown that is practically painted onto her, nor in a pair of leggings and a baggy shirt with her hair piled on top of her head. This looks is more simple, casual, and somehow it's become one of my favorites.

One of your favorites? You shouldn't have a single fucking favorite. Not only is she way too young and way too off limits she's...no. No favorites.

"You look perfect," Alec says, smiling at her like a fucking jackass. "These are for you."

"Sunflowers? They are my—"

"Favorite, I remember," he fills in with a smile that seems to turn Cassi to goo.

Are you fucking serious?

"I'll just go put these in some water and then I'll be ready to go," she says.

"Can I come in?" Alec asks.

I answer that for him.

"No," I say before slamming the door shut in his face.

She looks at me in outrage before rolling her eyes and moving towards the kitchen. My feet follow after her before my mind can talk them out of it.

"What crawled up your ass and died this morning?"

I go to speak when her words hit my ears fully.

"The fuck?"

She lets out a little cackle as she pulls down a vase and fills it with water before plopping the sunflowers into it. Once she's done, she wipes her hands onto a towel and starts back towards the door. Or at least tries to. I take a step in front of her, blocking her way.

"Where are you going?" I ask.

"Out," she says dryly as she attempt to step around me.

I block her easily, and then again when she tries to go the other way.

"With that little fucker?"

She pauses for a moment like she's trying to wrap her mind around something before she shakes her head.

"I'm sorry, who are you again?"

I don't respond to her sarcastic quip as she moves past me and for the door.

I sure as fuck make sure to stay hot on her heels though. When she opens the door, I see Alec leaned up against a motorcycle, his smile returning when she steps onto the porch.

"Absolutely fucking not," I scoff. "Do you know how dangerous those things are?"

"I've heard a story or two," Cassi says, not even turning to look at me as she practically skips towards him.

"Your parents are not going to be happy about this," I warn.

"Actually, my parents have always loved Alec. They'll know I'm in safe hands," she says, casting a look over her shoulder as Alec stands up, offering her a helmet.

She smiles in thanks as he slips it on over her head, clipping it into place before smirking. He mounts the bike, his own helmet in place as she climbs on behind him. I watch as she slowly slides her body against his, wrapping her arms around his chest before nuzzling into his back. Her face shield is up so I can't tell if she's looking at me but let me tell you, the move feels deliberate as fuck and has my pulse jackhammering.

Alec starts up the bike and they take off in a flash while I'm left staring as they go, fucking pissed. Adrenaline takes over as I storm inside, slamming the door shut behind me. I pace several steps, trying to regain control of my breathing. I should be in the shower right now, getting ready to get the fuck back to Boston. So why is it taking everything in me not to call an uber and order them to follow the punk on the tricked out sportster?

You don't even know her, Nico. What's the big fucking deal? She was a one night stand. She means, nothing. She is nothing.

I repeat this mantra in my head over and over again, but for some reason, the words won't sink in. Before I'm able to think this through, I'm climbing the stairs and slipping into Carly's childhood room. The bed is empty, just the faint sound of the connected bathroom echoing from the cracked door.

Slipping through it, I'm met with a wall of steam as Carly's silhouette is casted against the glass door.

"We have a problem," I say, the lie rolling off my tongue without a second of a hesitation.

Goddamn, I should probably feel bad about what I'm about to do but honestly, I've never been so sure about a gut made decision.

"What?" she asks as she opens the door slightly, poking her head out.

"The company plane is down for repairs in LA. They don't know when it will be operational again."

She looks at me in concern before shaking her head. "Can't they like, give us a rental plane?"

I stare at her for a moment, slowly blinking.

"No, Carly. That's not how that works."

"My insurance covered a temporary car when my engine broke last year, though," she counters.

I open my mouth to explain how many things are wrong with that statement, let alone the idea of trying to compare the situation of a personal vehicle to a private jet. Something in me just doesn't have the capacity, though. So, instead I just shake my head and move forward.

"Think your parents will mind if we stay here for a few more days?"

She wrinkles her nose up like she hates the idea of it.

"I mean, I'm sure they'd be thrilled but is that what I want? No."

I shrug at her as I rest my hands into my shorts pockets.

"We're stuck in Seattle until further notice."

"We could fly commercial," she offers.

I just stare at her for several seconds, her own words sinking in before she laughs.

"Oh my god I can't believe I just said that. We haven't flown commercial in years," she laughs like she just made the silliest joke.

It takes everything in me not to release the eyeroll that is queued up and ready.

"Talk to your parents, we can always get a hotel room if it inconveniences them."

She waves me off. "They'll be fine. Though, Dad will absolutely be forcing you out for a fishing trip. Good luck with that one."

I nod and begin to walk away when she calls out to me.

"Wait, Nicholas. Don't you want to come join me?" she practically purrs.

My eyes roam over her soapy body as she pushes the door open more. Carly is beautiful, don't get me wrong. A blind man would be insanely attracted to her. Right now, though, I'm just...

"Not in the mood," I cut brusquely as I turn to head back into the bedroom.

She scoffs and I hear mutter, "Since when?"

I choose not to respond, gathering some fresh clothes for the day and heading for the guest bathroom to get cleaned up for the day.

Chapter Eight
Cassi

My arms are wrapped around Alec's lean torso as he takes a sharp left turn. I lean with him as we speed down the road before we are upright once more. I haven't been on the back of a motorcycle since...god, I guess since him. It was the only thing about Alec my parents didn't love. They forbid me to ever ride with him, to which I promptly broke that rule every chance I got. Hey, I never claimed to be a good teenager. Who was?

Besides, they didn't need to worry. Alec was an excellent driver then and he clearly still is now. He loves to ride but safety is important to him, so is keeping me safe. At least, that's what he always said.

It's funny how sometimes, certain parts of your life, someone can mean so much and then over time they just sort of...fade. Not that I ever forgot about Alec. To this day I thought of him often, I just assumed he didn't want me in his life anymore and I guess I got over it. Though, now that we are here and now, I can touch him, see him, smell him, it all makes me remember why I fell in love with him in the first place.

As if he can hear my thoughts, he turns over his shoulder to look at me as we pull up to a red light. I can't see through him helmet but for some reason I just know he is grinning. I can't help but smile in response as I shake my head before the light turns green and we take off again.

I didn't make it ten feet out of the restaurant before I got my first text from Alec.

Unknown: Where do you think you're going with my heart like that?

I immediately couldn't contain my smile when I read it. It goes back to an inside joke we had back in high school. He'd always tease that when I left it felt like his heart was leaving too. Kinda intense now that I think about it, at least for a high school relationship. That's just how we were, though.

We burned bright and fast and then kinda faded out after we broke up. He wanted to stay together despite his parents having to move all the way to New York. I was the realist. He's a gorgeous guy who had college right around the corner. I didn't want to hold him back. I gave him all the typical shit of us staying friends, that if we were meant to be together we'd find our way back. My mind can't help but pull at that thought as we cruise through the early morning streets. Maybe seeing Alec was all for a greater purpose. Maybe me accidently sleeping with my sister's boyfriend will work out because if anything, it's given me great motivation to think about and do practically anything else. Lo and behold, I have the perfect gorgeous distraction right in front of me, and if memory serves, he loved eating pussy for literal hours so honestly, win, win.

After I went to bed last night, Alec and I texted for literal hours. When he suggested going out today, I assumed he meant at night since the text was sent at just after three in the morning. When I told him I was in he said 'great, see you in four hours,' and that was that. I could have laughed in his face because normally I would require way more sleep than that but honestly, it feels good to have someone desperate to spend time with you. So, I set an alarm for three hours, only leaving me an hour to do a bare minimum shower, makeup and outfit change before I was out the door.

God, what was with Nicholas this morning? Or Nico, whatever. He was such an ass. I can't tell if his problem stemmed more from issues with me or issues with Alec. I'm going to go out on a crazy limb here and say that his issue is with everyone. He seems like one of those rich, arrogant 'I can be mean to anyone because I can buy your entire life with a swipe of my credit card', types. Not like Alec in the slightest. Maybe that's why I was so eager to go out with my sweet ex-boyfriend. He is literally everything Nicholas isn't, which I've very recently realized is everything in a man I despise and want nothing to do with.

When I see where we are going, I literally almost pee myself laughing. Alec maneuvers our way into the parking lot of the sketchy breakfast restaurant we came to nearly every morning. It's sketchy because of the part of town, the overall dilapidated appearance and the less than pleasant customer service. It's amazing though for the food and the price. So, for a couple of high school kids on a budget, this place was date night material. Or in our case, date day.

Once Alec kills the engine, he takes his helmet off before helping me with mine. My hair becomes a static ball instantly and he smiles at me as he attempts to smooth it out.

"I can't believe Donny's is still around," I say with a shake of my head.

"Right? I drove by when I got back in town and was shocked. I thought they'd have knocked it down or maybe someone else had bought it by now."

Alec offers me his arm like it's 1860 and he is escorting me around the gardens, and I happily take it, laughing as we walk through the parking lot and slipping inside the restaurant. Once we choose a corner booth, we order our usuals like no time has passed as the impatient waitress rolls her eyes at us and walks off. Neither of us pay her any mind, though as Alec rests his forearms onto the table and leans forward, smiling at me with those beautiful bright eyes.

"So, how have you been, Cass?"

I smile and nod. "Good. I'm a receptionist at a dental office. It's not the most glamourous job but I'm happy."

"I'm so glad," he says, like he truly means it.

"How have you been? How is college?"

He nods as he leans back a little. "College was good. I graduated early and have a job lined up on the east coast once I'm done out here."

"Done?" I question.

Alec's smile fades as he nods.

"My grandma is sick. She was put on hospice, and I moved out here until she goes."

I frown at that, reaching out my hand to cover his. "Alec, I'm so sorry. I always loved her so much. Is she in pain?"

He shakes his head. "No, she has a great team that keeps her comfortable. I spend most of my days with her. Her memory is kinda going so a lot of the time she thinks I'm my dad, but it helps her, I think."

I nod at that.

"How does she do when you and your dad are in the same room? Or do you guys visit separately?"

No attempt at keeping his smile in check works. His face falls as his eyes drop to the table. He doesn't speak for several moments before he finally does, his eyes never moving up more than an inch or two.

"He, uhm. He actually passed away. Him and my mom."

"What?" I ask, unable to hide my shock.

"Yeah, it was last November. We all went up to Vermont to ski and we hit a patch of black ice. Threw us right into a semi and..."

The air between us is so heavy, I'm practically choking on it.

"Alec," I whisper, feeling my throat tighten with each passing second. "You were...you are okay?"

His eyes come to me as he nods. "Physically, I had a broken leg and some fractured ribs. The car sort of contorted into this weird angle that created a protective bubble for me. I don't know. The doctors were blown away I wasn't more hurt."

Normally, I wouldn't ask this follow up question, but it's Alec. He was at one point my absolute best friend, the one person I knew better than anyone.

"And mentally?"

He attempts to give me a strained smile as he nods.

"I'm hanging in there."

My heart aches for him, for all of them. I loved his family like he loved mine. We were all this funky amazing blended family. So many barbeques and lake days spent together. Holiday gatherings, birthdays. To think that they've been gone for months and I didn't even know. Grief strikes me hard and true, accompanied by a deep amount of empathy. What must he have felt like to wake up in the hospital and realize that his parents were gone? That he was the only one to survive? Then just a few months later, move back across the country to take care of his dying grandmother? The fact that he's even hanging on at all is a literal miracle.

"Alec...I wish I would have known."

He shakes his head and shrugs.

"I kinda kept to myself after the funeral, it was probably best that I lost your number. You would have had my drunk and depressed ass calling you at two in the morning every night," he laughs dryly.

"I would have answered," I say, causing his laughter to die as his heavy eyes look to me. "Every time. If you would have called, I would have answered."

I watch as his throat moves like he's swallowing before he nods.

"I know," he rasps, his hand twisting beneath my own before lacing our fingers together.

I give him a soft smile that he matches before letting out a heavy breath.

"Jesus, what a way to start a date."

My smile widens but I shake my head and roll with his obvious need to switch topics.

"I mean, screw breakfast. I'm wet and ready to go."

His look of appreciation flashes before it's gone in the next minute, a suggestive smirk touching his mouth as he leans forward once more.

"Oh really? Well, in that case. I'll meet you in the bathroom?"

A surprised laugh rips through me, echoing inside the restaurant as I shake my head.

"Not on your fucking life, buddy. I don't even want to know what we'd catch getting naked in there."

He frowns in mock disappointment but nods. "Fair enough. Honestly, I'm just impressed my game is strong enough to have you talking about getting naked two minutes into a date."

I roll my eyes and shake my head at him as he laughs. From there, the topics stay a lot lighter and a lot more flirty. Our lovely waitress brings us our food and we eat while catching up. He tells me about a few friends of his back in New York and I talk to him about Arianna and Naomi. He was shocked to find out that we are still friends, honestly, I don't get why. We have been friends for so long, we are in it for the long haul. Until we're old and grey.

After our nearly three hour breakfast date, the waitress finally came right out and said it was time for us to leave, which honestly had us cracking up. Alec quickly paid the tab and though I offered to pay my own meal, he just rolled his eyes and told the waitress she could keep the massive tip. Her eyes widened out of her head and for the first time since we were there, she looked almost kind, softened. She said thank you under her breath and quickly rushed into the back.

Alec smiled after her before standing up and offering his hand for me. I took it easily and together we made our way back to his bike. The drive back to my house went by faster than I anticipated. I closed my eyes as I rest my head onto his back and when I opened them again, we were there.

Pushing myself away from him, I step off the bike, taking the helmet he gave me off before handing it to him. He pushes his helmet off as well, running a hand through his blond hair before swinging a leg over so he's just leaning against the bike.

"Thank you for breakfast, or maybe it's now considered lunch?" I laugh.

He smiles as he reaches for my hand, pulling it up to his lips before placing a gentle kiss against my knuckles.

"It was my pleasure."

I feel soft butterflies flutter inside me as I look at him. Our eyes stay on one another for so long, you'd think it would be awkward. It's not, though. Nothing is with him. Everything is easy, simple. Comfortable. Like riding a bike, we have picked up practically right where we left off.

His hand tugs on mine gently, and I know what he wants without his having to speak. I close to the distance, coming to stand between his legs as his hands come to my hips, holding me in place.

Mindlessly, I wrap my arms around his neck as I smile at him. Even leaning down like this he's still at perfect eye level with me, which means I can see the way his eyes dart down to my mouth before back to my eyes. A silent ask of permission. I was always the dominant one in this relationship, though, and it looks like some things never change.

Leaning forward, I press my lips against his as one of his hands lift to the back of my head. He holds me tenderly as his lips move against mine, his tongue licking the seam of my lips before I part for him. He twirls his tongue against my own, letting out a soft groan as he does. I feel myself wanting to be closer and closer to him as I hold him tighter when he roughly tears himself away, letting out an almost pained groan.

"If we weren't in your parent's driveway in broad daylight, I'd bend you over this bike and show you just how much I've fucking missed you."

"If you knew how to have fun, I'd let you," I tease against his lips.

Another moan that sounds more reminiscent to torture than pleasure escapes him as he presses one more kiss to me. When he tears himself away, he shakes his head.

"You are fucking trouble Cassi Fischer."

"And you love it Alec Thompson," I smirk.

"Absofuckinglutly do," he says on a short laugh.

I smile at him as one of his hands starts rubbing soft circles on my lower back.

"Does this mean you'll let me take you out again?"

I pretend to think about it before he pinches my side, causing a laugh to squeal out of me.

"Yes, I'd love that," I nod.

"Good, because you actually didn't have a choice."

"Oh no?" I ask in amusement.

"Absolutely not. I got my eyes on the prize, babygirl," he says as he stands up, swinging his leg over his bike once more and starting it up.

I cross my arms over my chest as I lift an eyebrow at him.

"Keep looking. It's gonna take more than a short stack of pancakes and a good kiss to get this prize."

"Don't I know it," he says with a shake of his head before shooting me a wink.

I laugh at that as he slips on his helmet and gives me a wave. I wave to him as he takes off out of the driveway and down the road. I don't even realize that I'm still smiling until I'm inside, when I run straight into a hard chest.

That familiar scent fills the air around me, and I look up to see Nicholas glaring down at me.

"What? Decided to cut your porno short?"

I screw my face up in confusion at him.

"What are you even talking about?"

"That little display. I can only assume you were filming it, if you're hurting for money that bad, all you have to do is ask for help," he says dryly.

I honestly can't tell if he's being serious or not, mainly because his personality fucking sucks.

"Shouldn't you be in Boston? You know, far fucking away from here?"

And me.

Nicholas stares at me for several seconds before he speaks, his voice tight and short.

"Change of plans. We're staying through the week."

I can feel my face fall at his words.

"Why?" I ask, as if knowing the answer will somehow allow me to find a way to get him and Carly on a plane as soon as fucking possible.

"Does it matter?" he asks as he turns and walks away.

Yeah, it really fucking does

When I got back from my date with Alec, I decided to take a much needed day nap. Which I know sounds ridiculous since I went to bed at noon but it's my last day off before I start back at work tomorrow so I'm going to enjoy it.

I finally pried my eyes open and checked my phone to see that it was promptly five o'clock in the afternoon. Looks like I absolutely slept the day away and I have zero regrets. Scrolling through my text messages I see a few from the group chat talking about Arianna's upcoming date with her masked man from the club, Naomi shooting down any and all of Arianna's inquiries of her time Friday night and then finally a private text from Naomi.

Naomi: How did this weekend go? Is he gone?

I scoff, shaking my head as I type out my response.

Me: If by gone, you mean is he staying for an extra week, then absolutely.

Her response comes almost immediately.

Naomi: WHAT

Naomi: EXPLAIN

Naomi: NOW PLEASE

I decide it's better to voice note but I make sure to keep any names or details out of it in case someone is close by.

"Yeah, that's what I've been told. No explanation. No elaboration. Just point, blank. Clearly this entire situation isn't nearly as painful for him as it is for me. If I was in control, I'd get the hell out of dodge immediately. I'd already be gone. Like it's bad enough that he's here, but in my house?" I add on with a whisper. "He's such a fucking asshole. I take back everything I ever said. He's trash in every way possible. But, on a random bright side, you'll never believe who I ran into at dinner last night."

I pause for dramatic effect before continuing.

"Alec Thompson," I say, already hearing her squeal of surprise. "It's so fucking sad, Nay. His parents died, he almost did too, or could have at least. Now he's out here taking care of his dying grandma. My heart is broken for him. He picked me up this morning and took me to Donny's like old times. It was actually so nice. So like yes, I hate that *he* is here but the plus side of things is that Alec is kinda in the picture, at least for now. He said he was going to take me out again soon and let me tell you, sparks definitely don't dim with time," I say as I end the voice note.

Forcing myself out of bed, I decide to head downstairs and see what the plan is for dinner. I know Naomi will be blowing up my phone for the foreseeable future which will be hilarious to come back to. She always loved Alec and swore that we were endgame, she was almost more devastated when we broke up than I was, which is pretty crazy because despite me ending it, I was heartbroken. I knew that she would latch onto that piece of the story as soon as it left my lips. Maybe that's why I did it. Because if my journalist major bestie is focused on my former boyfriend who she adored, maybe she won't see that I'm lying through my goddamn teeth.

Okay, maybe that's an exaggeration. I wouldn't say through my teeth.

Am I happy I ran into Alec? Absolutely.

Do I think Nicholas is a trash human? Undoubtedly.

Am I feeling major sparks with Alec after one date that outshine what I felt with Nicholas for just one hour? Not even fucking close.

I wanted to. I really did. It was a great kiss, and there was... something that stirred inside me when I kissed him. To be honest, I don't know what to think. Is it in my head? Am I standing in the way of happiness because I'm so caught up with guilt and shame? I honestly don't know and I'm nowhere near emotionally mature enough to dive in and discover the answers.

So, I'm going to force it until an answer smacks me in the face. It's my own special brand of avoidance that works out for me about 33% of the time, which is not nothing.

As I make my way downstairs and into the kitchen, the smell of my mom's famous meatloaf fills the room. I don't know why meatloaf has such a bad reputation, maybe some people don't cook it correctly. If they had my mother's they'd never eat anything but again. My eyes roam over the kitchen to see that she also took the time to make her sweet rolls and mashed potatoes? Fuck me upppp.

"Hey sleepyhead," my mom smiles.

I give her a tired smile as I zombie walk my way over to the plate of fresh rolls. Stealing one and avoiding my mom's hand smack all in one. A talent, I know.

"Cassi, you know mom and I don't care what you do on your days off, but waking up at five in the afternoon?" my dad laughs from his recliner.

I smile and shake my head at him. "I took a little nap that turned into a long one."

"I heard some activity early this morning, what were you up to?" my mom asks.

Before I can respond, a cutting voice comes from the hallway before the owner steps into the kitchen. Nicholas is wearing a pair of slacks and a black dress shirt, way too dressed up for a lazy Sunday if you ask me but maybe that's why arrogant pricks like to wear on their days off. Who am I to judge?

"She had a date, with that waiter from last night."

His eyes cut to mine, almost in a taunting way. Does he think I'm twelve? Think he's gonna get me in trouble with mommy and daddy? To my delight, and his surprise, my parents react the way I anticipated.

"Alec? Oh sweetie, that's wonderful!" my mom says as my dad nods.

"I always liked that kid. How are his folks doing?"

A pang of sadness hits me and my eyes cut to Nicholas's before deciding he doesn't need to be privy to Alec's situation. He clearly has a distaste for him and therefore, doesn't deserve intimate details.

"Good," I say, keeping it short. "Can I help with anything, Mom?"

"You're okay. I just needed some more butter from the store and Nicholas was sweet enough to run out for me."

On cue, he reaches between us, handing my mom a box of butter with a smile that would charm any woman right out of her pants. Certainly charmed me out of mine when he aimed it at me.

"It was no trouble," he says simply.

My mom smiles at him lovingly in a way that has me resisting the urge to vomit. Give me a fucking break.

"Where is your girlfriend, *Nicholas?*" I ask.

"Nico," he corrects flatly, his tone brokering no argument.

Tough luck for him, I've officially found out what pisses him off the most, so as a little sister would, I will forever use it to bug the living shit out of him.

"Oh, I'm so sorry. Do you prefer, Nico? Carly always told us your name was Nicholas," my mom says.

His harsh stare towards me melts away when he looks to my mom.

"I do. Nicholas just feels too formal for me."

"Yeah, you are the picture of relaxation," I scoff with a shake of my head.

My eyes find my dad's who gives me a 'what the hell was that for' kind of look. I shrug my shoulder to him, looking anywhere else as my mom and Nicholas keep chatting.

"You didn't answer my question, where is Carly?" I ask, cutting into the conversation.

"Why is it any of your business, Miss Nosey?" my mom tosses out. "She's getting her nails done. Carly and Nico are going to stay with us through the week. Won't that be nice?" she asks with a smile that says be polite.

I give my best fake smile as I nod my head and look to him.

"Why yes, what joyous news."

My mom sighs, shaking her head as I move to the cabinet for plates.

"I'll set the table," I say as I gather up enough dishes for us all and head for the dining room. Not before I catch my mom's words.

"Sorry about her. Carly and Cassi have never gotten along very well. I'm afraid you're the enemy by association."

"Something tells me I've earned that title by my own merit."

Well, at least he's telling the truth for once.

Chapter Nine
Nico

Carly strolls in at the very last moment and sits down into the seat beside me at the dinner table. Her freshly manicured nails are on display as she goes into detail over the emotional torture she endured on deciding what color to select. I can't suppress a roll of my eyes. You're a grown ass woman, no one at this table cares if you chose ballerina pink or light in love. It's fucking pink.

Goddamn. I'm glad that most of my words these days stay inside my head because I have become quite the prick. I'd like to say it's because she makes me this way, that's not fair, though. Even if she is irritating as hell, that doesn't mean she is the reason I've become...well, my father. She certainly isn't helping the case, though.

Personally, I've never been a fan of meatloaf, but the instant I take my first bite, I regret all my prior notions.

"Mary, this has to be the best meatloaf I've ever had," I say.

Her smile practically lights up the room as she brushes me off.

"It's nothing really."

I see Cassi sitting beside Henry, shaking her head.

"Quit with the fake modesty, mom. Your meatloaf is literally the best ever. I used to ask to have it for breakfast."

"Really?" I ask in surprise and also partly in disgust.

"It's true," Mary smiles. "That girl will eat anything, any time of the day."

"Social constructs revolving around food are absolutely ridiculous. How can it be a right or wrong time of day to enjoy certain foods?" Cassi asks the table.

"I do love waffles for dinner on occasion," Henry agrees.

"But do you love it because you're not supposed to have it?" Mary challenges.

"I don't buy that, remove the taboo and it's still a delicious waffle, or a life altering piece of meatloaf, right?" she asks me for back up.

I hesitate for a moment, not sure what to say. Cassi's bright green eyes are practically begging me to agree with her and before I think otherwise, I'm nodding my head.

"Good food is good food, no matter if it's considered right or wrong to have it."

The instant my words are out, I want to take them back. Especially when I see the flare in Cassi's eyes followed by the deep breath that has her chest rising and falling. A chest I'm extremely acquainted with. One I've seen bare and donned with beautiful rope that made her look like an unwrapped gift for the taking.

I've come to the realization that I'll never be able to escape that night. No matter how hard I've tried, it has been etched into my brain. Every last detail of it, of her, there forever. To stand the test of time, I have no doubt of it.

"I've always hated meatloaf. It's so fatty and weird," Carly adds in, taking the conversation into a swift and sharp detour.

The mood feels instantly soured as everyone looks from one another, unsure of where to go. I watch as Mary's proud smile dims as she softens her voice and her head.

"It's okay, sweetheart. You don't have to eat it. I have some salad in the fridge if you'd prefer."

Carly moves to stand when I rest a hand into her lap, pushing her leg down so she's forced to sit. She looks to me in confusion as I attempt to control my irritation.

"You need to apologize to your mother and eat what she made."

"Have you seen this meal? Not a veggie in sight. Do you want a fat girlfriend?" she argues.

Jesus Christ.

"I want a respectful one. Apologize and eat, in that order."

She gives me a defiant look but ultimately caves, turning to her mom.

"Sorry, the food is good. I'm just watching my macros."

Mary gives her a tight smile paired with an understanding nod before everyone resumes their meal. I peel my hand away from Carly immediately and ignore her completely when she pouts. I know she's expecting me to dote on her and praise her for being a decent fucking human to the woman who birthed and raised her, and I don't have the energy or patience to point out how fucked that is.

Shaking my head, I focus on my meal as I recount how idiotic it was to decide to stay here. I can't fucking take this. I don't even know why I wanted to stay.

That's not true and you fucking know it.

Still.

I need to get home to Boston. Away from the entire Fischer family. They spell nothing but trouble for me.

"So, Nico, since you will be with us for a little longer, how about we head out to the sound? Do some fishing?"

"I've never been," I admit, "but it sounds like a good time."

Henry smiles like I've just made his day.

"What do you say, Carl? Your boyfriend is coming."

"Dad, I've told you how much I hate that nickname. Second, three of us piled into your dingy? Sounds awful."

Henry shakes his head and busies himself with his food. Okay, some of my guilt over spoiling Carly rotten is starting to dissipate because if this is how she speaks to her parents all the time, then maybe she was always like this and just put on a very convincing front. I can't help but feel completely conned.

"I could find us a boat for the day. Something we could take wherever we wanted to go, I'm sure?" I offer.

Henry looks up in hope that will convince his daughter and Carly returns my suggestion with a wrinkle of her nose as she stabs at the meatloaf once more.

"I'll go, Dad. We don't need a fancy boat, just some worms and beer, right?" Cassi says.

Henry looks to her and nods. "That's all you need for a good fishing trip. Nico has a point. The boat has a small crack in the haul from the last time I took her out. I'll go halves with you on it?" he says to me.

I shake my head before he can even finish his sentence.

"You have invited me into your home, for longer than you agreed upon. Please, let me."

"Yeah, dad. Let him, he wipes his ass with hundred dollar bills," Cassi snarks.

I look to her with a serious expression.

"I could never be so wasteful," I tsk before looking to Henry. "I use twenties."

Laughter erupts from the table, of course except Carly as Henry shakes his head.

"As any good man should."

Cassi is grinning so wide it actually catches me off guard. Her teeth are so white, so perfect. Her smile transforms her face into something...else. I don't know how to explain it. Like how people say someone lights up the room. She lights up an entire city block.

Light, and joy and...something else just radiates out of her. It's a look I've really never seen on the smartass twenty one year old. I didn't think she had it in her to look anything other than irritated by me. The fact that she's laughing, at a joke I made no less, it does something to me that I know it absolutely shouldn't.

The plan was to go out for some evening fishing tonight since everyone had to work. I did some things on my laptop and took a few conference calls but I have my VP holding down things well enough so my presence wasn't overly necessary. Carly set up a girl's day with some friends from high school and honestly, I'm grateful for it. She's been breathing down my neck since we've got here. I haven't so much as kissed her since our fight, and she can tell. I'm not sure why I haven't fucked her, she's my girlfriend after all. Maybe I just don't feel like it because I'm so goddamn irritated with her. Maybe by the day, her personality ruins her outer appearance for me more and more to the point where I'm losing my attraction to her altogether. Or maybe I'm shit scared that if I fuck her, I'll wish I was inside her sister.

Say anything you want about Cassi, fuck knows I've said it all in my head, but that woman is...something else. Her body was so responsive, flawless. Supple curves, silky skin and a pussy that felt like it was goddamn made for me. Carly is beautiful of course but Cassi is almost ethereal. Like a forbidden goddess. Something out of my reach, out of my grasp. Two things I am not familiar with.

The first thing I did this morning was have my assistant arrange a boat to take us out for fishing. She said she found the perfect one that came with a captain and had glowing reviews from CEO's to celebrities, even an NFL player for the Seattle Crusaders apparently used them. I told her that it sounds good enough and had her book it for today.

Katelyn Taylor

I'm not a huge water person. A beach house is about as involved as I get so this is definitely new territory for me but I like Henry, he seems like a good guy. The girls are lucky to have him, I'd have given anything to have the kind of dad I know he was to them. Seeing Carly shoot him down so easily bugged me and then seeing how Cassi swooped in to save the day in a sense opened my eyes. It had me watching her a little closer for the rest of the night. Every snide remark Carly would make to someone, Cassi would match it with a compliment. Every complaint Carly had, Cassi had something to thank for. Every turn, she was actively trying to right her sister's wrongs. It must have been fucking exhausting growing up like that.

Mary and Henry met me at the house and together we drove to the docks where our boat is waiting. I was surprised at first when Mary asked if she could join this morning. She didn't seem too interested last night but I'm glad she came. She has this warmth to her, something that reminds me a lot of my mother, and I didn't realize how much I enjoyed being around people that carry themselves in that way.

Cassi didn't get off work until four so she said she would meet us there and true to her word, she is waiting in the parking lot inside her silver Civic that has to be from the nineties at the newest. That color too, I can only imagine how completely invisible she becomes against the roads when it's overcast and raining out here. One bad accident in that thing and she's done, yet she seems completely unbothered by the tin can she rolls around in.

Cassi steps out of the car, huge sunglasses covering her face. She's wearing a pair of blue jeans and a cropped band t-shirt. Not exactly what I picture for a receptionist at a dental office.

"Did Carly seriously not come?" she asks as she looks between all of us.

I shake my head and she scoffs.

"Fucking bitch."

"Watch your mouth," Henry says, his words holding absolutely not heat in them.

"I'm just speaking the truth," she says, tossing her hands out by her sides before looking to me.

"Alright Mr. Twenties, lead the way."

I choke on my next breath as I look to her.

"Is that really going to be my nickname?"

She shrugs. "I haven't decided yet. It's a solid contender."

Letting out a heavy breath, I gesture for Mary and Henry to follow me as we make our way down the dock. At least, that's what my assistant told me to do. I have no fucking clue where I'm going but the water is this way, so it's a safe bet.

At the end of the dock, a man dressed in black dress pants and white captains shirt is standing with his hands clasped in front of him. When he sees us approaching, he smiles and reaches his hand out to shake.

"Mr. Sanders. It's a pleasure to meet you, my name is Darryl and I'll be your captain this evening. Who do we have with us?"

"Please, call me Nico. This is Cassi, Henry and Mary," I introduce.

"A pleasure. Right this way, I'll let you folks get settled and we'll depart momentarily. I heard we're in the mood for some fishing?" he asks as he gestures to Henry who is holding a fishing pole.

"Yes, sir."

"Well, we have four poles set up and at the ready for you at the stern, though I'd take a guess that's a lucky pole," he asks as he helps us onboard.

"You'd be correct, Captain."

"Just what we need," he smiles warmly. "If you folks need any food or beverage, Jackie is inside to take care of anything you may need."

"Thank you," Cassi says as she steps on before I follow.

"Thank you," I nod to him as we begin exploring.

I've got to be honest. I've seen some nice boats, acquaintances own nice boats. This isn't a nice boat. This is a goddamn mansion on the water. The craftsmanship is spectacular. The finite details make the entire space feel refined and elegant while still being functional. Plush seating, marble countertops and glossy wooden floors has me quickly forgetting where we even are.

An older woman with a pleasant smile emerges from the dining area as she speaks.

"Hello, my name is Jackie. Can I get you all anything to eat? Drink?"

"Do you have any beer?" Henry asks.

"We do," she smiles.

"Then we're in business," he says as he follows her towards a fully decked out bar.

Mary walks alongside him as Cassi and I exchange amused looks. Instead of following, she wanders over to the railing, staring out over the water as the sound of the engines fire up. I can't help but swallow roughly, taking a healthy step away from the edge.

"Step back," I tell her.

She frowns at me, looking over her shoulder.

"Why?"

"The boat is going to start moving. I'm sure we need to take our seats."

Cassi's head tilts to the side in curiosity.

"You're sure? Have you ever been on a boat before?"

"Yes," I snap.

No.

Her green eyes drill into me for a second longer before she smirks.

"You're full of shit. Are you...scared of the water?"

"No," I practically snarl. "I'm not scared of water, I'm not a fan of what lies beneath it. Especially in practically black waters like this," I say as I gesture around us. "Now will you please get away from the edge?"

She raises her hands innocently and steps away from the edge, heading inside the dining area before getting a glass of champagne.

"I'll have the same, thank you, Jackie."

Once we all have our beverages, we all fan out across the boat as we begin to move through the water. I opt for a secure recliner inside the dining area while the others are out on the decks. The view is just fine from in here, though.

I'm catching up on some emails on my phone when I hear someone sit down across from me. I don't have to look up to know who it is, though. I can practically feel them. Like my body knows it's them before even I do.

Not allowing her to distract me from my work, I continue typing out my response when she speaks.

"Are you going to hide in here the whole time? Kinda hard to fish from inside."

"I'll exit the dining room once we have stopped moving."

I hear her mutter something akin to 'big baby' and it has me setting my phone down in irritation.

"You want to know why I don't like the water? I was eight years old and I went out on a boat with my dad. We ended up breaking down and were trapped in the middle of nowhere. He decided to go swim for help and was eaten by a shark right in front of my goddamn eyes."

Cassi's eyes round with horror as she stares at me.

"Are you serious?"

"No, but imagine if I was? You'd feel pretty shitty for judging me."

Her mouth hangs open in shock before I'm assaulted with a pillow. She is smacking me over and over again and I can't help but laugh at her outrage.

"You're such an ass! Just when I started to feel sorry for you! Jesus, you're the fucking worst. So you're dad isn't really dead?"

"Oh no," I say. "He is, it was just too much whisky and cheeseburgers that took him out, though."

She stares at me in disbelief, shaking her head like she's in complete shock.

"Shouldn't judge others. Things aren't always so surface level, bunny."

"Bunny?" she asks with a wrinkle of her nose.

"Yeah, it's your new nickname. I can make them up too."

She scoffs and shakes her head. "Well, could you come up with one that makes sense? That's just stupid."

I cock my head as I lift my glass of champagne.

"Not really. You're a little rope bunny. I shortened it up. Unless you prefer the whole title."

Her cheeks instantly flush a deep red as she drops her eyes, a reaction that I know is a rare one for her.

"I thought we were going to forget it ever happened," she mutters quietly.

I lift a brow to her in question. "Have you forgotten?"

Slowly, her bright eyes come to me and all the answers I needed lay right there. That's what I thought.

"If I'm the rope bunny, you're definitely the rope master," she throws out, like she will somehow gain control of the conversation.

I take a considering sip of my champagne and nod.

"You would know."

Her eyes dilate and that flushing of her cheeks intensifies as she pushes herself to stand, shaking her head as she promptly exits the conversation. I can't help but be a little disappointed that she does, though. I was having fun riling her up.

Chapter Ten
Cassi

I had to walk away. I don't know what kind of game he was playing or is playing or whatever but I want no part of it. I can't fucking believe he got me with the fake dead dad story. Or I guess his dad really is dead, but the fabricated story was wild and had me feeling awful. That's like something I'd pull to prove a point and it has me feeling more than a little irritated.

We cruise for a little while before anchoring off in the middle of the sound. My dad instantly takes his post as lead fisherman, at least that's what I assume he refers to himself as in his head. My mom and I are sipping champagne in two of the lounge chairs overlooking the deck while dad attempts to show Nico how to bait and cast a line.

I can't help but watch Nico, he's so focused, hanging onto every word my dad says like it's the gospel. He strikes me as the type of man who doesn't do anything half ass and is determined to be the best in anything he attempts. Unfortunately, for him, it's looking like fishing isn't one of his strengths.

It takes Nico three separate times before he finally releases the line properly, allowing his bait to sink down into the water. My dad claps him on the shoulder in encouragement but the little wrinkle between Nico's eyebrows tells me he's more than frustrated with himself. Nico reaches over to his right, grabbing two beers from the galvanized ice bin, passing one to my dad before they fall into conversation about Nico's work.

I can't quite make out every word he says, but I don't need to. Watching his mouth move is more than enough for me, it is a gorgeous fucking mouth. I mean, I'm not really a fan of the asshole that's attached to it but still. He's a pretty face to look at, with a wicked tongue, steady hands and a huge—

"Enjoying the view, Cass?" My mom asks.

I startle for a moment, like I'm snapping out of a daze as I look to her.

"Hm?"

She gives me a mischievous smirk that looks far too much like one that I deliver regularly. I've gotta say, I'm not sure I enjoy being on the receiving end of it, though.

"Your sister certainly has excellent taste. Nico is a...fine young man," she says, giving me a knowing look.

I pretend to be unaffected by her words, despite me absolutely freaking the fuck out. I mean, it's not like she knows anything. She's just teasing me, attempting to be playful. Regardless, I want nothing to do with any of it.

"He's easy on the eyes but that personality could use some work," I say with a shrug before taking another sip of my champagne.

My mom's brows furrow as she cocks her head to the side.

"How do you mean?"

Doing my best to avoid her gaze, I set down my drink as I stare out at the water.

"He's just a little surly for my taste, serious. You have to admit, he's kind of an asshole. I mean, look how hard he's trying to impress you guys," I say as gesture around us. "Does he really think money can cover up what he's clearly lacking?"

"Wow, you seem to be really opinionated of someone you met only two days ago. I think you're being a little harsh there sweetheart."

I shrug my shoulders, wanting to be done with this conversation. Unfortunately, my mother doesn't seem to share the same intention.

"He seems good for Carly. He has a good head on his shoulders, stable career. Probably spoils her a little more than she needs if I'm being honest," she muses.

I snort in agreement to that. Yeah, maybe that's actually a con. My sister definitely doesn't need more people treating her like she's god's gift to the earth. She wears that badge proudly every day of her life without any help from anyone.

"They deserve each other," I comment under my breath, not really intending for my mom to hear it. More of just a statement to the universe.

She doesn't agree, though. To be fair, she doesn't disagree either. Instead, she quietly finishes her drink before standing and moving to my dad, plopping herself into his lap. He holds her with one hand easily, somehow simultaneously manning a pole and a beer. Name a more talented man to ever live, go ahead, I'll wait.

Some people can't stand parents that are still so in love with each other. I personally have always found it deliriously romantic. I mean, what could be better than being raised by the perfect example of true honest love? Maybe the only downside to having parents who are so nauseatingly in love is that it is a consistent reminder of what you haven't found yet.

Don't get me wrong, I completely grasp the fact that I literally just turned twenty one. I have plenty of time to find my forever person. Is it so wrong to wish they'd come along already, though?

As if his ears were burning, my phone pings with a text message from Alec.

Alec: How was work, beautiful?

I smile at the screen before typing out my reply.

Me: Absolutely riveting. You?

Alec: We were slammed from the moment I clocked in to when I clocked out. You'd think people would want to get their overpriced mediocre meals elsewhere once in a while.

I let out a laugh at that.

Me: Hey, don't hate on my favorite Italian restaurant. I was just starting to like you again.

Alec: When did you ever stop?

Smirking, I begin typing out my response when my phone is plucked out of my hands. My head whips up to locate the thief, and of course, I'm not at all surprised by the suspect. Nico's eyes trace over the screen, that perma-scowl he wears so well firmly in place before he looks back to me.

"Stop flirting with your boyfriend and come spend time with your dad. He's been trying to get your attention."

I look up to see my dad gesturing towards him, another fishing pole at the ready, presumably for me. Standing to my feet, I reach for my phone as I speak.

"He's my ex-boyfriend," I clarify.

Nico pulls the phone just out of reach as he lowers his face just a half an inch closer to mine.

"You sure about that?" his deep voice husks, almost like it's his attempt at a whisper.

My eyes pause on his, that rich chocolate color practically drowning me before I swallow roughly.

"It wouldn't be your business even if I wasn't," I say before snatching my phone from his meaty paws as I make my way over to my dad.

"Let's do some fishing, pops."

After hours of fishing I caught four blue gill, my dad caught six and one huge bass and Nico caught approximately nothing. Despite his frustrations and ever changing 'technique' the fish wanted nothing to do with him. I bet they could sense his shit personality from down there and said no fucking thanks.

Now we are heading back to the docks, a cooler stocked with fish and a smile on my dad's face that he couldn't wipe away if he tried. He loves being on the water, I swear if he could retire and live on a house boat, he would. I think him and mom would both really like that actually.

Some of my favorite childhood memories are fishing with my dad. Carly came sometimes but each time she did she ruined it with her whining. She didn't like the outdoors, the cold or anything outside of shopping, really. God, would you listen to me? I make her sound like a high maintenance vapid bitch.

...but I mean, if the shoe fits.

Mom and dad wandered inside the boat a little bit ago, though calling this mammoth a boat is honestly an insult. We could be out here for days and I don't think we could see every room on this thing. Okay, that's a complete exaggeration but you get my point.

I wandered around for a bit before I came to the bow. The breeze is gentle but constant, blowing my hair behind my shoulders as the sun begins to dip into the water for the night.

"Why do you insist on tempting fate?" Nico asks

I look over my shoulder to see him glaring at me, arms crossed while maintaining a healthy distance from the railing.

"Why do you insist on being such a coward?"

He scoffs at that but doesn't say more, and I don't feel the need to fill up the empty space with useless words. So, instead, I focus back on the sunset. My hands that have been gripping the railing loosen as I throw my arms out by my sides in the wind.

"You're being reckless," he warns.

I shake my head and smile to the sky, loving the feel of the ocean breeze through my hair.

"This is the part where you're supposed to reassure me that I'm flying."

"I'm not going to recreate a scene from a movie about a horrific watercraft accident."

Spinning around to face him, I frown.

"You really do have a stick up your ass, you know that, right?"

He doesn't respond, just continues staring at me with that impatient scowl. Before I can think better of it, a wicked thought crosses my mind and I rest my hands onto the railing once more before lifting myself up to sit on it.

"Would you catch me if I fell, Nico? Would you put that grumpy asshole schtick to the side in order to save m—"

My words are cut off as we hit a rough wake, the whole ship dipping to accommodate for a moment. Before I even start to lose my grip, he's there, closing the distance between us in a flash before scooping me into his arms and plastering me to his chest.

Instinctively, I wrap my legs around his torso and hold onto him tighter than what is probably needed. My heart is jack hammering inside my chest as I take several deep breaths before slowly pulling back to see him.

He's already looking at me, a wild look in his eyes as he looks me over from head to toe like he is expecting to find an injury or something.

"Are you okay?" he asks, his low voice rumbling through his chest and practically into mine.

"Yeah," I rasp.

"I told you that you were being reckless," he says, though his words hold no heat and his eyes hold no judgment.

I can't quite name the look on his face. It's just...intense, and something in me never wants to look away.

"You did," I agree,

"You could have gotten hurt," he says, his arms tightening around me almost instinctually as he speaks.

Swallowing roughly, I nod my head in response before chewing on the inside of my lower lip. An action he notices immediately. Nico's deep brown eyes snap down to my lips, a lustful look filling his features as his own part just slightly.

"You can put me down now, I'm safe," I say carefully.

Nico stares at my mouth for another moment before he blinks once and slowly lowers me to my feet. I won't deny that I take my time unwinding my arms from around his neck before I look up at him.

"Thanks."

He nods but doesn't speak, his intense gaze holding true. As bad as it would be, I want to push the limits, see how reacts, how I would react. The tension between us is palpable, even when we're arguing, it's always there. It's like the forbidden fruit dangling in front of one another, and with each resistance, a guarantee that the fruit sweetens with each time. I can practically taste it and based on the way he's wetting his lips, I'd say he is right there with me.

Knowing that if I act on my impulses, we will be fucking bare ass right here on the bow with my parents and the crew to witness, I take a step back and force a laugh.

"Are you painfully aware of all the rope that is within reach around us or is that just me?" I joke, hoping to ease the tension.

As if my words snap him out of whatever kind of trance he was in, his surly frown returns as his eyebrows furrow.

"What?"

"Rope. We're on a boat, you teased me about being a rope bunny. I teased you about being a rigger. I'm easing the sexual tension with a joke, get it?"

Nico takes a moment to respond before he tersely shakes his head.

"There is no tension."

Before I can respond, he storms off, and I don't bother to stop him because honestly, I'm not able to take a full breath until he is finally out of my vicinity. He can lie to himself all he wants, there is tension, and if he doesn't get the fuck back to Boston, and fast, well. I don't know what's going to happen. Whatever it is, though, I can only imagine it's going to be horrible.

And satisfying.

Definitely satisfying.

Chapter Eleven
Nico

I barely spoke to anyone once we docked. I thanked the crew, tipped them all heavily and went straight to the car. Cassi and her parents are a little slower behind me and I really fucking hate that I don't have my own car here. Maybe I should rent something, even if it's for a day or two. It's not like we will be here for much longer. This was a mistake to begin with. We should have gone home as planned.

Cassi wraps her arms around herself as the evening wind picks up, gusting through the parking lot and tossing her red hair over her shoulder. Instinctually, I take a step towards her. Like I can block the wind for her, like I can take away the cold in her bones. Then I take a breath and come to the realization that's a really stupid fucking thing to even think let alone do.

"I've got dinner in the slow cooker at home, Cass. You coming?" Mary asks as Cassi heads to her car.

"No, Alec texted me. Wants to grab dinner. I'll see you guys tonight."

"Drive safe, sweetheart," Henry says.

She smiles and nods as she opens her door, stepping inside before casting me a look.

"Thanks...for the boat. It was fun."

I don't have any words, none that are appropriate or eloquent or make any relative goddamn sense. So, instead of answering, I give her a terse nod. She returns it with a tight lipped smile before she's sliding into the drivers seat and taking off a few moments later to god knows where. With Alec.

I'm not sure what it is about the guy that makes me want to punch him in the fucking mouth. Maybe it's just the fact that he seems like the type of guy who has never had it, and is long over-due. Something is off about him. He's too...friendly, convenient. Or maybe I just fucking hate the idea that the little shit has had his cock inside Cassi.

That would be crazy, though, right? Crazy to be psycho jealous over an ex-boyfriend to a girl that isn't even my girlfriend. She's my girlfriend's sister. Admittedly, one that I've slept with, but still. I have no claim over her, and she should have no power over me. My head is clearly fucked up and I need to just go lie down or have a drink or do fucking something to shake off this weird mood that has suddenly taken over me.

"I swear, it's like she's back in high school all over again," Mary laughs lightly as Henry holds the door open for her.

She slides into her seat as I sit in the back and tilt my head.

"What do you mean?"

Mary turns in her seat to face me with a smile.

"When Cassi and Alec were together they were inseparable. We'd almost never see her. Mornings and nights, that's about it."

Henry nods his agreement as he fires up the car.

I frown at that. "Didn't that bother you?"

Mary shrugs. "She was in love. She always told us where she was and who she was with and Alec is a good kid from a good family."

She pauses for a moment, wincing with a shake of her head. "I can't believe his parents are gone. The poor thing has nobody. No one."

A feeling I'm uncomfortably familiar with, and Mary seems to sense it too. Her eyes widen slightly, and she reaches her hand out to me in apology.

"Nico, I'm so sorry. I know you lost your parents and—"

"It's okay, Mary. I get what you're saying, and you're not wrong. It's hard to grow up without a family, no matter how old we are."

She nods sympathetically before patting my knee.

"Well, you've got one now."

I smile at her words in thanks and nod as she turns around. I really like them, more than I anticipated. I knew that Carly was the spoiled one of her family, but I didn't realize everyone besides her would be so...kind, welcoming, warm.

Too many thoughts are buzzing through my mind, far too many for my comfortability so doing my best, I shove them all to the side and focus on the city lights zooming beside us as we head to the Fischer family home.

Once we get back to the house, Mary finishes prepping dinner and Carly shows up just in time. When she leans in to kiss my cheek, for once in the last week or so, I don't pull away. Forcing myself to lean into her affection is good, it's what I need or at the very least what I should do. The whole point we came out to Seattle was to meet her family. Because we have been together for so long and if our relationship would ever go any further, introductions were absolutely the next step. Somewhere along the way that idea got distorted, it happened between the breakup at the airport and having the most incredible night with her sister if I had to guess.

I know, I know. I'm a real fucking class act.

"Did you have a good time with Hannah and the girls?" Mary asks Carly as she begins setting the table.

Surprisingly, Carly lends a hand, taking the plates from her and setting them at the dining room table.

"Yeah, we went to that new spa that opened in town. We drank way too much champagne, laughed way too hard. It was perfect," she says with a smile as her eyes move to mine.

There is a sparkle in them. One I haven't seen in a long fucking time. Maybe it's just because she's buzzed, maybe it's because she was able to get grounded at her roots. Or maybe it's a one off, honestly, you never know with this girl.

"What about you guys?" Carly asks, her eyes coming to me. "How was the boat?"

I nod my head once as I respond.

"Good."

"It was better than good!" Mary cuts in. "Nico rented an entire yacht. Can you believe it? We had wait staff coming out of our ears with delicious food and drinks! And your father caught so many fish!"

"It was a great day," Henry agrees as he carefully takes the job of scooping the hot food out of the slow cooker and into a serving dish.

"Well, had I known it was a yacht I probably would have come," Carly says, though her words lack the usual bratty under-tone. Instead, she's smiling to me like it's an inside joke of sorts. Like I would find her comment amusing. I don't know what the hell is going on with her but it's putting me on edge. Did the spa do body transplants or something? Because I suddenly am very unfamiliar with my girlfriend of three years.

I grab the pan of fresh rolls out of the oven before Mary can attempt to before I gesture towards the table.

"Sit, I've got it."

She smiles at me gratefully and moves to take her seat, Henry sitting beside her next. Carly takes a seat as well as I set the rolls onto a serving plate and bring it over. There are two open chairs at the table, one across from Carly and one beside her. Though instinctually, I want to go for the further one, I decide to sit beside her. The simple gesture isn't lost on her, either. She practically beams up at me, pressing another kiss to my cheek before her hand rests on my thigh.

Guilt and confliction war inside me. It feels wrong to have her lips on my skin when mere hours ago I almost snapped and crushed my own to her sister. It feels wrong to sit beside her willingly because I know that if Cassi was here, I'd have taken every opportunity to sit beside her. She's not here, though. She's out. With *Alec*. And I'm here, with Carly. As we both should be.

Dinner goes by actually quite lovely. Henry and Mary tells us some stories about when they were young and living in this house and Henry tried his hand at some do it yourself handy work around the house. Suffice it to say, they ended up calling a service each time. Carly also surprisingly stayed quiet for most of the dinner. She didn't feel the need to fill the space with empty jabbering, she didn't need the spotlight on her. She was...nice. It felt good. Like I hadn't wasted the last three years of my life with an ungrateful brat.

After, she helped clear the table and Henry and I tackled the dishes before the girls went to the back deck and chatted. Once we were finished, we joined them and I'm proud to announce I only found my eyes watching the door, waiting for Cassi to be back from her *date* three times. Which, if you think about it, isn't that much.

Eventually, Mary and Henry head to bed for the night and say goodnight to us before leaving Carly and I alone, bathed in moonlight and porchlight. Her hand comes to my thigh as she rests it gently and smiles.

"That was really nice of you to take my family out today. You didn't have to."

I shrug.

"It was nothing. I enjoy them...your dad especially," I tack on.

Carly grins, a smile that reminds me of a thousand memories as she nods.

"He's the best, and he adores you too. So does my mom, she might even be more in love with you than I am," she laughs.

She sobers for a moment before shrugging one shoulder.

"My sister, she's a hard one. She's hard to get along with honestly. I wouldn't break my back trying to please that one if I were you."

I don't respond because this suddenly feels like dangerous territory and with us having a nice night, so far, I don't want to ruin it.

"I want you to know, Nicholas, how much I appreciate you. I've never taken our relationship for granted but I also don't think I've been as communicative for my appreciation of you as I could have been. I'm sorry."

Skepticism has officially entered the conversation. This has to be an act of sorts. She's laying it on too thick. Too sincere for Carly. What kind of spa was that again? Did she spend time in the exorcism room?

"I know, you might not be able to ignore all of this shit I've pulled over the last few years but I want to start over, if that's okay," she continues, her eyes practically glittering with emotion as she looks at me.

Before I can respond, she's slowly standing, slipping into my lap before winding her arms around my neck. I don't wrap my arms around her to hold her closer, then again I don't push her away either. Instead, I stay neutral allowing her to control this moment as my rattled inner thoughts scramble to decide what to make of all of this.

Carly smiles at me once before leaning in, her pillowy soft lips brushing against mine. I'm unreceptive for one kiss, two, and when her lips pull against my own for a third time, I decide what the hell. Wrapping one arm around her back while using my other hand to cup the back of her head to me, I crush myself against her.

She moans into my mouth as my tongue comes to twirl around her tongue, her pussy grinding against my hardening cock. I haven't kissed her in what feels like so long, I'd almost forgot what she tastes like. Biting her lower lip, I push us to stand as Carly wraps her legs around me and I carry us through the back door, across the house and up the stairs.

I open her bedroom door easily in between kisses, kicking it shut behind me before dropping her onto the bed. She falls with a plop and I take advantage of her disorientation, pushing up her mini skirt to her hips, leaving her only exposed with her white lace thong. Grabbing her legs, I push them back so I can see her spread open for me and my cock throbs as I do. Fuck. She may be an entitled bitch but she has a beautiful pussy not as beautiful as her sister's, but that's the fucked up thoughts I won't be allowing tonight.

Tonight is all about me and Carly. My girlfriend. No one else will enter the conversation or my head. Tonight, I'm putting everything into this, to us, and I'm finally going to shove that stupid fucking One Night Stand out of my head.

Grabbing the string of her thong, I pull it to the side before leaning forward, licking my way through her before my tongue pauses on her clit. She lets out a low moan before quickly covering her face with a pillow as I revel in the taste of her. I proceed to eat her fucking soul out of her cunt before she begins wiggling and squirming against me. I feel the moment she has her first orgasm of the night. Her legs tremble, her moans turn to a whimper before her pussy throbs. I lick every drop of her release up before moving to stand.

Carly looks to me in disorientation, half naked as I begin undoing my pants. It takes me no time at all to get naked and when I am, I begin stroking my cock as I look at her. She's beautiful, stunning, every man's wet dream. When my eyes close for half a second, though, I don't see her. A messy head of red curls and rope digging into soft pink flesh comes to the forefront of my mind and it's so goddamn irritating.

Gritting my jaw, I force my eyes open, practically demanding my head to stay in the moment. Cassi is probably getting raw fucked over the side of that stupid fucking motorcycle. She is not here and is not yours.

Carly sits up, easily sucking my cock into her throat without me even having to ask her. She knows what I like. There is no discovery between us, no learning. We've been together long enough to know what each needs, and she does a fine job of sucking the life out of my cock.

Her slurps and moans are hot as fuck, and have my cock jerking in her throat. Even more so when I tip my head back and close my eyes and yet again that green eyed redhead appears, now the total cause of my pleasure.

I could keep fighting it, or I could succumb to whatever the hell my subconscious is conjuring currently. It's just fantasy. I'm fucking my girlfriend, so what's the harm in indulging, right? When I've decided to say fuck it, I pull away from her and speak without looking.

"Hands and knees, poke that ass out for me."

She does as I ask, practically scrambling to her hands and knees before I line myself up to her. I push inside her pussy slowly, inching my way in as her head falls forward with a satisfied moan. Even better. Now all I see is a smooth back, a round ass and my cock buried inside. She could be anyone beneath me and now, she is. I keep my eyes closed as I begin fucking her, reliving the little sounds and faces Cassi made that night in the club, doing my best to replace Carly's in real time. It's shocking how fast my mind is able to do so, like it takes no effort at all.

The idea of being inside Cassi again is one that fills me with confliction and pleasure, so much goddamn pleasure. Fucking her again is like having a drink of water after sixty days in the desert.

It's like coming up for air when I was left abandoned on the ocean floor. And this is me just imagining the woman beneath me is her, I can't even comprehend what it would feel like to actually take her again.

Not that I'll ever find out.

This is fantasy.

It's not real. It's just a release.

"Nicholas," she moans.

"Call me, Nico," I grit through clenched teeth.

"Nico, oh my god! Nico!" she cries out.

"Yeah, good girl. Come for me again," I say as I lean forward, rubbing tight circles against her clit.

She bucks at the feeling but I only press myself against her deeper, not allowing her to move an inch as our bodies work together until I pinch her clit. She cries out, a cry far too loud to not be heard through every inch of the house. Right now, I couldn't give a fuck, though.

I drive into her deeper, practically jack hammering her gspot before I find my own relief. My balls draw up before my cock begins to jerk, euphoria washing over me as I let out ragged breaths with my orgasm.

Once I'm finished, I collapse on top of her and we lay in the dark for several moments. When I finally decide to get up, I look to see Carly is already asleep, a satiated smile on her face. Slowly, I pull out of her before standing and making my way to the bathroom. I clean myself up a bit and grab a pair of boxers sliding them on when a series of dings comes from Carly's purse. Followed by another set. Jesus, I cannot sleep with that shit.

Moving to her purse, I reach inside and pull out her phone, flicking it to silent when my eyebrows pull together. Text messages appear on the front screen of her phone, what looks to be a group chat absolutely blowing up with the most recent from Hannah.

Hannah: Did the whole obedient girlfriend thing work for you, Carly?

Hannah: Please tell me you're getting dicked down right now.

Hannah: If you are, I'll be accepting my thanks in the form of booze or cash.

Hannah: I told you, these powerful men just want to feel taken care of. Lay it on thick about being grateful and they'll eat it up every time...and you up! Hahahaha

I scoff, tossing her phone back into her bag as I shake my head. Makes sense that it was just an act, it was too much of a personality change to be anything else. Shaking my head, I scrub a hand through my hair as I grab a pillow and a blanket and head for the couch. No way in fuck am I sleeping in bed with a snake like her.

Chapter Twelve
Cassi

"You have to choose or your whole family will die," Alec says.

I let out an exaggerated sigh. "Alec, I'm sorry but that's the stupidest thing I've ever heard. Why would my whole family die if I don't choose if I'd rather stick my hand in a hornet's nest or fight a bear."

"It's part of the game," he insists.

I can't help but roll my eyes as I line myself up to the dartboard and sink it into a triple twenty. Writing down my mark, I reach for the beer to my left as we continue to play the dumbest version of would you rather in this little dive bar.

"Fine, I'd probably take the hornet's nest."

He looks at me like he's disappointed and shakes his head.

"What! I'm allowed to make my own choice," I laugh in outrage.

"Well, yeah, but I thought you were going to choose right."

My eyes bug out of my head. "You want me to fight a bear? A fucking bear?"

He shrugs, his eyes running over me slowly. "You could take him."

I laugh at his ridiculousness as he begins to chuckle before lining up for his shot. He misses pathetically so and I can't help but tease him a bit.

"God, is it painful to be losing by *this* much?"

"I'm slow playing it," he shrugs as I grab my darts and throw mine.

I get a sixteen, an eighteen and a one. Still doing better than he is.

"You're no playing it, Alec," I laugh.

He smiles, pushing his golden blond hair out of his face as he nods.

"Alright, I'll make you a deal. Sudden death. First person to make a bullseye wins."

I tilt my head to the side and smirk.

"Oh yeah? And what do I get when I win?"

"Whatever you want," he says with a shrug.

I think on this for a moment. I mean, this is a high pressure moment. I can't waste this opportunity.

"Your leather jacket," I smirk.

He looks down at it in faux outrage.

"Don't you have enough of my jackets? I'm fairly certain you have enough from high school to make an entire exhibit."

"I don't have one since you got...taller," I say as I look him up and down.

He has gotten taller, and wider, more muscley. His jaw line is sharper, his eyes more observant. Alec was cute in high school, now he's fucking hot.

Alec closes the distance between us, taking his time as he lets his words draw out like he has all the time in the world.

"Yeah? Taller? Is that what I've gotten, Cass?"

I swallow and nod once, causing him to grin as he comes toe to toe with me. Slipping his hand into my hair, he begins gently playing with it in a way that has my eyes fluttering closed for just a moment.

"Deal, if you win you get my jacket, but if I win..." he pauses, forcing my eyes to open and meet his gaze.

I look to him expectantly and he smiles down at me with a look that is equal parts sweet and spice.

"Then I get to take you home and show you how much I've missed you."

My breath stalls in my chest. I don't know why it does. It's not like Alec and I haven't slept together a million times. He took my virginity for fucks sake. He's only gotten hotter and I'd be a liar if I haven't been a little curious if he still has that...touch about him. Maybe even some new moves from the years. Honestly, there is only one thing holding me back and it's a pair of deep brown eyes flashing into my head. I haven't been with anyone since him. If I sleep with Alec, it almost feels like I'm erasing the memory completely. Like it never happened, which actually is a good thing, right? Right.

"Okay, deal," I breathe out with a nod.

Alec's mouth hooks up in the left corner, delivering a devastatingly delicious smile. He takes advantage of how close we are, pressing his lips to my own before pulling away.

"Ladies first," he whispers against my mouth.

Butterflies rush through me as I nod and grab a dart, blowing out a breath as I line myself up. I'm torn on making it or missing on purpose. This guy doesn't have a chance in beating me and I am more than curious to find out if we have that spark still. Then again, I'm extremely competitive and absolutely hate to lose so fuck that. He has to earn it.

Tossing the dart, it spirals in the air for a moment before sinking into the green bullseye. Not technically a full bullseye but it's close enough. I shout in celebration as I begin victory dancing while Alec laughs. He nods his defeat, slowly peeling off his leather jacket as he wraps it around me. I take it happily, not so subtly inhaling the musky scent of leather and him.

"Congratulations, so glad to see that you're still a miserable winner," he teases.

I grin at that and nod. "I'll never change, baby!"

His smile lifts even higher. "I hope not."

Picking up a dart, he keeps his eyes on me and that smile on place as he lines up without looking and sinks his dart straight into the red bullseye. Like directly in the middle. It couldn't be more in the middle if he fucking tried, and he did it without looking.

My jaw is on the floor as I turn to face him, a shit eating grin donned across his features.

"Are you...you fucking hustled me," I accuse.

"In my defense it was for a good cause," he says as his grin turns guilty.

"What's that? My panties?" I scoff.

"No," he says as if he's offended. "What's under them."

I smack his arm and he laughs before shaking his head.

"I'm teasing, Cass. You know we don't have to do anything you're not comfortable with."

I let out a dramatic sigh like I'm so inconvenienced as I shake my head.

"I'm a woman of my word. C'mon Alex Thompson, let's dust off your dick and give you that orgasm you've been waiting for since you left me."

He laughs at that and smiles, grabbing me into his arms as I turn to walk towards my car.

"I have been waiting for this ever since we broke up. You may have not been my last but you've always been my first, Cass. You've always been here," he says as he rests a hand over his chest.

I melt, okay? Like into a fucking puddle in the middle of this sticky and dark dive bar. Wouldn't you? Jesus this guy is good.

"No need to lay it on thick, you're already getting laid

tonight," I say with a dramatic eyeroll, attempting to cover up the massive melting that is going on over here. Alec laughs and presses a kiss to my cheek before grabbing his motorcycle helmet and dropping a twenty on the table we were using for a tip as we head out of there.

I follow Alec to his childhood home, though I could have easily led the way. I practically lived here all of high school. Even when my parents thought I was out with Arianna and Naomi, I was always here.

The driveway is empty, though, the house dark. It's such a stark contrast from how I remember it. So full of life and love. I can't believe his parents are really gone, and his grandmother is on her way as well. When she's gone, he will have...no one. My chest aches for him at the idea of that. Of how unfair it all is.

When we park, Alec swings off his bike and comes to my door, opening it for me as I shut the car off. He holds out his hand for me and smiles as he intertwines our fingers.

"We don't have to sneak you in the back like before."

I smile at him.

"I mean, I'm not sure I know how to use your front door, but I'll give it a go."

Alec laughs as he unlocks the house and turns on a few lights before shutting the door behind me. God, it's just like I remember it. Perfectly preserved in time.

"Do you want some water or anything? I think I have—"

I rest my finger on his lip to stop his hosting habits as I shake my head.

"A deal is a deal," I say as I head up the stairs, his leather jacket still wrapped around me.

His heavy feet follow after me quickly as I turn and head for his bedroom. The only new thing in here is that there is a bigger bed, meaning less walking space. Which, honestly is fine because what else do you do inside your bedroom but sleep, really?

Alec steps inside the room behind me, shutting the door as he closes the distance between us, his hands cupping my face tenderly as his breath brushes against my lips.

"I'm giving you an out, Cass. We don't have to do this."

I raise an eyebrow as I take a step out of his hold. Steadily, I shrug off his jacket before peeling off my shirt. I unclasp my bra and push down my shorts and panties until I'm standing completely naked.

His eyes roam over me like a man who has been starved, lust completely drowning any color he used to have.

"Does it look like I want an out?" I ask.

Alec practically pounces on me in the next moment. Our mouths battle for dominance as I fall backwards onto the bed, his body quickly covering mine. He tears his mouth from my own, peppering my neck with rushed and passion fueled kisses before his teeth nip at the sensitive skin. I gasp at the feeling and can literally feel his smirk against my neck as he does it again and again, sucking on it as if that will ease the bite.

"You're gonna give me a fucking hickey," I moan on a laugh.

He pulls away for a moment, those blue eyes boring into mine as he smirks.

"Good, now there will be no question that you're mine."

Alec begins kissing his way down my body before nudging my legs apart. He makes himself perfectly at home as he tosses my legs over his shoulders and goes face first into my pussy. He groans in pleasure almost louder than I do. Almost. Like no time has passed, his tongue eagerly tastes me, swirling and flicking through me as he slips a finger inside.

"Fuck, Alec," I moan.

"I love my name on your lips," he mumbles against my clit, sending a rush of pleasure through me.

"More," I beg, winding my hand through his thick hair.

Doing as I say, he slips a second finger inside me before he begins massaging my gspot. Pleasure is building inside me and I know I don't have long before I come undone. I don't want to come like this, though. I want rough, raw, passion filled fucking. I want to be pinned down and made into his own personal sex doll.

"Fuck me, please," I beg.

Alec comes up for air, releasing my clit with a wet pop before he smiles. He wastes no time in pushing off his pants and boxers, discarding his shirt in the next moment before he lays on his back.

"Ride me."

Disappointment flickers inside me. Not because I don't enjoy being on top. It's fine, I'm just not really a dominant person in bed. I think maybe I was more so a switch when Alec and I dated. After I got a little more experience, though, I quickly realized how much I crave being a sub. How good it feels to relinquish power to someone else and then experience how they take care of you in reward.

It's not Alec's fault, though. I haven't communicated that, he's falling into old routines where I was almost always the initiator. He's rekindling something, reliving it, and just because I get on top this time doesn't mean it'll be every time. Hell, I don't even know if there will be more times after this. I know he said that there is no question that I'm his, but I'm not sure how that sits with me. Which is honestly so unfair because do I have any reasoning as to why I wouldn't want to give it another try with him? No, not really.

"You okay?" he asks, and of course he did. I've been spiraling in my own head about my sexual desires and our impending label for at least a minute. Way to make things awkward as hell, Cass.

Climbing on top of Alec, I slowly lower myself down onto him and he moans in approval. The feeling of him inside me is amazing and I draw back up when I realize something.

"Condom," I practically choke out.

Alec's eyes widen for a moment before he reaches for a bedside table, fumbling around before grabbing one. He tears it open in no time and pushes me off for a moment before rolling the latex down his cock. When he's ready, he pulls me back down onto him.

I'll admit, it really doesn't feel as good as going bare. You know what else doesn't feel good? STDs.

Though I'm on birth control, I don't know what Alec has been up to over the last few years, or even the last few weeks. It's a topic we will obviously have to discuss later since my dumbass just sat right on down with no questions.

That's a later thing, though.

I begin gyrating my hips as my hands come to rest on his chest for stability. Alec's hands settle on my waist and he holds me tight as he helps guide my movements.

"Fuck, Cass. You feel so good. I've missed you so goddamn much."

"I've missed you," I pant.

I've been on top for roughly seven seconds and I'm already exhausted. I'm convinced it's more strenuous for girls than it is for guys because goddamn, being on top kinda sucks.

Pushing through the burn in my thighs, I keep on pace as my eyes fall closed on a moan.

God. This feels so good. I've needed this release, this pleasure. Now that I have it, I can finally erase Nico from my head once and for all.

Though, thinking of Nico in this moment was probably the worst thing that I could have done. Instantly, my mind conjures his face. That barely there smile, those intense brown eyes. His large hands, my god. I never thought I would be attracted to hands but watching them tie rope effortlessly, seeing the way he grips my skin firmly, keeping me in place until I'm exactly where he desires me. Fuck, it's like a drug, and my pleasure doubles from just the thought of it.

By it's own free will, my mind keeps playing a fucking highlight reel from that night with Nico. The feel of his lips on my skin, his touch, the look in his eyes when I gave myself over to him so completely. The tension, the aching, the pleasure.

Before I know what I'm doing, I'm falling over the edge, riding the cock inside me like it's Nico and I'm desperate for just one more time with him.

"Oh my god. Fuck! Yes!" I moan as I fall over the edge, circling my hips over and over to pull out every ounce of pleasure possible.

"Cassi," he calls out beneath me, instantly shifting my reality.

My eyes fly open as understanding dons on me. That wasn't the deep gravely voice I've become way too familiar with these last few days. That was an old one from the past, a familiar one. Alec.

He smiles up at me like he just had the best time of his life, meanwhile my stomach turns in an instant at the realization of what I've done. I fuck faced him. I had sex with him imagining he was someone else. I'm despicable, I'm disgusting. I'm....

"That was amazing," Alec smiles as he gently rolls me off of him, wrapping his arms around me tightly like we have all the time in the world.

"Yeah," I rasp, struggling for my smile to meet my eyes.

He can tell too. His grin begins to slip as his gaze fills with concern. Doing my best to slip on a content smile, I press a gentle kiss to his lips that seems to lower his guard.

"I have work in the morning, I should probably head home."

Disappointment touches his features but it doesn't last long before he nods.

"Let me get dressed and I'll walk you out."

I nod as he disappears into the bathroom while I get dressed as fast as humanely possible. I feel dirty, ashamed and so morally corrupt.

By the time Alec is out of the bathroom, condom disposed, I'm already dressed and heading for the door. He barely has time to grab a pair of boxers before he's chasing me down the stairs and to the front door. I'm barely able to make it to my car door before his hand comes to rest on my car.

"So, that's it, just gonna hump and dump me?" he teases.

My eyes come to his and find that he's one thousand percent kidding. It still doesn't erase the ugly guilt that is gnawing at my insides.

"I'm sorry," I say, leaving it open ended because I'm sorry for way more than leaving quickly.

"I'm kidding, Cass. As long as we're good. Are we good?" he asks, forcing my eyes to his.

I give him a small smile and a nod which allows his shoulders to relax fully.

"Good. Text me when you get home, okay?"

"I will," I say as he leans in to kiss me.

I don't pull away, though I don't engage too much either. When we break apart, I give him a smile and a nod before slipping into my car. Alec watches me start the engine and back out of the driveway, giving me a slow wave as I take off down the road.

My house isn't too far from his which means I'm not nearly done mentally berating myself by the time I pull into my driveway. So stupid. I was having a nice night, with a good guy, and then Nico fucking Sanders had to come along and ruin everything per usual.

Actually, to be fair, I think I kinda ruined everything for him originally.

You know what, fuck that. I didn't ruin anything. I'm the one who has been single the whole time. He's the slimy loser. Fuck him. What was I thinking? Defending a man? Who have I become?

Slamming my car door shut a little harder than necessary, I walk up to the front door, unlocking it quickly before stepping into the dark house. Glancing at my phone I see that it's just after midnight and I have to be up for work at five thirty. Awesome.

Moving to the kitchen I flick on the light to grab a protein bar or something from the cabinet when movement comes from my left. I practically jump out of my skin as I let out a shriek and see a disheveled looking Nico on the couch. His hair is pushed up in an untamed way I haven't seen before, his eyes barely open as he squints to me.

Seriously? Half asleep and he still looks like he belongs on the cover of a magazine. He's so fucking annoying.

"What the fuck? What are you doing?" he grouches.

"What am I doing? Getting a snack, what are you doing sleeping on the couch?"

He just glares at me, slowly wiping the sleep from his eyes as he stands.

"I figured it was better for the night."

"Better than sleeping with my witch of a sister? Well, can't blame you there. At least you've woken up to the devil in your bed," I scoff as I open a cabinet and rifle around until I find what I'm after.

The chocolate peanut butter goodness is practically calling my name but I don't get to unwrap it before my neck is being ripped to the side, two large hands holding me in place.

"What the fuck is that?" Nico practically snarls.

I'm barely able to look at him with the way he has my neck craned but I'm able to see his nostrils flared and his jaw clenched tight before his eyes come to me. It takes me a moment to figure out what he's referring to before it dons on me.

The hickey.

"What does it look like?" I say with a shrug as I push myself out of his hold.

He lets me go easily as his hands return to his sides, balling up tighter and tighter by the moment as he speaks.

"I know what a fucking hickey is. What I want to know is who gave it to you?"

"How is that any of your business?" I challenge with a lazy raise of my brow.

Nico's jaw tenses once more before he blows out an irritated breath.

"It was that little prick, wasn't it?"

"If by little prick, you mean my ex-boyfriend, then no."

Nico's brows furrow. "No?"

"Yeah, no. As in, no, I won't be answering your out of pocket line of questioning, but thank you so much for playing," I say with a roll of my eyes as I step past him.

Or at least, try to step past him.

His wide body blocks my escape easily, taking step by step until my back hits the wall. Nico's hands come to cage me in, his head angled down to keep eye contact with me.

"So, what? You come strolling in after midnight looking freshly fucked by that little nobody?"

My face screws up at that. "What is that supposed to mean?"

He scoffs as me as he shakes his head.

"C'mon, Cassi. You could do a lot better than that guy. What does he have going for him? Does he have a nice pension at the fucking Olive Garden rip off? I'm sure his salary is substantial and his real estate assets are probably overwhelming," he says with a sarcastic drill.

I blink at him slowly like he's stupid, because he sounds like it right now.

"Do you honestly think money or assets would factor into my decision of who I fuck, even a little? Do you truly believe that is how a persons worth is measured?"

His misplaced anger seems to ebb for a moment or two before I'm the one to scoff.

"Maybe that is how your world operates but that's not how I live my life. I'm far more interested in literally anything else besides how many zeros someone has in their bank account. Stop projecting your weird elitist shit on everyone else and go crawl back to my gold digger sister."

I go to take a step away but he matches my move, blocking me in once more. His eyes haven't left mine, honestly, they feel like they never will as he stares at me in silence for several seconds.

"I can't," he says, his raspy voice practically rumbling the walls.

"Can't what?"

Those deep brown eyes come to me, so much intensity in them it's almost hard to breathe.

"I can't go back to her when you've infiltrated my goddamn head. You've wormed your way in and I can't fucking get you out," he snaps like he's furious with me.

I'll be honest, it feels validating to know that I have the same effect over him that he does over me. Not like I'm going to share that piece of information willingly, though.

Shrugging a disinterested shoulder, I look away from his heavy eyes as I speak.

"I don't know what to tell you, maybe you should have left for Boston when you had the chance. Or better yet, maybe you should leave now."

I'm met with silence for several moments before I feel a gentle finger press against my chin, slowly forcing my gaze back to his, surprised to find his mouth only inches from mine as he speaks.

"I'm confident there isn't a land far enough where you would escape my thoughts. I could travel to the ends of this world, and it wouldn't be far enough to get you out of my head."

I'm shook to my core, frozen in place. Goosebumps race against my skin and my feet turn to led. How does one respond to that? How do I even know how I want to respond to that?

Nico's eyes scan my own, as if he was searching for something, whatever it is, it seems like he finds it as he leans in closer and closer. So close, that I abandon every bit of freewill or determination I possess as I close my eyes and wait for the inevitable.

Instead of the familiar feeling of his lips on mine, though, I feel his forehead pressed to my own.

"You're going to be the very death of me Cassi Fischer."

Chapter Thirteen
Cassi

I got the hell out of there. I mean, I had to. The moment was too intense, his words were too perfect. I could still feel where Alec sucked on my neck while I rode his cock and there I was standing in my family's kitchen ready to risk it all with my sister's boyfriend. I had no choice, I bolted away from him before he could say one more perfect thing and took off for my room.

I ended up tossing and turning for over two hours before I was finally able to fall asleep. Unfortunately for me, my alarm came way too fast and the deep dark circles beneath my eyes are proof of that.

Despite taking a practically cold shower in hopes it would wake me up, I'm dragging my feet through the house as I put on my makeup with barely open eyes and slip into an outfit for work. Jeans and a short sleeved blouse is more than dressy enough for my boss. He's pretty laid back unless my shirt hangs down a little too low. The man is a prude to say the least, which is odd because I didn't think men had it in them, I thought they were all whores who thought about sex all the time. Not David, though. A little cleavage to him is like garlic to a vampire.

I was grateful I was the first person up this morning but even knowing that, I wasn't going to run the risk of going to the kitchen for anything. I don't need a repeat of last night.

Heading straight for my car, I start it up as I glance at my phone for the first time. A few concerned text messages from Alec because I didn't text him that I was home safe last night. Shit. Guilt gnaws at me as I quickly type out an apology and let him know that I'm on my way to work. His reply comes way too fast to be coincidence. He was waiting for me, and now I feel like a fucking ass.

Alec: I'm glad you made it safe. Have a good day at work. I had the best time last night.

I smile at the text, though I can tell it's not a full smile. It's a tight one, a sad one, because I had a great time last night too...right until we got to his bedroom. It's not that it was bad. I came, he came. It was fine. It was the context behind it, the underlying thoughts and desires that has the encounter soured in my mind. This messy web of feelings, illicit desires mixed in with an old flame has me feeling like I'm brewing up my own personal Molotov cocktail than starting an actual relationship.

I also see that I have a missed text from Naomi and one in our group chat from Arianna saying the cell service is shit out at the family lake but she can't wait to talk to us soon. I heart Arianna's message and decide to Facetime Nay for ease.

Clicking my phone into the window holder, I back out of the driveway as I head to work. The call rings and rings before she finally answers.

"Do you know what time it is?" she rasps.

"Ass crack of dawn, but your alarm goes off in ten minutes anyways."

She glares at me through the phone. Despite the room being practically pitch black, I still see her nose wrinkle in irritation as she wipes the sleep from her eyes.

"You know how blissful those last ten minutes are?" she groans as she rolls over in bed.

"About as good as an orgasm, oh wait, you wouldn't know what that's like, would you?" I ask.

She doesn't respond, just scoffs and shakes her head. I can't help but poke fun from time to time. I mean, she's twenty one and a virgin. By choice too! Guys have been breaking down her door since her ass came in and her tits filled out Freshman year of high school. Still, she's wanted nothing to do with it, or men in general. Ari and I have asked her several times if she's sure she just isn't attracted to men. Nay always says she is, she's just not ready and leaves it at that. Ari drops it but I definitely pick at the subject more than I should, I mean, c'mon. She's gorgeous, and sex is great. My bestie is missing out and she doesn't have to be.

"What has you looking like death this morning? Late night?" she asks, throwing it back to me.

I can't help but enjoy the verbal spar. I like mean Naomi.

"I went out with Alec last night. We went down to Charlies, had a few drinks and then...went back to his house."

"Okay well you could have started with that," Naomi says as she practically presses her face against the screen. "Tell me everything, did you guys do it? Was it as good as it used to be? Better?"

"You sure your delicate virgin sensibilities can handle it?" I tease.

She rolls her eyes as I continue.

"It was...good. Kinda like coming together after a long break. Easy. Everything sort of clicked into place like a puzzle."

Naomi nods. "Well, that's kinda great! You were so in love with Alec. Now you can officially shove your sister's piece of shit boyfriend far out of your head once and for all."

"Yeah," I agree as I keep my eyes on the road.

"Cass," she says gently.

"Sorry, I'm at work. I gotta go," I say before hanging up the phone.

I still have a twenty minute drive but I'm not ready to talk about what happened last night. In my head at Alec's or in the kitchen with Nico. It's messy and confusing and honestly I don't even have any answers to it, nor explanations. It's all just...messy.

Grabbing my phone and my purse, I step out of the car and head for the front door, unlocking it and turning on the lights of the waiting room. A rustling sound comes from the back and I already know it's Maddie who is this morning's opener dental hygienist.

Moving to the break room, I drop my purse in there and poke my head into the back where she is gathering supplies.

"Morning," I say.

"Morning," she calls out before turning to face me. "Oh shit!"

I frown at that. "What?"

"Dude, what story are you using? A curling iron mishap or a vacuum that went rogue? Because your neck is looking sluttttty."

Her words take a moment for my brain to comprehend before I'm rushing to the bathroom and looking in the mirror. Oh fuck. I forgot to cover the hickey. I mean, how could I honestly? The thing is an ugly red and purple monster. Honestly, I know Alec thought he was being cute and possessive but honestly, it screamed high school. People have jobs and lives. No one is marking each other up anymore. At least not for others to see.

"Shit, shit, shit," I mutter as I run for my purse and begin rifling through it.

Sometimes I will have some concealer in here or something. Unfortunately for me, I come up empty.

"I have a scarf I keep forgetting to take home," Maddie offers.

I stare at her blankly. "It's seventy two degrees outside."

She tosses her hands out and shakes her head.

"And your other options areeee? You know if Daniel sees that he's going to send you home."

Letting out an irritated sigh, I hold my hand out and she moves behind me and grabs the purple and grey scarf that has been floating around the breakroom since February. I tie it around me neck and turn to face Maddie for approval. She lets out a choked laugh and shakes her head.

"I mean, paired with the short sleeved blouse and sun streaming in through the doors, it's definitely a look."

I roll my eyes and scoff. "You're a bitch."

She cackles at that as I head to my desk, firing up my computer for the day. She's not actually a bitch. I really like Maddie. She's the perfect work friend. We get along, work well together and she also likes half priced margaritas on Monday down at the restaurant on the corner.

Daniel walks through the door, nodding in greeting before he pauses. His eyes glance to my scarf as a tint of confusion colors his face.

"Is that your scarf that's been in the breakroom all this time?"

"Oh, no. It's Maddie's. I was a little cold and forgot a jacket," I say with a shrug like it's the next obvious solution.

Daniel nods slowly before moving to the back while I turn around in my chair and shake my head.

Once the workday is done, I pull out my phone and see a few missed texts from Alec and my mom.

Alec: How is your day going?

Mom: What time will you be home tonight?

Alec: Are you doing anything tonight?

Mom: We are taking Nico and Carly to Pike Place Market if you want to join us for dinner?

The idea of having dinner with Nico and Carly is enough to have any semblance of appetite gone in a moment. Maybe with a little bit of a buffer, though, it won't be terrible. Besides, two birds one stone. Besides, I can't let Nico think that his behavior or presence has any sort of affect on me. The more unaffected I can behave, the better. So, yeah. A buffer is definitely needed.

I give my mom a quick call to find out where they are at currently before shooting a text to Alec for him to meet us. He agrees almost too quickly and I head for my car before battling traffic through the city towards downtown.

Mom said they already finished up at Pike Place and shot up to Capitol Hill to one of our favorite Mexican restaurants. It takes me at least twice as long as it should to get up there but when I do, I only have to circle the block twice to find an empty parking spot. Lucky me.

I strategically pull my hair to one side, conveniently concealing the rapidly darkening mark that Alec left on my neck. Not like anyone at dinner would care, but it wasn't like I was going to wear Maddie's scarf into the night.

Stepping through the doorway of Poquitos, I spot my parents in the back instantly, excitedly waving to me. I can't help but smile at the absolute dorks they are as I weave my way through the beautiful restaurant. Gorgeous lights, stone flooring and a fireplace warm up the fusion restaurant, creating a warm and comfortable atmosphere. And I could literally eat my bodyweight in their guacamole so, win, win.

Looks like they secured a long table with six chairs. My mom and dad are beside each other with Carly beside my mom and Nico across from her. I hesitate between the two empty seats. Do I take the one beside Nico or the furthest one away? Am I overthinking this? Definitely, it's not like anyone cares where I sit. Wherever I'm most comfortable, right?

As soon as Nico's chocolate eyes look up to me, practically locking in on mine, though, the anxiety inside me only amplifies.

"Sit down," he says.

His words are harsh or brash, but they are firm. It's not quite a command but it isn't a request either. For some reason, I do as he says, slowly sinking into my seat. Conversation picks up organically with my dad asking Nico something but I still can't take my eyes from him because my god I can't figure this man out. He carries such a large presence about him. He's quite yet steady, firm but gentle. He's a fucking anomaly in every aspect and as much as I hate myself for it, I'm completely enamored.

"Do you need something, Cassi?" Carly snarks, snagging my attention from, well, her boyfriend.

My eyes snap to her, embarrassment filling me for half a moment before I decide I don't give a fuck what Carly thinks of me. Kinda makes me want to look at her man more, honestly. Just to piss her off. Though, pissing my sister off is like coming at a hornet's nest with a bat.

"I've got my loving family, what else could I need?" I smile with the biggest fuck you smile.

Smoke practically billows out of my sister's ears and before she can pop off, a hand touches my shoulder. I look up to see Alec smiling down at me.

"Hi everyone," he smiles to the table before pressing a kiss to my forehead as he takes his seat.

Everyone says hello back, except Nico who is staring at my forehead with a glare. His eyes slowly move to Alec, a disinterested look passing across his face before he looks down at the menu.

"So glad you could join us, Alec," my mom smiles.

"Thank you so much for having me," he nods happily.

Our waiter comes over and takes our menus before my dad strikes up conversation with Alec.

"So, you mentioned before that you have a job waiting for you on the east coast. You must be pretty special for them to wait on you like this."

Alec shrugs with a gracious smile.

"I'm really grateful that they have been so understanding during this time. Technically, I've already started onboarding and have begun doing some light training remotely."

"What is the company called again?"

"Sanders & Son. They are based in Boston. Their reputation is impeccable and they are ranked one of the best places to—"

"Are you shitting me?" Nico cuts in.

All eyes turn to him as he stares at Alec with a lethal edge.

"Sorry?" Alec asks, defense sharp on his tongue.

"You work for Sanders &Son? You were hired? Who do you report to?"

Alec's brows furrow in confusion as he looks to me before back to Nico.

"Lawrence Jennings, why?"

"You're the new IT prodigy?" Nico scoffs like he can't believe it.

"I'm sorry, I'm lost," Alec admits.

"Sanders & Son is Nicholas's company," Carly says. "You work for him."

Chapter Fourteen
Nico

Are you fucking kidding me? What are the goddamn odds that the new hire Larry wouldn't stop yammering about is Cassi's ex? Or maybe he's her current. With the fucking bruise left on her neck from his sloppy mouth, who knows what they are.

I can't stop my hand from tightening into a fist in my lap. Awesome. Even when I leave Seattle, I'll have a permanent reminder of *her*. As if there was ever going to be a reality where that wasn't the case but now it'll be a physical reminder. A living breathing string bean piece of shit who has had his mouth, fingers and probably limp dick on or inside her.

"You're kidding!" Mary says, like it's the most wonderful circumstance. "Is that true Nico? Is that your company?"

"Yes," I answer tightly, forcing myself to relax as I look to her.

"Well, looks like Alec has you to thank for being so understanding of his delayed start," Henry says as he takes a sip of his beer.

"Guess so," Alec says before looking behind Cassi, conveniently wrapping his arm around her chair as he looks to me. "Thank you, it means a lot."

My eyes narrow at him. I don't like this kid. At all.

His thumb begins gently rubbing the bare skin of her neck, pushing through the curtain of hair that is strategically hiding the hideous mark he's marred her skin with. It's a taunting gesture, as if he wants my eyes to move towards it, like he wants me to know his claim has been staked. My gaze doesn't falter for a moment, if this little shit thinks he intimidates me for even a second. If I wanted his girl, I could have her. In a heartbeat.

Normally, id think a statement like that with zero hesitation. When it comes to Cassi, though, I can admit that I'm not one hundred percent confident in that statement. It felt like I almost had her last night. Hindsight, I'm grateful she stepped away when she did, because I was two seconds away from picking her up and fucking her raw on top of her mother's kitchen island.

My cock stiffens at the thought of it. Being near her is so goddamn intoxicating. All rational thought and logic flies out the window. Even now, the subtle smell of vanilla and cinnamon is pulled off of her, filling my senses and dulling my mind. It takes everything in me not to lean a little closer and bask in...her.

"Of course, besides, any friend of Cassi's is a friend of mine," I say, pulling Cassi's attention.

I feel her eyes on me and as much as I'm tempted to look down at her, I'm too invested to break this sort of pissing contest her little boy toy has started.

"Appreciate that. Though, Cassi and I are definitely way more than friends these days, right, babe?" Alec asks, pulling her into his side slightly.

She looks visibly uncomfortable, and it takes all of the restraint I possess not to rip her from his grip.

"Uhm," Cassi starts before Mary sweetly cuts in.

"Oh, are you two officially back together?" she asks, a hope tinging her words that instantly rubs me the wrong way.

I can't be the only one that sees this asshat for who he is, right?

"Like we were never apart," Alec answers for Cassi, smiling to Mary. "I knew what I had when we were together. Life had other plans but it also brought her back to me, and now, I won't let her go for anything," he smiles, though his eyes are only on hers for half a second before they come to me.

Before more can be said, our meals come and the table chatter is quickly silenced with the sounds of forks against plates and eating. Once we are finished, Harry attempts to pay the bill, but I beat him by a mile. Thankfully he doesn't put up much fuss, giving me a quiet but appreciative thank you instead.

"Well, I think we are going to head home. Are you two staying out for a bit?" Mary asks Cassi and Alec.

Alec is already nodding as he looks down at her.

"We could go shoot some darts again, or go back to my place and watch a movie?" he asks, his true meaning crystal clear.

I don't even think before I'm speaking.

"Carly and I could go for a round of darts."

Cassi turns to me with disbelief as her eyes move to her sister.

"Since when does Carly play darts?"

"I went to college, Cassi. A lot of the local bars had plenty of dart tournaments."

"You dropped out of college," Cassi highlights.

Carly's face pinches at that as she leans forward across the table.

"And you're the loser who couldn't even get in to anything worthwhile," she snarls.

"Hey," Henry snaps sternly. "Enough."

The table goes quiet for a moment before Alec and Cassi stand. I'm quick to follow as does the rest of the table. We all say our good-byes to Mary and Henry as Carly comes to my side, whining and pulling on my arm like a toddler.

"Baby, I don't want to stay out. I wanted to go home, take a long bath. Maybe have you join me," she smirks.

I can't even pretend to act interested in her. I'm not in the slightest. It was challenging enough to push myself last night but then to immediately realize that it was all a ploy. She's despicable, and I truly don't know why I'm wasting one more second with her.

That's a lie.

I know one reason. One curvy, green eyed red headed reason. If I dump Carly now, there would be no reason to stay in Seattle. Though we are leaving in two days anyways, that's two more days here. With her. Nothing will happen, of course but the idea of leaving before that is...unsettling. I don't like it. Am I staying with my toxic selfish girlfriend so that I have an excuse to spend more time with her sister? Fuck, I guess I am.

"C'mon, we will play a game. Have some drinks, it's almost time to go home. We're on vacation," I persuade, though I don't need to do much convincing. With each word I speak, a smile grows across her face until she's nodding, practically skipping down the road.

"Fine, come on! I know this place with the best slippery nipple shots."

I can't help but let out a short scoff and a shake of my head as Alec and Cassi follow behind Carly, their hands lacing together. Irritation flickers inside me as I look away, scanning our surroundings in attempt to look literally anywhere but right in front of me when we come to this bright pink and purple bar. The music is loud, the décor is over the top and the people inside are eating it the fuck up.

Carly bounces to the counter and orders herself two shots before I come to stand beside her and get a beer. I see Cassi and Alec moving to order separately when I shake my head and gesture for them to order.

"I've got money," Alec says almost defensively.

A smile touches my mouth as I nod.

"My money, it sounds like. Mixed in with some tips? Just

order," I say as I make a spectacle out of pulling my black card out of my wallet. Honestly, for no other reason than to be an asshole.

Cassi takes note of it too and gets an evil grin on her face.

"What's your most expensive bottle?"

The bartender frowns at her before scanning the back wall. He shows Cassi a thirty five year old scotch and she smiles and nods.

"That's perfect. Put it on Tony Stark's tab," she says as she points to me and takes the bottle from the guy.

The bartender looks to me to make sure it's okay and I roll my eyes as I nod and hand him my card.

"Tony Stark?" I ask as I grab a few glasses and follow Cassi and Carly over to an empty table.

"Yeah, if you were blond I'd call you richie rich but I figured with the dark hair and dark eyes and overall unpleasant demeanor, Tony Stark would do," she says.

Alec cackles at that while I shake my head.

"You and your fucking nicknames," I say as I crack open the bottle and pour myself a heavy drink.

Carly knocks back her two shots before looking to me.

"Okay, where is this fucking dart board?"

We all stare at her for a moment blankly before Alec speaks.

"We don't know. You led the way, remember?"

Carly instantly dissolves into a fit of giggles before she nods and stands.

"I forgot. God their drinks are so good. Anyone else need anything?" she asks before moving to the bartender before we could answer.

"There is pool," Alec says as he looks at the empty pool table in the corner.

I shrug as we stand and bring our drinks over there. Alec sets up the table and when Carly comes back, it's time to play.

"Prepare to lose, Sanders," Cassi says as she lines up for her first shot, absolutely crushing two balls into pockets.

My eyebrows lift in surprise as Carly giggles and grabs the stick.

"My turnnnn!"

Jesus she's a lightweight.

She doesn't even hit the ball, she misses it completely, shrugs and bounces over to a group of girls that are dancing in the corner. Alec watches her go, shaking his head with a laugh before he takes his turn. Overall, we are all pretty evenly matched, but of course I'm playing solo so the fact that we are currently neck and neck means that I'm way better than that little shit, right? Right.

With each play, the contents of that bottle of scotch dwindle, really between Cassi and I. Alec only had one glass before saying he has to drive his motorcycle home. I'm gonna be getting a ride, though, so I'm saying fuck it and getting smashed.

I fill up another glass well over halfway and begin gulping it as Cassi stumbles towards me for another. I catch her with one hand easily, and she looks up at me with a relaxed smile.

"Quick moves."

I smile down at her, blissfully unaware of the audience we have for two seconds before he clears his throat.

"I think it's time to get you home, babe. You have work in the morning, right?"

"Shit," Cassi groans. "That's right. I fucking hate working, you have to get up and be nice to people who are mean to you or you don't get to live. What kind of bullshit is that?"

Alec laughs and nods. "Life, unfortunately."

I look down at the unfinished table of pool and shrug, taking one last drink from the bottle before setting my glass down.

"I've got her," I say as I come toe to toe with Alec.

He sharply pulls Cassi out of my reach and scoffs.

"I think you have your hands full enough as it is."

Looking over to the direction he points his head, I see Carly slumped over a table while people around her are still dancing. Shit. Is it bad that I forgot she was here?

Sighing to myself, I walk over to her, hauling her up and over my shoulder as I begin walking out of the bar. Alec and Cassi are behind us as I pull out my phone and call a ride.

"Thanks for the drinks and dinner," Alec says before pausing, "And I guess in a way the job," he laughs though there isn't much humor to his tone.

He takes a half of a step away before Cassi pulls her hand out of his.

"I don't feel confident riding on the back of a bike right now. Little too buzzeded," she slurs. "I'll text you."

Alec frowns like he doesn't like that as I look to him and nod.

"She'll be safe."

He narrows his eyes slightly like he's not sure he believes me before looking to her.

"If you're sure."

She nods and he cups her face, pressing a kiss to her lips that has me looking away roughly. Fuck. Why does that stab me in the goddamn chest.

When they pull apart, Alec gives a lazy wave before heading off in the direction of his bike. Our driver pulls up in the next minute and I carefully set Carly into the back before holding the door open for Cassi. She scooches in and I take the front seat before the driver takes off.

It doesn't take long to get back to their house and I carefully lift Carly's snoring ass out of the car and carry her into the house. Cassi unlocks the door for me and I thank her before moving upstairs. I lay Carly down into her bed before turning the light off and shutting the door. Still not fucking sleeping with her.

Making my way downstairs, I see the back porch light on and Cassi sitting out there looking up at the sky.

"What are you doing?" I ask.

"Just hanging out," she says. "What about you?"

I shrug.

"You good? You seemed a little buzzed at the bar."

She shakes her head. "I may have been laying it on a little thick."

Frowning at that, I lean against the doorway.

"Why?"

She moves her head from side to side like she's contemplating actually answering me before she speaks.

"Alec is wanting to move fast and I don't know if I'm ready for it, with him."

I do my best to remain my composure but when she tacks on the with him part, a small piece of me wonders what she means by that. If she really means just him, if she has someone else in mind... fuck, would you listen to me? I'm pathetic.

"Are you saying he's been pressuring you?" I say, forcing my attention on the far more alarming bit of information she's shared.

Cassi shakes her head. "No, I just...he's ready to pick up where we left off and I don't know if I can...or I want to."

I don't say anything for a moment before I cross the deck, taking a seat on the other side of the sectional.

"Have you told him that?"

She shrugs. "No, feels silly to do so. Him basically telling my family we are dating though when we haven't really discussed anything tells me it might be time for a talk, though," she laughs bitterly.

"So, you're not together?" I hedge gently.

She cocks her head to the side slightly.

"Are you asking out of curiosity or personal interest?"

"Does it matter?" I throw back.

"To me," she says as she tilts her head the other way.

I roll my lips together. I can feel the effects of the scotch. My guard is lowered, my filter practically nonexistent and the words are tumbling from my lips before I can stop them.

"I'm interested, are you together?"

"Kinda, I guess," she answers.

My stomach turns. I don't like that answer. Not at all.

"Are you and my sister together?" she asks, catching me off guard.

"What do you mean?"

"You two seem...distant with each other. Did something happen or...is that just how your relationship is? Like are you two just putting up with each other or are you together?"

Recycling her words, I look her straight in the eyes as I speak.

"Kinda...I guess."

Disappointment colors her features as she nods and looks away. It's the most emotion I've seen her express towards me apart from anger since...that night in the club really. Something about having her attention on me, her desire on me has me scooting a little closer, softening my voice just a little.

"I still can't...stop, though."

Those green eyes come back to me once more as she tilts her head to the side.

"Stop?"

"Thinking...about you," I say over the ball that has suddenly formed in my throat.

My words seem to have stolen the breath from her lungs for a moment before she swallows.

"Me too," she rasps. "Fucked up, huh? Thinking about my sister's boyfriend?" she laughs bitterly.

"Not sure it's as bad as me thinking about my girlfriend's little sister."

She blinks, unwinding her arms from around her legs and inching just a hair closer to me as she nods.

"True, you really are a piece of shit."

A surprise laugh escapes me as I shake my head at her. A breathtaking smile consumes her features and I can't help but marvel at how she looks like this. I'd do anything to keep her like this forever. Peaceful, happy, fucking beautiful.

Her smile slowly falls, her eyes quickly scanning across my face as my own smile begins to fade. My body is practically screaming to be closer to her, while my mind reminds me what a terrible idea that would be. I'm facing an internal war within myself and I don't know how to stop it.

Cassi lets out a heavy breath and goes to stand. Disappointment flares inside me because yet again, I've blown it and she's fleeing. Before I can come up with something, anything to convince her to stay out here for just a little longer, she takes a step towards me, and then another.

One leg lifts, resting her knee onto the cushion beside my thigh before she lifts the other and does the same until she's straddling me. She hasn't sunk her full weight onto me but when she winds her arms around my neck, my own instinctively wrap around her waist, pressing her down into my lap.

I feel her brush against my hard cock and based off the gasp she lets out, she feels it too.

"Nico," she breathes out.

I pull one of my arms away from her, pushing my fingers through her hair so I don't miss a second of her beautiful face. Her wild red locks look so fucking perfect interwoven in my fingers. Like they were always meant to be.

"We shouldn't," she says, as she grinds herself against me.

"I know," I say with clenched teeth, cupping her ass with my free hand and dragging her against me.

Her mouth parts softly and I want nothing more than to bury my cock between her pouty little lips as I speak.

"Tell me to stop. Tell me to let you go. Tell me to walk away, and I will."

Her breathing is ragged as her eyes flick between my own before she shakes her head.

"Don't walk away."

Fuck it.

Slipping my fingers to the nape of her neck, I drag her towards me and crush my mouth to hers. She moans against my lips and a guttural groan sounds from inside my chest as we grind and move together. Her silky tongue wraps around mine as her hands run through my hair.

Kissing her feels better than I even remember. Taking a breath for the first time or having a drink in the middle of a drought doesn't even come close to describing the euphoria I feel in this moment.

It doesn't matter that she's not mine. It doesn't matter that I'm not hers. Right now, in this moment, she's the only thing I crave, the only thing I desire, and so selfishly, recklessly, I'm taking her.

Holding her tight to me, I flip her around until her back is pinned against the couch. My mouth moves across her cheek, peppering her neck until I come across her hickey. Anger rages inside me and I can't stop myself from sinking my teeth into her. She hisses out a pained groan as she snaps at me.

"What the hell?!"

"Punishment for letting that little fucker mark what's mine."

She shakes her head as I continue kissing across her chest, licking her cleavage as my hands move to her pants and wiggle them down before pulling my cock out.

"I'm not yours, Nico. This is just a one time thing to break the fucking tension between us."

I pause all movements for a moment before I line my cock up to her waiting pussy with one hand and grasping her throat with another as I speak.

"We'll fucking see about that."

With no warning, I thrust inside her, forcing her to let out a sharp gasp that sounds equal parts pleasure and pain. My cock throbs at the feel of her bare pussy as I withdraw my hips and snap back into her even harder.

"Fuck! Nico! Con-dom, condom," she says choppily, her voice ragged as I loosen my hold on her a little.

"I don't have one on me, babygirl. I can pull out and go to the store."

She looks up at me and shakes her head as her arm pulls my head to her.

"Fuck that."

Her tongue licks the seam of my lips and I allow her full control of the kiss as I begin thrusting the ever loving shit out of her. All she can do is hold on because this has been almost a week of pent of sexual tension that I have to let out. If she thinks one time will be enough for either of us, she's severely fooling herself. I'm a logical man, and though logic feels like it has no place in this moment, I know that once of anything when it comes to Cassi Fischer will never be enough. Ever.

"Shit," Cassi moans as she wiggles on my cock. "You fuck me like you hate me."

"I do," I admit. "I hate that you've wormed your way under my skin. I hate that you've consumed my every thought since the moment we met. I fucking hate that you've been fucking that asshole," I practically snarl.

"And I hate that you're my sister's boyfriend," she throws back.

Touche.

Pushing my cock as deep as I can go into her, her mouth drops open on a silent moan.

"Do I feel like your sister's boyfriend, right now, Cassi?"

"Fuck," she mutters as I do it again and again.

"Do I?" I ask, rubbing my tip against her gspot as she shutters.

Those green gems come to me, swirling with lust as she shakes her head.

"Not tonight."

Fuck. I should feel a hell of a lot more guilty for this but how can I when it's so fucking hot? When it's her and she's so hot? When this thing between us is as effortless as breathing.

My hand trails down her body, moving to her clit as I begin rubbing her. She squirms in my lap as she reaches between us and grabs my balls, massaging them in a way that has me cursing.

"Fuck. I'm gonna come, Cassi."

"Good," she says. "Come thinking of me and only me. Come thinking about how good it feels to be buried in my cunt and how you never want to stop," she says as her eyes roll into the back of her head and her mouth lets out a whiney moan.

I'm quick to cover it with my other hand as I feel my own orgasm take over me. Her pussy spasms and squeezes me as my cum floods her. My thrusting doesn't slow as I fuck it deeper and deeper only pausing when I'm fully spent as I collapse on top of her.

We lay there for several seconds, breathless and drained before I slowly lean up to look down at her. Before I can ask her if she's okay or anything she leans forward, pressing her lips to mine before she whispers against me.

"Let's go to bed."

Chapter Fifteen
Cassi

My eyes softly pull open at the sound of a vibration against my bedside table. A hand reaches over me, turning it off before running fingers through my hair gently. My gaze moves to look for the owner of the magical fingers, and for a moment I'm surprised. For one moment, I forgot about last night. Then, it all comes flooding back to me in an instant. The kissing, the touching the...shit, can we call that fucking? It felt so much more than that. The ruining, yeah, that's more like it.

I told him that we should go to bed and he agreed, followed me up to my room and when I asked him where he was going he said, "with you," like it was obvious. I can't lie, that pulled a cheesy as fuck grin out of me.

So, I let him stay the night. We stripped off what little clothes we had left, crawled under the covers as he pulled me until I was on top of his chest before he scratched my head, effectively putting me to sleep. He must have set an alarm on his phone once I was out so that he could get up before everyone else. Smart, considering if my sister walked in on us like this, she'd likely burn the whole fucking house down.

"I better slip out of here before someone sees," he says quietly.

I nod as I lean into his touch, savoring every last stroke of his fingers in case this is the last time I'll ever feel them. Disappointment starts to eat at me at the thought of that and he's quick to catch it, tugging my chin up the instant my eyes drop as he forces my gaze onto his.

"I don't regret last night," he says, his low voice practically rumbling against my chest as he speaks.

He rolls his lips together like he wants to hold back his words before he lets them go anyways.

"This...us...It's complicated," he says, pulling a dry sarcastic laugh out of me as I nod.

"But I can't stay away from you, Cassi. I don't *want* to."

My heart practically does a backflip in my chest as the sound of a bedroom door opening down the hall startles us both. We look at each other with wide eyes before he leans down, cupping my face as he steals one more kiss before he's slipping on his clothes and sneaking out of my bedroom.

I lay there, my head still spinning from his kiss alone, never mind his confession. What the hell am I supposed to do with all of that? I know what a good sister would do, a good person. They would not engage. They would tell them that it's wrong and that they need to go sort their shit out. Leave me out of it. I know myself far too well to know that is not what I'm going to do, though.

After I manage to pull myself out of bed and take a shower, I comb through my wet hair before throwing it up into a bun for work. Looking down at my phone, I realize how early of an alarm Nico must have set. We were barely asleep for three hours before it went off. Who the hell was up this early, then?

I get my answer as soon as I step into the kitchen and find my mom humming to herself, making what smells like pancakes as Nico flips bacon. A soft smile plays at my lips. You can tell how much he likes my parents, and they like him. He fits so well into our family. So effortlessly. If I was the one that brought him home, everything would be perfect. Unfortunately, that's not even close to how all of us came to be under one roof.

Complicated is an understatement, this whole situation is messy as fuck.

"Good morning, sweetheart," my mom greets me as she turns away from the stove, bringing a stack of pancakes to the dining room table.

Nico looks back, gracing me with by far the warmest smile I've ever seen him possess.

"Morning," I say before my eyes pull back to my mom. "Anything I can help with?"

She shakes her head.

"Nico has been a love and practically taken care of everything. Can you believe he was up and at it even before me?"

I nod my head. "That is something, you're the earliest riser I know."

She smiles at me and presses a kiss to my cheek as my dad strolls into the room.

"Good morning, how is everyone doing?"

"Good, you're just in time for all of the food and none of the prep," my mom teases.

My dad grins at her.

"Sounds like I have excellent timing, then."

She rolls her eyes, swatting at his shoulder as Nico speaks.

"Morning, Harry. Coffee?" he asks, gesturing towards the fresh cup he is pouring.

"Would love some, thanks, Nico," he says as he crosses the room, taking the cup with an appreciative head nod.

I walk over to the cabinet, grabbing plates and forks for everyone before we all take a seat at the table once the food is brought over. Mom and dad sit together on one side and surprisingly, Nico takes a seat beside me. He must be able to read my thoughts, I swear because he turns to look at me with a barely there grin before his hand comes to my leg, resting on my bare knee.

I can't help but clear my throat as I shift, attempting to pull my sleep shorts down as if I can make them seven inches longer. As if having my knees covered with something other than Nico's bare skin would help dilute the fire that has sparked inside of me and is currently raging from his touch alone.

Apparently, my discomfort is amusing to him as that smile stays in place as he takes a bite of his bacon.

"How was your night?" my mom asks.

Though, at first I don't hear her, too transfixed with the way Nico's thumb is gently rubbing against my knee, back and forth, back and forth.

"Huh?" I ask, shaking my head before looking at my mom. "Sorry, what was that?"

She gives me a funny look before speaking again.

"How was your night? Did you guys do anything fun?"

"We did," Nico answers. "Carly took us to this bar down the road and we played a little pool. It was a nice evening, right, Cassi?"

I look to him, his teasing sitting in plain sight. If his idea is to play things cool, I'll tell you, he's failing miserably. If he doesn't care about being discreet, then he's a dumbass.

"It was alright."

"Did you go home with Alec? Or did he come here?" my mom asks.

"Mary," my dad groans with a wrinkle of her nose.

"What?" she asks. "C'mon, Henry. It's not like we don't know she has sex."

"Ah ah! I'm eating," he grumbles.

"I'm with dad on this one, mom. My sex life is not breakfast discussion," I quickly add on.

She looks disappointed for a moment as Nico cuts in, staring at his plate as he stabs a piece of pancake with more force than necessary.

"Besides, she could do much better than that tool."

"You don't like, Alec?" my mom asks.

Nico looks up to her, pausing for a moment before shrugging his shoulders.

"Haven't spent enough time around him to know anything about him, really. Just a feeling I get."

"He's a good kid," dad chimes in. "His parents were wonderful too. They did a good job with him. He's going through a lot right now, that's probably what it is."

Yeah. Or maybe it's his intense jealousy that's clouding his judgment, either way.

"I'm really happy you two are giving it another chance. I always thought you guys were going to be those high school sweethearts who got married and lived happily ever after," my mom says.

I feel Nico's grip on my leg tighten slightly at that and I know it's in warning, to choose my words carefully. I'd love to see what he does if I don't though. So, I push his buttons a little bit.

"It feels like a fresh start, who knows where it'll take us."

The inside of my thigh is suddenly pinched and I can't help but yelp in reaction. My parents give me curious looks, followed by a faux one on Nico's face.

"You okay?" he asks.

I grit through my teeth as my eyes shoot daggers at him.

"Yeah, bit my tongue."

He nods. "Maybe you shouldn't talk so much while you're eating."

Ass.

Why do I kinda love it, though?

That gesture right there told me everything I needed to know. He's far more affected by the idea of me and Alec than even he wants to admit. It drives him fucking crazy. Almost as crazy as the idea of him and my sister drives me, I'd wager.

As if I summoned the devil herself, she walks into the room like a zombie, her hair a mess, mascara smeared across her face and she's still wearing the same clothes from last night.

"Rough night, hun?" my mom asks, though I can see she's holding back a smile.

"Coffee," she answers in response, numbly walking into the kitchen.

I feel Nico's hand slip away and I can't help but feel a sting of jealousy from it. Logically, I understand why he did it but illogically, it pisses me off that he stops touching me when she comes into the room.

After Carly pours herself a cup of coffee, she comes to the table, slumping into a seat between Nico and my mom.

"You two have any plans for the day?" my mom asks Nico and Carly.

"Sleeping," my sister answers as she rests her head onto the table.

Nico nods his head. "We had talked about doing some underground tour thing downtown? Looks like maybe today will be a workday," he says as he gestures to Carly.

"Oh, I haven't done the tour in years. How late do they run, I wonder?" she says, turning my dad.

"The latest starts at 6PM. We could probably make that, if it's not an imposition," my dad tacks on as he looks to Nico.

Nico shakes his head. "Not at all. Cassi, are you interested?"

The way he says my name has my cheeks flushing, which is stupid because he's said my name lots of times before. Actually, not two days ago the sound of him saying my name sounded like nails on a chalkboard. Or maybe I just willed myself to believe that in attempt to shove away the glaring tension building between us.

"Uhm, yeah. It's pretty cool. I'd be down."

"It smells horrible down there. Literally, I'll puke. Count me out," Carly says as she grabs her cup of coffee, stealing a piece of bacon from Nico's plate as she stands and stumbles out of the dining room and back upstairs."

"Four tickets it is," my dad says to himself as his fingers move across his phone. "Locked in."

"Thank you, Henry. You didn't have to do that."

My dad scoffs. "Oh yeah, I didn't have to do that while you've been insisting on paying for every meal, renting a private goddamn yacht just so we can go fishing."

"Henry, you're allowing me to stay into your home. It's the least I can do."

You can tell that was the perfect thing to say in my dad's eyes. He gives him a grateful smile and a nod.

"We've loved having you. We're sad to see you guys go. You're welcome back anytime, we mean that too."

Nico swallows roughly, like his words mean more than my dad could know.

"I really appreciate that and will be taking you up on that. You all are welcome to Boston anytime. You name the day and I'll make the arrangements."

"When are you leaving again?" I ask.

He looks over to me, his expressions generally neutral.

"Tomorrow evening. I have to get back for a board meeting and I've extended myself away from the office for as long as I can for now."

"Well, we appreciate you wanting to spend time with us with so little time left in Seattle," my mom says.

Nico nods and smiles at her before cutting me a quick look.

"It's time well spent."

Chapter Sixteen
Nico

W as it ridiculous of me to rent a car the last full day that I would be in Seattle? Yeah. Is it worth it so that I could drive to Cassi's work to pick her up and spend an extra twenty minutes of alone time with her? Fuck yeah it is.

When I stroll into the dentist office, my eyes scan the waiting room. It's clean, organized, though a little outdated with some soft jazz music playing through the speakers in the corners. The front desk is empty as I stroll up to it.

A perky blonde is walking down the hall behind the desk looking down at her phone when her eyes catch me and she pauses. A slow smile spreads across her face as she tilts her head to the side.

"Well, hi there. Can I help you?"

"I'm looking for Cassi," I say.

Her eyebrows lift in surprise. "Wait, are you the hickey man?"

My pleasant expression vanishes in an instant, my voice curt.

"No."

She takes instant notice to the shift in my demeanor and nods.

"I'll go grab her."

Not five seconds later, Cassi steps out from the back, her wild

185

red hair tamed by a bun. I want nothing more than to let it out and bury my fingers into it, though. Suprises passes across her face as she rounds the desk and comes to me.

"Hey, is everything okay?"

"Yeah," I nod. "I figured I'd drive you to the tour."

She cocks her head to the side in confusion.

"Why? I drove to work?"

"And now I'm driving us to the tour," I say simply.

"What am I going to do about my car?" she counters.

I shrug, not at all concerned with the details. "We can come back and get it later."

"But why wouldn't I just take it now so I don't have to back-track later? Besides, what are you even driving?"

"A rental."

"Why would you rent a car when you're leaving tomorrow?"

Letting out a heavy sigh, I shake my head before looking around, ensuring we are alone as I cup her face and bring her lips to mine. She goes speechless the instant we touch and when I pull away, I rest my forehead against hers.

"Because I wanted to spend more time with you, where it's just the two of us. Now will you stop being so goddamn argumentative and get in the fucking car."

She looks up at me dazed before roughly swallowing.

"I still have ten minutes on the clock."

I nod. "Then I'll wait."

Dropping my hold on her, I turn and take several steps towards the chairs in the waiting room. Sitting down, I rest one foot against my knee as I gesture for her to continue with her day. She falters for a moment before moving to her desk, taking a seat as her mouse begins clicking. Her fingers fly across the keyboard occasionally before she makes a few phone calls about past due bills which I can immediately tell is a huge discomfort for her. As I sit back watching her, I can't help but have a million thoughts run through my mind.

Does she like her job? Does she wish she could do something else? What are her dreams? Her desires? It's just now hit me that besides where she lives and works and her proclivities in the bedroom, I really know nothing about this woman. Yet, she's entranced me from the moment our eyes met in that club and no matter how hard I tried to fight it, I knew it would be a losing battle from the start.

Once her shift is over, she moves to the back, grabbing her purse and coat before turning the lights off in the waiting room. The girl from before who she calls Maddie pokes her head out and says goodbye, eyeing me suspiciously. I hold the door open for Cassi, resting my hand on her lower back as I guide her towards the rental car.

"You rented a Porsche?" Cassi asks is disbelief.

I shrug my shoulders. "I like the way they handle. I have the same one at home."

"How does it feel to have money coming out of your ears?" she asks as I open the door for her.

My mouth twitches at that but I don't respond as she slides in because I'd be an ass if I said it feels really good.

I round the car and slide into my seat, firing up the car before I look to Cassi. She looks beautiful in my car, even if it's not actually mine. It's the same one I have back in Boston. My mind flashes with images of what she'd look like in my home, my bed, my space. She fits so well. Perfectly, actually. Like that is where she belongs. The only trouble is she is three thousand miles too far.

"Do you like your job?" I ask.

"Hm?"

"Your job, do you enjoy it?"

She shrugs. "It pays pretty well. Decent hours, holidays off. Can't complain."

"You don't love it, though," I gather as I back the car out of the parking lot.

"No, but that's okay. Not many people love their job. Sometimes just a paycheck with reasonable conditions is enough, right? I mean, I don't want to live to work, you know?"

I grunt at that. "No, my whole life is consumed with my business. I think this week has been the most 'living' I've done in twenty years at least."

She frowns at that before a laugh bubbles out of her. "That's actually really pathetic."

A surprised laugh escapes me as I scoff. "Thanks."

"No, no, I just mean. Damn no, never mind. It is pathetic."

I shake my head as she smiles and tugs on my arm in a playful way.

"Seriously, you have more money than you know what to do with. You never spoil yourself? Take a random trip? Buy something stupid expensive for the sake of it?"

Shrugging my shoulders, I turn on my blinker as we approach a light.

"I'm too busy making more money to spend any of it, I guess. Your sister usually handles that part for me."

The energy in the car shifts when I bring up Carly, and I want to kick myself for it. Cassi's body goes rigid, her demeanor shuts down and I worry that I've ruined the moment. Suprising me, though, her words are spoken with a more relaxed tone than I anticipated.

"What a gold digging bitch."

A sharp laugh tears out of me once more as I turn to look at her.

"That's exactly what my mom used to call her."

Cassi grins at that. "I think I would have liked your mom very much."

"She would have loved you."

Her smile softens, a look of sadness touching her features as she reaches out to me, resting her hand on my thigh much like I did at breakfast to her. Though while my touch was meant to be teasing and playful, hers is soft, comforting, warm. Covering her hand with my own, I squeeze it once before keeping my hand in place as we turn, with no intention of releasing her.

"Carly really isn't coming to the tour?" Cassi asks, a hint of hesitancy in her voice.

I glance at her and shake my head as I weave through traffic.

"No, she's still sleeping off her hangover, I think."

Cassi nods to herself before she speaks.

"So, with your girlfriend gone does that mean you're going to try to make a pass at her sister?"

I swear to christ I almost crash the fucking car. My head whips over to her so fast the wheel turns along with me, forcing me to overcorrect just to stay in our lane. Cassi is watching me with a smile that practically says I dare you. If she has any guilt about sneaking around behind her sister's back, it isn't in the car with us. Which, to be fair, Carly is a shit sister to her, so I don't really blame her. If I was a better man, I'd stop this whole thing before it went further, but then I remember how I fucked her raw last night on her parent's back porch while my girlfriend was asleep upstairs and decide there really is no further to go.

Moving the hand not on the wheel, I move to Cassi's leg, sliding it across her thigh as I begin brushing my fingers against the seam of her legs. She spreads them instantly, inviting me further. My cock jerks in my pants as my hand begins rubbing against her jean covered pussy, a soft mewling sound coming from her before she's quickly unbuttoning her jeans and pulling them and her thong down her legs.

"What are you doing?" I ask as I keep my head on a swivel between the road and her.

"Seeing what kind of a multitasker you are," she says with a smirk as she once again pulls her legs apart.

I can't help but lean forward, looking down to see her pussy spread open for me. Holy fuck. I waste absolutely no time, cupping her pussy with my hand as I grind the heel of my palm against her clit before dipping a finger inside her. She's fucking soaked already, practically dripping down my finger as I slip another inside her.

"Shit! Nico," she hisses.

My cock throbs again, just my name on her lips has me ready to fucking nut in my pants. I pull my fingers out, earning a whimper from her before I suck on my fingers. Her taste instantly greets me like my favorite meal. I lick my fingers clean before pushing inside once more, this time from a different angle so I can finger fuck the hell out of her gspot.

"Rub your clit, I want you to make a mess all over my fucking seat," I command.

She happily obliges, one hand coming down to her clit as I continue pumping my fingers in and out of her.

"This what you wanted? Wanted me to spread you open and have my way with you while no one is looking?"

"Yes," she moans, her eyes rolling into the back of her head as she does.

"The only thing that could be better is if I had you tied up. Subdued and submissive all for me."

She moans again.

"Would my little bunny like that?" I ask.

Her eyes fly open, desire practically drowning her beautiful emerald color.

"Yes," she pants.

I give her a crooked smile as I turn my eyes back to the road.

"Prove it. Soak my fingers, babygirl."

Her hand moves faster against her clit before her pussy is tightening around me and she's screaming out her release.

"FUCK! Nico! Shit, shit, shit! Yes!"

I keep my rhythm finger fucking her through her orgasm until she practically collapses into her seat. Withdrawing my fingers, I immediately begin sucking on them, my cock aching so hard I feel like I'm going to explode. Pulling my fingers away, I groan with frustration as I clench the steering wheel with all of my might.

Cassi reaches over in the next moment, palming my hard on as she begins quickly rubbing me through my pants.

"Shit," I hiss through clenched teeth, resting my head against the headrest as I check the GPS.

Quickly, I take a right, turning us onto a side road. It says our ETA is five minutes out. I won't fucking last five minutes though and there is nowhere in this goddamn city to pull over.

Cassi continues stroking me and it takes everything in me to keep my eyes on the road.

"Fuck! I'm gonna come. Take my cock out and suck it," I say.

She gives me a wicked smile as she shakes her head but continues stroking me.

"I'm not fucking kidding. I'm gonna come in my goddamn pants if you don't stop."

"Good," she smiles. "I want you to come in your pants for me. I want you to be so desperate for me that you can't hold yourself back."

I attempt to pull her hand away but she just comes back with the other hand, increasing her efforts as I breathe through my nose.

"Cassi, I don't have any extra pants. You're going to make me come and then I'm supposed to go walk around a fucking tour with your parents?"

"Sounds like a hell of a story," she laughs.

I'm about to bitch her out when she leans towards me, whispering into my ear as she nibbles on my earlobe.

"I want to feel you come for me, do it for me."

Her voice is breathy and desperate and fuck me I'm powerless against it. I come fucking hard. My cock jerks and I moan as cum quickly soaks my pants. Cassi only stops when I practically melt into my seat before she looks at me with a triumphant grin.

I however, am not happy. The GPS announces our arrival and I quickly eye a parking spot that I whip into before unbuckling her seatbelt.

"Wha—"

She begins to ask but I don't allow her to finish before I'm grabbing hold of her bun and shoving her face into my lap.

"Clean up your fucking mess. Suck me clean."

"Your pants?" she questions as she attempts to look at me.

I push her down until she is nosed against the cum stain as I speak.

"Lick it up, now."

To my surprise, she does as I say, stroking her tongue against the wet material before she begins full on sucking on it. I'll be honest, I expected more of a fight. Some hesitancy. Instead, she is sucking on my stained slacks like I'm her favorite dessert. A soft moan even escapes her and she doesn't come up for air for over a minute before she looks at me with a grin.

"I think me licking it up made it worse," she says as I look down at the stain that has now doubled in size easily.

"Maybe, but I feel a hell of a lot better," I say as I crush her lips to mine.

She smiles against me before we tear apart, and I look down to see her pants still around her ankles. Reaching forward, I spread her pussy with my fingers to get one more look before I spank her clit. She bucks at the move as I readjust my cock and turn the car off.

"Put my pussy away, I'll be dealing with her later."

Chapter Seventeen
Cassi

I do my best to hold back my laugh as Nico attempts to dry off his pants before he gives up altogether. A large wet stain is laying right there on his upper right thigh. A combination of his cum and my saliva.

Fuck.

That was so hot. Easily one of the hottest things I've ever experienced. Road head is one thing. It's practically vanilla. Jerking off my sister's boyfriend through his pants until he comes while driving down the road, then him making me suck his pants clean? Yeah, that is going down in my top five sexual moments ever.

Nico shakes his head before I hear him mutter, "fuck."

He rifles around in the backseat floorboard before pulling out a water. He stands up and gets out of the car before dumping the bottle of water across his lap. My eyes widen in surprise as he finishes, tossing the now empty bottle into the car. His eyes come to mine and he lifts an eyebrow like he's questioning why I'm confused.

"You spilled the water into my lap like the brat you are."

I watch him consideringly for a moment or two before I grin.

"That does sound like something I would do."

He nods, a half of a smile spreading across his face before he shoots me a wink and shuts his door, rushing around to my side. I can't fight the smile or the flush that spreads over my cheeks from that wink alone. Before I can even open my car door, Nico is there, pulling it open before offering me his hand.

"Quite the gentleman," I quip.

"When I want to be," he says as I take his hand and step out of the car.

He shuts the door behind me before locking it as we look around and see the signage pointing towards the start of the tour. We take a few steps before I realize Nico hasn't let go of my hand yet. I wiggle my fingers, attempting to free myself when he gives me an almost irritated look.

"What are you doing?"

"Trying to get my hand back," I laugh.

"Why?" he asks, his stupid perfect face full of confusion.

I let out a short laugh before I realize he's being serious. My head whips all around us as I speak.

"We don't know if my parents are already here or not. If they see us like this..."

My words trail off and Nico begrudgingly releases my hands, sighing as he pockets his into his dress pants and continues leading the way. Not two seconds later, we round a corner and see my mom and dad standing there waiting for us. I look up at Nico pointedly, as if to say 'see'. Of course he ignores me, turning up the charm to an eleven when he sees my parents.

"Long time no see," he says as he gives my mom a hug.

She laughs like it's the funniest thing and I'm almost embarrassed for her. Mom needs to cool it, her crush on her daughter's boyfriend is showing. I wonder if mine is too?

"Nico, hun. What happened to your pants?" she asks with a

laugh as she looks down at the huge water stain. (Or what can be assumed is water.).

He looks down and scoffs, shaking his head.

"Your klutz of a daughter dumped her entire bottle of water in my lap. My guess is it was on purpose," he whispers conspiringly in a way that has my mom teetering.

"It was not," I say as I smack his shoulder.

He gives me a disbelieving shrug before turning to shake hands with my dad. They begin bonding over how bad the traffic was. Such an old man thing to gripe about but they fall into step with each other as they lead us to the start of the entrance.

"How was work today, sweetheart?" mom asks.

"Good," I nod. "You?"

"Just fine," she smiles.

The tour leader scans the tickets from dad's phone and gestures for us to head down the stairs and wait at the bottom. As we do, the brightly lit area soon darkens until you can hardly see a hand in front of your face apart from the dim yellow lights installed every few feet or so on the walls. I haven't done this tour since my seventh grade field trip but the instant that smell hits my nose, I can't forget it. It's hard to describe and uniquely foul. Damp, rotten soil? If you can call it that. Really, it smells more like sewage than anything.

I look over to see Nico's nose wrinkle in displeasure. For some reason, that sour look brings a smile to my face.

"You're not enjoying the aroma of old Seattle, Mr. Twenties?" I tease.

He rolls his eyes, turning to face me.

"Will you stop fucking calling me that?"

I shrug like I'm helpless. "Afraid not. It's too perfect for you, it just might be the winner."

Nico sighs, shaking his head as he falls back into conversation with my dad. My mom laughs by my side, looping her arm through mine.

"You two fight like siblings I swear. He's like the brother you never had."

My look of disgust comes too naturally, I can't even hide it. Brother? If my mom knew the things we have done together, then she would know using the term brother should be illegal. If we were related and we did everything we have, we'd be locked up for sure.

"Mom, gross," I say with a wrinkle of my nose.

"What? I mean, if him and Carly ever get married he will be your brother in law, so it's practically the same thing."

My stomach turns at that.

"They are not going to get married," I say, almost defensively.

Mom shrugs. "Carly was talking about how it's the next step for them just yesterday.

"Yeah?" I laugh. "Does the groom know of her plans just yet, I can guarantee he's in the dark on this."

My mom gives me an odd look at that and I instantly realize I need to shut the fuck up. Attempting to play it off, I give her a shake of my head and a sigh before the tour guide thankfully comes down the stairs.

"Welcome to what used to be the main street of Seattle! Settlers first came to Seattle in 1851..."

His voice grows quieter as he moves deeper and deeper into the tunnel. About thirty of us are down here and slowly, everyone begins moving along with him. Several people are taking pictures or recording while the tour guide rattles on about the Seattle fire and the way of life back in the day.

Slowly, my mom catches up to my dad, trading in my arm for his as she holds onto him. He looks down at her before placing a loving kiss against her forehead. She smiles into him and for some reason, it weirdly chokes me up. They are so in love after over forty years together. They still light up when the other walks into the room. I think when you grow up with parents who are so in love with each other, you just think it's normal but then you become an adult and realize how much of a gift it actually is. You understand how hard they have had to work at that love over their life and how precious it is.

"They love each other a lot," Nico says into my ear, scaring the ever loving shit out of me.

I yelp in surprise, earning scolding looks from the rest of the tour goers before the guide continues his speech.

"You scared the fuck out of me," I whisper.

"Don't be so skittish," he shrugs.

I roll my eyes, though I doubt he can see me do it.

"We are in a dark and creepy abandoned tunnel where this old as dirt city used to be built. You know how haunted it probably is down here from all the people that died in the fire?"

"If you were paying attention to the story, no one died in the fire, surprisingly. So your basis of a haunted tunnel is weak at best."

I give him a flat look that tells him to shut the fuck up and he raises his hands in surrender, smiling as he backs away. Asshole.

Focusing back on the man's words, I catch the part that he says about how the fire spread out of control because all of the sidewalks were made of wood as well as the water pipes and spouts. Hindsight, that was a terrible fucking idea. Then again, what do I know about infrastructure back in the late nineteenth century.

My phone buzzes in my pocket and I stop walking for a moment to check who it is.

Alec: Hey beautiful, I miss you. Can I see you tonight?

I wince at the text. Alec. Fuck. I've almost completely forgotten about him. He's so sweet and kind. We have so much history together and he used to be an incredible boyfriend, but he doesn't...

Before I can finish that thought, a hand wraps around my mouth before an arm yanks me back into a dark alcove. I try to scream but it's too muffled by the hand pressed against me.

"Shh, shhh, it's me," Nico rumbles into my ear.

Irritation fills me as I turn to face him in a flash. He lets me go easily and I can just barely see his features in the darkness as I glare up at him and whisper.

"What the fuck! Are you hell bent on scaring the ever living shit out of me or what?"

Before I can say more, his hand slips behind my neck as he pulls me in for a kiss. His mouth crushes to mine and for a moment I push back. There are people everywhere. This is so fucking stupid! Yet, when his tongue swipes against the seam of my lips, I'm a goner.

I melt into Nico's hold, sighing softly as I wind my arms around his neck. His other hand comes to rest onto my hip before he's tearing himself away.

"C'mon, little bunny. We gotta catch up before someone comes looking for us," he rumbles low.

"That nickname is weak at best. You keep trying to make it work, but it's not working."

He gives me a challenging look before he pushes his hand into my pants, moving past my panties as he slips a finger inside me. He pumps in and out of me just twice before pulling out his practically dripping finger. Nico pushes his finger into my mouth and I let him, willingly as I begin sucking my taste off him.

Though I can't see very well down here, you'd have to be blind to miss the way he's staring at me. Lust and want practically consuming him as I suck on his finger like I'm sucking him off before releasing him with a pop.

He attempts to regain his composure, clearing his throat before he speaks.

"Trust me, it works."

With that, he pushes on my lower back, guiding us back to the crowd. When we catch up enough, we create some distance and just in time for my dad to turn around, looking relieved when he sees us. My mom turns around too and smiles as she nods before facing forward once more.

Nico and I stay a little behind everyone and here and there our hands will bump into each other. A fluttering fills my stomach with each touch and I look up at him to find that he's already looking down at me.

Fuck. I am so screwed. This man has the capability to absolutely ruin me, and God help me, I'd let him every day of the week.

Chapter Eighteen
Nico

Once the tour was over, Mary suggested we grab some dinner at the waterfront. Not wanting anything with going back to the house and being around Carly, I agreed that it was an excellent idea. They settled on a seafood restaurant that overlooked the water and that was fine with me since my only requisite was sitting beside Cassi.

Despite there only being four chairs at the table, a flicker of excitement and ease filled me when she took the seat beside me. I didn't hesitate to slip my hand onto her knee under the table. She didn't look at me or squirm like she did this morning, instead, she placed her hand over my own and slid it up higher and higher until I was practically cupping her pussy under the table in front of her goddamn parents. I gave her a squeeze that forced her to slam her mouth closed, like she was about to moan right here and now otherwise before returning my hand to where it belonged. Mainly because if it raised another few inches I'd rip her goddamn pants off and feast on her right here and now for everyone to see. Yeah, absolutely couldn't lose control like that.

"Thank you so much for coming out to Seattle, Nico, and for

staying longer. It's been a real treat. We've missed Carly so much and we have been so anxious to meet you. We were half convinced she had made you up," Mary laughs.

I set my menu down and smile, nodding thankfully.

"I so appreciate you two opening your home to me so willingly. This has been...a trip of a lifetime," I say, not being able to help my eyes from drifting to Cassi, just a for a moment, before I look back to Henry and Mary.

They both smile thankfully, none the wiser to how close I am to throwing their youngest over my shoulder and hauling her out of here so I can claim every inch of her.

"You're welcome anytime, I know you don't have much family but you've got us. Even if things don't work out with you and Carly," Henry says, surprising everyone at the table.

Mary seems to pinch him under the table as she hisses at him to mind his own business.

I take no offense, actually breathing a sigh of relief. Honestly, though I didn't expect it, I really like Henry and Mary.

Everyone looks to Cassi expectantly, waiting for her to say kind words about me or the idea of me returning soon. She stays straight faced, though, before she looks around the table and shrugs.

"What?"

I can't help but smirk as Mary shakes her head in disappointment.

"I told you, like damn siblings," she grumbles to Henry.

My face twists up at that as I look to Cassi with a face of horror. She has her lips mashed together in a tight line as she nods her head as if to say 'yeah, you heard that right.'

The horror across my face quickly melts away to amusement because what I'm going to do to Cassi tonight is so far beyond brotherly.

After dinner, Cassi and I drove back to her work so she could pick up her car. We made out in my car for a solid ten minutes before I'd even let her get out. Then, I walked her to her car door and lifted her into my arms before we kissed for another few minutes. I know that I was being ridiculous, that we were literally returning to the same house a handful of miles away but I can't help it. This woman is like a drug, and I'm so goddamn addicted.

I let her take off first, following quickly behind her as she led the way back to her house. When we got there, I was actually relieved to see that the extra car wasn't there. That means that Carly borrowed a car and isn't here. Perfect. It's the last night that we are in Seattle and once we are back in Boston, I'm going to sit her down and tell her it's time for us to call it quits once and for all. I can't keep doing this with her.

We've both been checked out of this relationship for a long time. I think the biggest reason I've held on for so long was because of how amazing she was when my mom passed away. She never left my side and I think I developed a sort of duty to her. Like I owed her for her kindness, when in reality, it's what any decent human would have done.

Unfortunately, that was one of the last times I saw Carly be a decent anything. It's time to rip off the band aid once and for all, and no, I'm not saying that so I can jump into bed with her sister guilt free. That is absolutely the plan, though. As horrible as it is to think, I'm going to be jumping into bed with Cassi Fischer regardless because not only do I not want to stay away from her. I can't. The white flag is raised. I give up.

Cassi and I step into the house together and hear the TV on in the living room. Shit. Despite it only being nine o'clock, I was really hoping that Henry and Mary had went to bed for the night. For one, I've been sleeping on the couch since I saw Carly's texts. Well, except for last night. Two, now alone time with Cassi is off the table and I do my best to hide my upset at that little truth.

She looks up at me like she had similar hopes before I rest a reassuring hand onto her lower back and nod for us to head into the living room. There, Tom is sitting on the couch watching today's baseball team. The Seattle based team has been crushing it this year, there is already talks of them going all the way to the World Series, though it's too early to tell for sure. I'm not a huge sports guy, but Henry is, and he educated me all about the legacy and future for Seattle baseball. He was so enthusiastic about it I couldn't do anything but listen attentively and nod.

"This seat taken?" I ask as I walk around the couch and gesture to the seat beside him.

"Not at all, please!" he says. "The girls never wanted to watch sports with me as kids so this is a treat."

"Uhm, excuse you. I've watched plenty of games with you," Cassi corrects.

Henry rolls his eyes. "Want to, not have to, Cass. You watched out of pity and we both know it."

"What do you think Nico is doing right now?" she challenges.

I turn around and send her a look that tells her to back down and let her dad have this. To my surprise, she rolls her eyes but obliges. Interesting. Maybe she's less of a brat than I had her pegged as. Since getting past our dislike for one another, or should I say, her dislike for me, we haven't really explored...dynamics...too much yet. I was already looking forward to one on one time with Cassi but this little development just made things all the more interesting.

While Henry and I watch the game, I hear Cassi and her mom laughing as they chat. From time to time I'll turn around to check on them and see them pouring glass after glass of wine as they put together those ready to bake cookie dough packs you can get from the store.

"Why not homemade?" Henry griped at one point, which earned him a quick smack to the back of the head as Mary shoved a cookie in his mouth.

"Be grateful for what you have."

He chewed over the hot treat as he grinned at her.

"Yes, dear."

I couldn't help but smile at their interaction, and honestly. I was kinda disappointed when the game was over and they went up to bed. Cassi was still lingering in the kitchen while I was on the couch when not two seconds later, Carly came stumbling into the house, clearly drunk. Again.

"Oh my goshhhh you're still up!" she smiled as her heels clicked against the floors before she practically side tackled me off the couch.

I catch her easily as he dress rides up around her hips, fully displaying her with the only thing protecting any kind of modestly is a pair of crotchless panties. Classy.

My hear turns to see Cassi watching with a disgusted look before she rushes off upstairs. I want to call out to her but what am I going to say?

Cassi's footsteps thunder upstairs and I sigh in disappointment as Carly drunkenly crawls into my lap.

"I missed you, baby. I'm so tired of us fighting all the time. Can we just make up already?" she whines.

"You're drunk," I say pointedly.

"Soooo what are you gonna do with me?" she grins as she leans down and begins kissing my neck.

I roll my eyes before standing up, holding her in my arms as I carry her up the stairs. She continues kissing on me, an excited giggle escaping her as I push open her bedroom door and lay her down onto her bed. She pulls up her dress to fully expose herself but I keep my eyes on her.

"Get some rest, Carly."

Anger immediately takes over her.

"Are you fucking kidding me? You're sleeping on the couch again? What the fuck is your problem, Nicholas!"

"We have to leave midday tomorrow. Make sure you're packed," is all I say before closing the door.

A few explicits fly out of her mouth, followed by a thump or two against her door. Sighing, I shake my head as I look to the closed bedroom door to the side of her. Is it totally fucking stupid of me to leave one sister's room to go into another? Yeah, but it doesn't stop me from trying the door handle. When I find it locked, I frown, and lightly knock against the wooden door. I stand there for several seconds before letting out a sigh of disappointment and making my way down to the living room.

Grabbing the bag of clothes I've been keeping down here, I rifle through it until I find a t-shirt and a pair of sweatpants, getting changed in the bathroom before setting up my 'bed' on the couch. If Mary or Henry have noticed that I've been out here instead of in Carly's room, they haven't said anything. Then again, maybe that's why Henry made that comment at dinner. At least it won't be a surprise to them when we break up. They have eyes, they are intelligent people. They know their daughter. It won't be a surprise to anyone.

Pulling out my phone, I scroll through before finding Cassi's number. Typing out a text, I re-word it about ten times before I hit send.

Me: Are you up?

Real fucking original, Nico.

Her response comes faster than I anticipate.

Cassi: No.

Okay then.

My fingers begin moving faster than before as I type out my reply.

Me: Are you upset with me?

Cassi: Wow, so fucking observant. Someone get this guy a trophy.

I frown at her words, trying to figure out how to phrase my next text when another one comes in from her.

Cassi: This is all a mistake. You're not mine and I'm not yours. We should stop this now before someone gets hurt.

Like me. That's the part she left off but I can read it plain as day, because despite only knowing her for a little less than a week. I feel like I've known her for a lifetime. There are several ways I could handle this topic, but the only way I think will give me a chance in hell in talking her down is in person. So, I egg her on.

Me: Say it to my face if you really mean that.

I wait for several minutes with no response. I'm half convinced she's fallen asleep before the next text comes in.

Cassi: The door is unlocked.

Say no more. I'm up and on my feet in half a second, rushing up the stairs as quietly as I'm able before coming to her door. I hear the soft sound of snoring come from Carly's room which is good. It means she let the alcohol take over and effectively knock her the hell out.

When my hand grips the door handle and it turns, a feeling of relief fills me, though when I step through the door and see the hardened look on Cassi's face, that relief vanishes in an instant.

Shutting the door behind me, I make sure to lock it before crossing the room. She's sitting in the middle of her bed, legs crossed, arms folded and an unimpressed look on her face as she whispers to me.

"This is all a mistake. You're not mine and I'm not yours. We should stop this now before someone gets hurt."

Yeah, scratch what I said before. Cassi Fischer is absolutely a fucking brat. One I can't wait to tame.

I take several steps towards her, not stopping until I'm at the edge of her bed. Leaning down without getting on the bed, I press my nose to hers as I look into her eyes.

"Say it again."

She falters for a moment before that stubbornness flares in her eyes.

"This is all a mistake—"

Cassi doesn't get to finish her sentence before my lips are on hers. My hands dive into her hair, digging into her wild curls as I tug on them hard. She gasps into my mouth as I pull away.

"Say it again," I warn.

She looks up at me dazed and I think I have her, until she opens that smart fucking mouth once more.

"You're not mine and I'm not yours," she says as I push her onto her back, gripping her sleep shorts before dragging them down to her ankles.

I peel off my sweatpants and boxers, kicking them to the side before shoving myself between her legs. She cries out, covering her mouth to muffle her sounds as I groan into her neck. Fuck. It's like heaven every time with her.

"Say. It. Again," I say through clenched teeth.

Her eyes flick back and forth between mine, worry and indecision clouding her beautiful gem colored gaze.

"I'm scared I'm going to get hurt," she admits, a raw vulnerability to her tone that has my chest cracking open at the sound.

My hand comes up to cup her face as tenderly as I'm able as I shake my head.

"Never. You hear me? I will never let anyone, or anything hurt you ever again. I promise, Cassi."

She swallows roughly as she looks up at me.

"I'm not worried about anyone or anything, I'm worried about... you."

I frown at her words and I don't know how to put her mind at ease because there is no way to do it. I'll just have to try to prove myself. Every day if that's what it takes.

"I'm here, Cass. I'm not going anywhere. You'll have to send me away yourself before I even take a step back. Even then..." I trail off, shaking my head. "I'm *here*," I emphasize.

She softens at my words, nodding gently before her hand comes to the back of my head, pulling me towards her. I go easily, like a sailor called to a siren at sea. Slowly I begin rolling my hips into her as our bodies move together. This tender sweet love making isn't my usual style. It isn't our usual style but in this moment it feels so necessary. So right.

Cassi tears away from me, moaning as she speaks.

"I'm sorry. I got jealous and—"

"Shh," I say, resting my finger against her lips. "It's okay. I'm here, Cass."

She nods like that cements her ease that much further as she lifts her hips, meeting me thrust for thrust.

"I'm gonna miss you, miss this," she moans, softening her tone when she realizes she's being too loud.

"Me too, babygirl," I grunt into her neck, peppering it with kisses. "So fucking much," I mutter against her skin.

Cassi's hand moves down to her clit as she quickly begins rubbing it and I pull back slightly to watch. Fucking hell. I love it when she touches herself. Being inside her while she pleases herself is the ultimate fucking turn on. Any man afraid of a woman who knows how to get herself off is a fucking bitch in my opinion. When I feel her orgasm begin to creep in, all I can think about is pulling the next one out of her.

"Fuck. Fuck, fuck! Nico!" she mutters into her hand before she bucks and grinds against me.

I put everything into my thrusts, effectively fucking her into the goddamn mattress as her pulsating pussy begins literally pulling the cum out of me. I wasn't even close to finishing a minute ago but now I have no choice. She gives me no choice ever. I lose myself inside her, my cock twitching and jerking as I fuck my cum deeper and deeper into her.

When my orgasm passes, I slump against her, our ragged breathing the only sound in the room before I roll off of her. She looks over to me in concern like I'm going somewhere but I quickly put that fear to rest when I drag her on top of me, pulling the blankets over us as she nuzzles into my chest.

We lay there for several minutes, so long that I think she's already asleep when she speaks.

"You have to let me up so I can get the cum out of me."

I pull back, giving her a disbelieving look as my grip on her tightens.

"You try to get my cum out of you and I'll spank your ass fucking bloody."

Her eyes widen in surprise in that and I force her to lay back down, holding her extra tight as I bury my nose into the crook of her neck and inhale. Fuck. She's perfect. She's everything. In this very moment, the creeping thought that I was fearful of is officially confirmed. I won't be letting this woman go for anything, no matter what happens, no matter what it costs. She was dead wrong. I am hers and she is mine.

Chapter Nineteen

Nico

I wake up the next morning to the sound of a door opening and shutting, followed by light conversation. My eyes slowly lift before I take in my surroundings. Pale pink walls, delicate feminine décor and a woman that is absolutely not my girlfriend.

Fuck. Fuck. Fuck.

Pushing Cassi to the side as gently as I can, I rush for my clothes, glancing at the time on her phone.

8:15am.

Son of a bitch.

I forgot to set an alarm on account of me leaving it on the couch and coming running upstairs last night. She literally said jump and I was already in the air. Goddamnit, how did I let this happen?

A sleepy looking Cassi sits up, her bottom half still completely naked as she murmurs.

"What's the matter?"

"We slept in. It's a quarter after seven."

Her dazed look vanishes, her eyes bugging out of her head as she looks at her phone.

"FUCK! I'm gonna be late for work," she says as she rushes for that bathroom.

I intercept her before she can and hold her in place for a moment before stealing a kiss.

"I leave before you get off work but I want you to text me throughout the day and let me know when you're safe."

"Okay," she says as she attempts to get past me.

"And I want you to come see me in Boston. Soon. I'll send the plane, I'll come and get you myself if that's what it takes."

"Really?" she asks, pausing for a moment.

I can't help but let out a short laugh as I shake my head and press a kiss to her lips.

"Really. Promise me you'll come? We can just...be."

Her face softens at my words as she nods.

"I'd love to."

A huge smile spreads across my face before I can stop it as I dip down and scoop her up for one last kiss, holding her face like I'm being shipped off to war and this could be the last kiss we ever share.

She tears away from me with a goofy smile as she playfully shoos me away and rushes to the bathroom, shutting the door before the sound of the shower turns on. I find myself still staring after her grinning. I know for a fact that wasn't our last kiss, though. I'll be making sure of it.

Turning to leave her room, I carefully open her door, looking from side to side before I step out. I only make it a step or two before I crash right into Mary. I steady her quickly as she startles.

"Oh!"

"Shit, I'm sorry. Are you okay?" I ask.

"Yeah, I'm fine. Did you come out of Cassi's room?" she asks, confusion coloring her expression.

I falter only for a moment before I shake my head.

"Half asleep from the bathroom trying to find my way back to

Carly's room. You'd think after a week here I'd be more acclimated," I laugh.

Mary looks at me like she doesn't believe my shit for one second but for some reason, she lets it go, nodding her head in agreement.

"Been there. Can I whip you up some breakfast before I head to work?"

"Absolutely not," I say with a shake of my head. "You're too kind, really. Besides. I still need to pack and nag Carly for the tenth time to do the same," I say with faux irritation that seems to finally put Mary at ease.

She laughs at that and nods. "Good luck with that."

"Thanks, have a good day at work!" I say as I shake my head and move towards Carly's room.

When I open the door, I expect her to be asleep still. All she has done since we've been back is sleep and party, I swear. To my surprise, though, she's up. Not only is she up but she's dressed, make up on and hair curled. She's also standing next to her luggage along with another bag she didn't bring with her originally.

Carly turns to look at me, her nose wrinkling in disapproval.

"You look like shit."

I scoff and shake my head but don't say anything as I move to the things I left in the room and begin gathering some new clothes.

"I didn't expect you to be up and at it so early. Our flight isn't until two."

"Yeah, change of plans, actually," she says.

I turn my head to look at her as she shrugs.

"Danielle's loser boyfriend dumped her and they were supposed to go on a cruise to the Caribbean so she invited me."

"When is this?" I ask.

"We leave today, like, right now actually," she says as she looks down at her phone and begins wheeling her luggage past me.

"What? You're not coming back to Boston?" I ask.

She pauses at the door and turns.

"I will when I'm back. It's just a ten day cruise."

"Were you going to tell me?" I scoff.

"Well, I would have but you wanted nothing to do with me last night," she says, gnashing her teeth in my direction.

I don't even attempt to play into her dramatics as I shake my head.

"Carly, we have to talk."

"I can't talk right now. I'll call you when I land in Miami and if I have service I'll text you here and there. Love ya," she says as she leans in and presses a kiss to my cheek before strutting out of her room and down the hall.

I stand there practically speechless for a moment before I shake my head.

What the fuck ever.

I called the office and had my meeting pushed back to Monday, giving me the entire weekend free thankfully, and I knew exactly how I was going to spend it. After a few more calls with my pilot, I was able to make all of the arrangements and accommodations for the trip and now I just had to run the final errand.

At 5:02PM, I open the front door just as Cassi is walking out of her job, pausing when she sees me.

"What are you doing here?" she asks. "Wasn't your flight at two?"

"Change of plans, c'mon," I say, holding my hand out for her.

She frowns, slipping her hand into mine as she speaks.

"Where are we going?"

"To Boston. I said soon, you agreed."

Her eyes widen in surprise as she shakes her head.

"What about Carly?"

I shrug. "She took off on a girls trip with Danielle and I pushed my meeting to Monday. The jet is waiting for us."

She blinks as I walk her towards my car.

"My car is here, my parents won't accept me just disappearing without a trace."

"Leave it here and tell them you're spending the weekend with some friends."

She pauses before arguing once more.

"What about clothes? A toothbrush?"

"Believe it or not, Boston has these state of the art places called stores," I smirk as we get to the passenger's side of the car.

"But—"

She starts as I pull her in for a kiss, instantly silencing her as I pull back and smile.

"Stop trying to come up with reasons why you can't go, and get in the fucking car."

Cassi looks up at me before a small smile crosses her face and she nods.

Opening the door for her, I let her slide in before shutting it, not able to wipe the excited smile off my face. An entire weekend with her, just the two of us in my city.

Chapter Twenty
Cassi

Holy shit. I can't believe we are doing this. There are at least a hundred reasons shouting in my head of why this is wrong. Yet, here I am, casually strolling across the tarmac as I board a private jet. Yeah...a private jet. What kind of backwards twilight zone universe have I stepped into?

When I step inside, my mouth drops. Honestly, I feel my jaw hit the fucking floor because this isn't a tiny little four person plane. No, this thing has twelve seats that look more like recliners than an airplane seat. The floors are a plush carpet without a single stain or strand out of place. My eyes move up to the ceiling where strategic lighting is placed in soft browns and light whites that make the entire thing feel...luxurious.

Slowly, my head turns to see Nico watching me with a knowing smirk. He knows he's a rich son of a bitch. He knows that just stepping foot on one of these things for someone like me was so far out of my wildest imagination. And now we're flying on it across the country? Just like that?

"Good evening. We are about ready to take off. Can I get either of you a pre-flight refreshment before we do?" a leggy stewardess with the whitest teeth I've ever seen asks.

"I'll take an ice water, what about you, Cassi?"

"Uhm, an ice water would be great. Thank you," I say.

Nico frowns as he looks down at me before looking back to her.

"Bring us a bottle of champagne when you have a moment too."

She smiles happily and moves to the galley as she grabs out our glasses. Nico rests his hand onto my lower back as he begins guiding us deeper into the plane before stopping on a loveseat. He takes a seat before tugging me down with him, though I don't fall into the seat. I land in his lap.

His arms are like tentacles, wrapping around me with ease as his face buries into my neck and inhales gently. Nervously, my eyes flick to the stewardess. I mean, I'd assume Nico uses her often, he doesn't just have a horde of them, right? Which means she knows my sister and probably assumes I'm some sort of floozy on the side. Which...well, technically, aren't I?

She doesn't look at us, though. Not until she's walking towards us and even then, she's looking in our direction but not at us, if that makes sense.

"Thank you, Jackie," Nico says, not even having to look at her to know she's beside us as she sets down our drinks.

"My pleasure. The captain told me we will be taking off now. If possible, please fasten your seatbelts for takeoff."

"We will need a seatbelt extender if it's not too much trouble?" he asks, moving his eyes away from me for a moment to look at her.

She gives him a small smile and nods her head before moving back to the galley, returning quickly with a seatbelt extender. Before I can ask him what it's for, he's hooking it up and wrapping it around us, effectively locking me in against him.

I look down at him with wide eyes as he smirks at me.

"Has anyone told you how fucking ridiculous you are?"

"No, they've never had the guts."

I scoff. "You're not intimidating, Mr. Sanders," I say with a faux posh accent.

He lifts a challenging eyebrow as he pinches my cheeks with one of his hands as he speaks.

"That's what you think, Miss Fischer."

Before I can quip back, he brings my face to him, my squished cheeks pushing my lips out for him and he eagerly takes advantage of the opportunity. The plane starts to move but we don't break apart. Instead, our kiss deepens as our tongues intertwine with one another. My hands are in his hair, his are in mine. I couldn't even tell you how long we stay there for, just making out like a couple of teenagers. It's long enough for us to line up and take off, though because pretty soon I feel us lift into the air, the small windows showcasing us slicing through the clouds as we ascend through the sky.

I pull back for a moment as Nico begins kissing up and down my neck as I look out the window. I haven't been on a plane in a while and I've never been on one like this. A few moments later, the captain comes in through the intercom, quietly telling us that we have reached cruising altitude and we are free to roam about the cabin.

That is all the permission Nico needs. Without pulling away from me, he unbuckles our seatbelt and stands up, me still firmly grasped into his arms as he begins walking me to the back of the plane.

"Where are we going?" I ask as his lips silence me.

He doesn't answer me as he continues walking before he lets go of me, and I'm free falling. Well, only for a second before I land with a bounce on a bed. I look around to notice that we are in a bedroom of sorts. A large bed, two side tables, a mini closet and a private bathroom is all around us. Nico turns, shutting the door and locking it before facing me once more.

Excitement and nerves rattle through me.

"Are you a member of the mile high club?" he asks.

I shake my head quickly and he smirks.

"You're about to be, but first, strip."

I hesitate only for a moment before I begin peeling off my clothes until I'm laying on the bed completely naked. Nico's eyes roam over me, a ravenous look to them and I expect him to pounce on me. But he doesn't. Instead, he moves around to the side of the bed, pulling something out before he moves to the next corner and the next until finally, he is by my side, pulling out a strap and wrapping it around my wrist. I look up at him with concern as he simply moves to my ankle, strapping that down as well.

"What are you doing? Are these—"

"Under the bed restraints? Yes," he answers as he straps my right ankle down before moving to my other wrist.

"Does your board members know they are sleeping on top of your kinky fetishes," I laugh, though I'm honestly trying to hide how fucking turned on I am right now. I swear to god I'm leaving a wet spot on the bed.

Nico pauses his work on my wrist, his eyes coming to mine as he lifts a single eyebrow.

"I had it installed this morning before our arrival," he says, fastening my wrist tighter than the others.

A sharp gasp escapes me at the move. Not in pain but more so in surprise.

I watch as he takes several steps back, watching me as if he were assessing the scene as he tilts his head to the side.

"Try to move."

"What?" I ask.

"Move, pull against the restraints. Try to get away."

I feel my heart begin to thunder inside my chest as I nod softly and begin tugging at the restraints. My arms are lifted and above my head and my legs are spread out pointing towards each corner. I honestly look like a human star fish. And I can't budge more than an inch on any restraint.

A satisfied smirk crosses Nico's face as he begins unbutton his shirt, shrugging it off his shoulders before moving to his pants. When he pulls his cock out, he strokes it a few times, looking down at me with a look of hunger that has me desperate to rub my thighs together. Unfortunately for me, I can't.

He seems to take notice of my desperation as he slowly crosses the space between us, kneeling onto the bed between my legs before leaning down. His face is a few inches away from my pussy and I attempt to bridge my hips to get him a little closer but the effort is futile. Nico looks to me with a smirk before he inhales deep, continuing to stroke himself as he speaks.

"You smell like heaven, little bunny. All tied up and helpless, looking like my most delectable meal on display."

"Then fucking eat me," I grumble desperately.

He flattens his tongue out and looks up at me as my body begins to practically shake with anticipation before he pauses and speaks.

"No."

I could cry. Literally. Disappointment and frustration slam into me and suddenly I'm fucking pissed. I pull against the restraints violently. If he's not gonna touch me, I'll touch myself. I hate being edged and I know that's exactly what his game is right now. I'm not having it.

His eyes widen in surprise as I pull against the restraints, an amused smile on his stupid face.

"Are you sure you're the girl from the club? She had a lot more patience. She enjoyed being teased and played with. She was a good little sub for me as I tied her up and fucked her into the mattress."

I stop fighting for a moment before I look up at him with a huff of my breath.

"She didn't know what it was like to be with you. I do and...I want it. There is no time for patience."

He smiles sweetly before coming around to the side of the bed. His hand reaches out to my cheek, gently cupping it as his thumb softly strokes my skin.

"Babygirl...you're not in charge here. I suggest you get used to it."

Without any warning, he leans forward, pushing his cock into my mouth. It takes me by surprise and I barely have time to ready myself before he's forcing himself down my throat. I gag for a moment before he withdraws and does it again and again, ruthlessly fucking my face as his hand still holds my cheek, softly rubbing it before delivering back to back smacks that have him groaning. I'm not sure if he's getting off on the smacks to my cheek or the way it feels against his cock. I don't care, though, because if I was leaving a wet spot before I'm leaving a goddamn river by now.

I could come with hardly any assistance at all and for a moment I wonder if I said that out loud because I feel his body stretch, leaning over my body before giving my clit a sharp pinch. Pain greets me first and my face tenses at it before pleasure suddenly blooms from the top of my head to the tips of my toes. I moan and buck against his touch as my orgasm rips through me like a fucking tidal wave.

As soon as my orgasm begins to fade, I realize that I've been essentially screaming in pleasure with the only thing muffling me being Nico's cock. I'm sure that was intentional.

Pulling away from me, Nico begins stroking his cock as he walks around to the end of the bed once more, pausing when he looks between my legs and smirks.

"Babygirl, you're making a fucking mess of my bed."

"I'd say I'm sorry, but I'm not at all," I reply.

His smirk widens to a full blown grin, his eyes dancing with a dark desire as he crawls onto the bed, covering my body as he lines his cock up to me.

"Me either."

Nico pushes into me with a hard thrust that has my back bowing. His hips snap into me with no mercy, they are almost painful with how deep he is going but there is no where to escape. I can't move an inch, left with no choice but to lay there and let him do whatever he wants to me.

It's like the instructor said in the club, sharing a dynamic like this takes a lot of trust. It's about giving up control and letting your partner have free range, trusting that in the end they will take care of you. That they will act with your best interests in mind. Or at least, they'll make you come after they fuck you raw. Which is good enough for me.

Nico's hands come up, pinning my wrists down to the bed as he fucks me deeper.

"Fuck!" he barks out before groaning. "You're just my little rope bunny, aren't you?"

I nod my head as pleasure slams into me over and over again. I can't believe I'm ready to come again already but that's what this man does to me. It's like I have no control over my body whatsoever. When we are together nothing else exists and we are surrounded by...pleasure.

"Nico, Nico," I whimper.

"Keep begging for me just like that," his low voice grumbles.

"Please don't stop," I beg.

"Couldn't if I wanted to, babygirl. I need you like nothing else in this world."

I can't help but get pulled from the moment, instantly sobered by his words as I look at him in surprise. Does he actually mean that? Surely it's just the lust talking, right?

He senses my shift in mood as his eyes come to mine and he cradles my face once more.

"Don't look so surprised."

With that, he crushes his lips to mine and slams into me deeper than before, forcing me to shout against him as his cock throbs, my pussy becoming filled with his cum as my own orgasm practically tears me in two. Our bodies jerk and grind together, wringing out every bit of pleasure possible before we collapse.

We only stay like that for a moment or two, catching our breaths before Nico stands up, releasing me from the restraints as he begins gently massaging the tender skin on my wrists and ankles. I look to him with a soft smile and he returns one all the same before pressing a kiss to my forehead as he whispers to me.

"Thank you for trusting me, I'll never take that trust for granted."

I melt inside. Literally, turn to goo from his words alone as I nod.

"Thank you for being worth it."

He gives me a small nod as his smile grows before he gathers me into his arms and lays us down. His fingers begin slowly tangling through my hair, massaging my scalp until my eyes begin to flutter. Before I even know it, I'm drifting off to sleep in the arms of a man I have no business being near, on our way to his home across the country while his girlfriend, my sister, is gone for the week. I shouldn't feel nearly as good about my decisions as I do.

Yet, here I am, in fucking bliss.

Chapter Twenty One
Cassi

Once we landed in Boston, we were immediately escorted to a town car where Nico's bags were already being loaded into the trunk. I've always heard people say that once you fly first class, you can never go back. I really hope the same can't be said for private. No stress, no hassle. Just ease, comfort and everyone around you treating you like you're their favorite person. Is this what it's like when you have money? It's a mixture between awesome and wildly fucked up.

"So what's the plan?" I ask.

Nico looks up from his phone as he glances at me, squeezing my thigh as he speaks.

"What do you mean?"

"Where are we off to?" I clarify. "Are we going to your apartment because I'll be honest, not sure how I feel about hanging up my clothes next to my sister's lingerie," I say with a dry laugh. "I mean, not like I have any clothes to hang up," I say, pulling at my shirt because I literally only have the clothes on my back with me and my purse.

Nico frowns for a moment before it melts away and he nods.

"We aren't going to the apartment. We're going somewhere else."

I nod at that as I look out the window, gorgeous historic buildings coming in and out of my view as we zoom through the city. Remember how I said that I feel no guilt? That was a lie. I feel really fucking guilty. No matter how much I try to convince myself that what we're doing is okay because my sister is a bitch who doesn't deserve Nico, and I've the fact that I've never felt this way about anyone before, it doesn't ease the guilt. I'm sick to my fucking stomach.

I try to push it aside, I try to enjoy the moment and yeah, maybe I'm a shitty person because the idea of sneaking around is kinda hot. The underlying guilt is there, and it's all more than a little overwhelming and majorly fucking with my head. Just wait until Ari and Nay find out. Fuck, I'm actually kinda scared for their judgment.

Who says I have to tell anyone, though? This is a fling. We had a one night stand that turned into a couple of hook ups. Just because he flew me across the country doesn't mean I'm worth much more than a call girl to him. He has the steady girlfriend bit with my sister, I'm just the side piece, which means I don't need to tell anyone about it, right?

As gross as it may be, for some reason, that puts me at ease a little bit. Maybe if I pretend that I don't have rapidly growing feelings, that butterflies don't tear through me the instant Nico's eyes meet mine, that I don't secretly wish he'd dump my sister and profess his undying yearning for me, I'll come out of this unscathed. Unlikely, but possible. So, I'm going to hold onto that for now because what the hell else will keep me grounded when a man who looks like him and fucks like him scoops me up and takes me away on a whim?

"Fuck," I say, pulling out my phone before I click on the text thread with my mom.

"What's wrong?" Nico asks.

"I forgot to message my parents. It's been hours since I was supposed to be off work."

Me: Hey! I'm staying the weekend with Naomi and Arianna at Arianna's cabin up north. Just wanted to give you a heads up.

I hit send and my mom's reply comes almost instantly.

Mom: Thanks for letting me know. Me and your dad were starting to worry about you. Love you, be safe.

Nico leans over my shoulder to read my text, nodding his approval.

"You're an excellent liar, Miss. Fischer."

I lift an eyebrow at him as I turn to face him.

"I know that was anything but a compliment."

He shakes his head with a soft smile at his lips as his hand lifts, running his fingers through my hair.

"Just as long as you never turn that talent on me, we're good."

"I could ask the same," I quip.

Nico looks at me seriously, his fingers pausing momentarily.

"I'm not sure it would be possible to lie to you. There is something about you that just..."

His words trail off and instead of searching for the right ones, he shakes his head and drops his hand from my hair. I'm still sitting on the edge of my seat, waiting for him to finish his thought before I realize he won't be doing any such thing.

Damn.

My phone buzzes with a notification and I cringe when I see who is texting me.

Alec: Hey. I haven't heard from you in a little. Is everything okay?

Fuck. I'm an asshole.

Me: Hey! I'm so sorry. I suck. I'm doing a girls weekend with Arianna and Naomi up north. Service is spotty out here. I'll text you when I can!

Alec's response comes quickly, and it sours my stomach instantly.

Alec: No worries. I was just worried about you. Selfishly, I'm disappointed I can't see you but I get it. Be safe, I'll be thinking about you. Love you, Cass.

Love you.

It's innocent enough. A phrase that can be exchanged between close friends, family members, or in this case I guess, ex-boyfriends? It's all about the intent of use, and unfortunately I know Alec well enough to know he is not saying or doing anything platonically. I can't let this thing between us go on any further. I've let it go far enough. Did I seriously consider giving us another chance? Absolutely. That was when I was doing anything and everything to keep my mind off my sister's boyfriend, though. Now that I have apparently decided to abandon all of my morals...well, I guess I can cut the safety net loose, which yes, I know how gross that is to refer to someone as wonderful as Alec like that.

I look up from my phone to see Nico deeply engrossed in his messages. Good. I have no doubt him reading Alec's message would send him into a foul mood. For this being a casual forbidden fling, he's most definitely the jealous type and I don't feel like arguing the entire time I'm out here. Then again, if we hate fuck, I could end up tied up again as he takes his anger out on my body. Hold up, maybe this could work.

Before I can make a decision on poking the bear or not, the car stops and the driver gets out promptly, opening Nico's door before I slide out through it. The driver grabs our bags and Nico slips him a few bills and nods.

"Thank you, George."

"Always a pleasure, Mr. Sanders."

I look around us, my eyes stopping on a large brownstone. With his bags in tow, Nico gently ushers me up the steps to the front door before taking out his key and unlocking it. It opens into a cozy foyer with a wooden hand railed staircase leading up to the second floor. The floors are a deep cherry oak and the trim throughout the home is a bright white, complimenting to the cream walls.

Slowly, I begin moving through the house, stepping through the formal living room with a huge fireplace before coming into the kitchen. It's clean, crisp and open, though the entire place this far feels a little...empty. Like no one has lived here in a long time. There is minimal decorations and the house feels more like it's staged to be sold than to be lived in.

"You live here?" I ask as I turn to Nico.

He shakes his head.

"I bought this place years ago. It was pretty run down at the time but a great deal. I fixed it up and planned to flip it but...I don't know. I got attached, I guess," he says as his hand runs along a carved door. The intricacy of the design make it very easy to believe it was hand carved, too. The entire place just oozes charm, but lacks occupancy.

"Come here," he says as he guides me past the kitchen, deeper through the house. "This is my favorite part."

He opens a pair of french doors that open to a private outdoor patio. Red brick cover the ground as well as the similar brick siding boxing us in. One side is slightly lower, allowing a beautiful view of a body of water. It's breathtaking.

"I've been meaning to fix this up but I don't really know what to do outside of what's been done," Nico shrugs as he points to the patio furniture that looks like it belongs on a balcony of a high rise penthouse, not a historical buildings patio.

"Maybe some lights? "I suggest. You could string them above

and it would warm it up back here. And you don't have any plants. We are outside and I don't see a spec of green anywhere," I tease.

Nico looks around and nods.

"What else?"

I step around the area, a million different ideas flickering in my mind as I point to the middle of the patio.

"Maybe a firepit? One of those gas ones or something with the glass rocks? That would be really pretty and would be a nice conversation hub."

My hand traces over the slate grey couch as I shake my head.

"I hate to say it, but this all should go too."

Nico frowns at that. "Why?"

I shake my head. "This place is a historical gold mine. It's a moment of history frozen in time and you're watering it down with millennial grey," I tease.

He scoffs at that as I shake my head. "Think warm colors. Browns, creams, nudes. Maybe a pop of greens or reds here or there."

My head keeps swiveling around, more and more ideas bubbling to the surface before I realize Nico hasn't responded, and I've no doubt offended him like a complete asshole. I mean, this place has to be worth several million dollars and I live at home with my parents. Who the hell am I to judge anyone?

When I look to him, though, I don't find judgment or irritation. Instead, he's watching me with a considering eye as he nods.

"I like it, your vision. It seems nice. Warm."

I nod. "I'd always take a nice cozy house over a sleek modern place any day of the year."

"Yeah, me too. I think that's why I couldn't let this place go."

"So, what? You just sit on it for fun? Bring your ladies of the night here?" I say with a waggle of my eyebrows, though, I'm only partially kidding.

Nico gives me a flat look before he closes the distance between us, running his fingers through my hair like he seems to always do. He does it so often I'm starting to wonder what the driving force behind it is. Is it the control? The connection? Or maybe he just has a kink for red curly hair.

"You're the first person I've ever brought here."

My teasing smile falters as I look at him seriously.

"How long have you had this place for?"

"Seven years," he says steadily.

Seven years. He's had this place longer than he's even known Carly, and he never brought her here. Yet, he brought me here the instant we touched down in Boston. I'm trying not to read more into it, but fuck, he's making it really hard not to.

"Wow, if you're not careful you're going to make me feel like I'm special or something," I tease.

"You are," he answers quicker than I ever would have imagined.

My throat tightens and I do my best to swallow through it before clearing my throat. Nico seems to sense my unease and he slowly unwinds his hand in my hair, placing a chaste kiss to my lips before he speaks.

"So, let's see what we can do about getting you some clothes and that toothbrush."

Yeah. Some clothes and a toothbrush my ass. Silly me, why did I assume that when he said we were going shopping for some essentials, that we'd be going to the local grocery store or something. No, this man takes us to Newburry Street. At first, I didn't know what that meant. It only took us passing by four luxury brand name stores for me to piece it together, though. We even walked by a sign that literally said the "Rodeo Drive of the East Coast".

After three bags from Chanel, two from Prada and four from Dior, I call it.

"Okay, what's the deal?" I ask as I'm standing on basically a runway in the dressing room of the Versace store.

"Hm?" Nico asks as he glances up from his phone.

"Why are you buying me enough clothes to outfit an army? You know I'm already sleeping with you, right? You don't have to try hard anymore."

Nico smirks as he waives me towards him. Of course I go to him, moving as carefully as I can in this silk black gown that I have absolutely no where to wear it to. He gestures for me to straddle him and I glance to the associate who has been circling us like a hawk as she smiles and shuts the curtains, effectively closing the dressing room off from all other customers.

Climbing into his lap, I loop my arms around his neck as he holds my hips.

"Do you not like it?"

"Like what?" I ask.

"Me spoiling you."

I laugh. "Sir, you passed spoiling about twenty thousand dollars ago."

He shrugs. "So what's twenty thousand more?"

Nico leans in and begins kissing my neck, moving down to my collarbone as I shake my head.

"It's forty thousand dollars total, you know, a brand new car. Or a downpayment on a freaking house? Look, I know you're used to throwing your money around to get your way but I don't need it."

He pulls away, looking at me tenderly as he nods.

"I know, that's why you deserve it, though."

I shake my head. "I don't need it, though. I'm not interested in what's in your wallet."

"Just what's in my pants?" he guesses.

I point to him as I nod. "Exactly, now you're getting it."

We both laugh at that before I shake my head.

"Seriously, I appreciate it more than you know. I feel like I'm having a pretty woman moment right now. You do know I'm a receptionist/college student, not a hooker, right?"

He furrows his brows in confusion.

"Fuck, I do this every time."

My mouth drops open, and I smack his chest as he laughs. "Asshole."

He grins as I try to push away from him, pulling me closer as he presses my mouth to his. I haven't really seen this side of him. This relaxed, playfulness. It's a complete 180 from how he was in Seattle, how he was around Carly. The naïve little voice in my head says I'm the thing that's bringing it out in him.

"Seriously," he says. "I hope I'm not making you uncomfortable. I just...I want you to like it out here. I want to make you comfortable and I may or may not be trying to sway you into coming out to Boston more than just this once."

"Really?" I ask.

He shakes his head like it's so obvious.

"Cassi, I'd move you out here right fucking now if I thought you'd let me."

I blink at that, more than a little stunned. Okay, maybe the fling thing was a little too built up in my head. No doubt from a point of self-preservation or something. Then again, maybe he wants his side treat on the tap, easy access and all that.

"We barely know each other, Nico."

He nods. "And I hate it. I want to know every single thing about you, and I want your zip code to be the same as mine while we do it."

My heart squeezes at his words and before I can respond, he continues.

"But, I know that isn't our reality right now, so I'll settle for stealing you away for moments like this."

"Until Carly comes back," I unhelpfully add, effectively ruining the moment.

Nico frowns as he shakes his head.

"It's not like that."

"It's okay, Nico. I get it, and I'm having a great time. I followed you across the country knowing what this this. I'm a big girl," I say as I stand and head for the dressing room, shutting the door behind me as a nasty wave of guilt and self-deprecation slam into me. Though, I don't get to revel in my misery for longer than a moment or two before the door comes swinging open, and a pissed off looking Nico is standing in front of me. I startle for a moment and go to ask him what he's doing but before I can, he's lifting me into his arms, pressing my back against the wall of the dressing room.

"What the fuck did you just say?"

"What...I—"

He cuts me off, shaking his head.

"No, what the fuck did you just say? That you know what this is? Tell me, Cassi, what is this?"

I can feel myself practically curling within myself as I shrug.

"I don't know. I just...I don't want to read more into this...thing then there is."

"Read away, babygirl. This thing between you and I is so fucking messy, so intensive, so epic, it's like galaxies colliding. It's important, it's real, and I'm not letting you go anytime soon. So, don't you dare try to diminish it, don't try to diminish yourself or who you are to me. I've known you for one week and yet it feels like you've been by my side for my entire life."

I'm speechless, actually fucking speechless. That was more romantic than any book, movie or poem I've ever seen or read in my life, and it was just delivered by the world's sexiest man to me. Honestly, what do I say to that?

"I wanted this weekend with you but I want so much more

than just one weekend with you, Cassi. I want all of the weekends with you. I want...you."

"What about—"

"You. Just you, do you get that?" he asks, his eyes practically begging me to agree with him.

So, what's a girl to do?

Slowly, I nod my head, and what looks like relief fills his gaze before he closes his eyes and nods, pressing a kiss to my lips.

Chapter Twenty Two
Nico

Before we got back to the Brownstone, I made a grocery delivery order, one of those items of course being tooth-brushes and toothpaste, as well as some essential items for the weekend. I haven't stayed in this house...ever actually. It's main-tained by a weekly cleaning company though that I keep on retainer for all of my properties.

The place is immaculate because of it but it's never really felt lived in. Not until Cassi literally stepped foot through the door and suddenly it felt like the entire property shifted before my eyes. Instantly, I was ripped back to my childhood, in a home that felt warm and light. Where laughter was filling every space better than priceless art and statement furniture pieces ever could. She feels like comfort, like happiness. She feels like home.

I honestly couldn't tell you what has happened to me. Eight days ago, I would have laughed if someone told me I was thinking what I'm thinking, feeling what I'm feeling. Here I am, though.

When the car stops out front of the house, George gets my door and I slide out before offering Cassi my hand. I tip George and rest my hand against Cassi's lower back as we move to the front steps.

"So, is George like your personal driver or something?" Cassi asks.

I nod as I come to the grocery bags that are waiting for us, bending down to pick them up as I offer my keys to Cassi so she can unlock the door. She does so wordlessly as I speak.

"He's one of several, though he's my favorite so I try to only use him when he's available."

"You don't know how to drive yourself from one block to another orr?" she says dryly.

I roll my eyes at her smartass comment, but I can't hold back my smirk.

"I can, but have you not noticed parking is in short supply around here? It's just easier sometimes."

She shrugs and I can't tell if it's because she agrees or because she doesn't feel like disagreeing with me. No, that can't be it. I swear, disagreeing with me has to be one of her favorite past times. For some odd reason, I kinda like it too.

When we step inside, I kick the door shut before moving into the kitchen and setting down the groceries onto the island. Cassi begins helping me unload the bags and she pulls out several items before giving me a puzzling look.

"Bread, cream cheese and jam...Nico Sanders, is this your ego salvaging way of saying you are actually intrigued by the idea of my late night treat?"

I do my best to hide my amused smirk as I shrug my shoulders.

"I know you like them, I figured if you're here for a few nights, the least I could do was have your favorite snack on standby."

"Be still my heart, that's romance right there," she says with a dramatic sigh as she places her hands over her chest and bats her eyelashes at me.

I shake my head at her theatrics as I finish unpacking the rest of the groceries.

"I figured we could order in for dinner tonight, if you'd like."

"Well, since you flew me out all this way to have your way with me, the least you could do is feed me, yes?" she smiles teasingly.

For some reason, the joke sits sour on my stomach, though. I pause what I'm doing as I look down at her, cupping her face as I shake my head.

"Didn't we just go over this? I didn't bring you out here to fuck you, I could have stayed in Seattle for the weekend and done that. I brought you because I wanted you here, not your pussy. You."

She blinks at that like she's surprised, but even with my words, I can tell she doesn't believe me. Sighing to myself, I shake my head as I press a kiss to her forehead.

"You're an incredibly irritating woman, do you know that?"

When I pull away, her green eyes are practically glimmering up at me as she nods.

"I've been told that a time or two, yes."

A laugh rips through my chest as I run my hand through my hair and sigh, pulling out a stack of take out menus that have probably been here for over a decade as I drop them onto the counter.

"Pick a place."

An hour later, we are laying on the couch, our tikka masala long forgotten as we watch some early 2000s comedy that Cassi picked. She also convinced me to build a fire, which honestly was harder than I imagined. I thought I was going to lose my man card there for a minute.

Cassi is engrossed by the show, laughing and giggling every few minutes, glancing up at me from time to time to make sure that I'm still awake. I am, of course. I'm just not the least bit occupied by the show.

Instead, I'm paying acute attention to the way her heart sounds as it beats against me. The soft rhythm of her breathing, how it perfectly matches mine so effortlessly. I can't focus on anything when her soft curves press against me like they were always meant to. I've absolutely lost my goddamn mind, and I couldn't care less. I'm not just into Cassi Fischer, I'm enamored. I'm infatuated. I'm flirting with a line that is far too close to love for my comfort.

Out of practically nowhere, she bounces to her feet, looking down at me before she pulls me to stand.

"Where are we going?" I ask.

"To the kitchen. It's grilled jam and cheese time."

I laugh at that. "How are you still hungry? Those portions were huge."

She pauses, turning to me sharply as she watches me closely.

"Nico, in case you weren't taught this as a child, there is never an appropriate time to tell a woman when she has had enough food."

Recognizing the dangerous waters I'm drifting in, I lift my hands in surrender as I nod.

"Yes, ma'am. My apologies."

She nods like all is well before stepping into the kitchen. She gathers all of the ingredients and slips into a routine all her own. I can't help but lean against the wall, admiring her as I do. She's so effortless in the way she lives life. So unapologetically herself. She can make herself at home anywhere she goes. It's authentic and refreshing and I swear to god, I'm addicted to it.

Grabbing out a pan and some butter, she begins heating it before setting her slop of creations onto the buttered pan. The bread sizzles in a way that has her doing a little happy dance. I push away from the wall, closing the distance between us before I wrap my arms around her waist, holding her close to me.

She smiles as she looks over her shoulder at me.

"Can I help you?"

I shake my head.

"I'm good right here, thanks."

Cassi tosses her head back on a laugh as she glances at me once more.

"How lovely for you. I, however, am busy creating culinary art, so if you could give me a little space..." she trails off, gesturing for me to release her.

I only hold her tighter, though, burying my head into her neck as I inhale her scent slowly and sigh. I hear an irritated groan that doesn't sound irritated at all, really, before she continues her extremely important work.

Once the sandwiches have been flipped and properly grilled on each side, she cuts each diagonally and slides a plate in my direction. I don't release her, so she settles for turning in my arms to face me.

"Bottoms up, big boy," Cassi says as she holds out her piece.

I pick one up, grimacing as I look down at it.

"I think that only applies to drinks."

She shrugs. "Says who?"

Cassi taps her sandwich with mine as if we were cheersing before taking a bite. She moans in pleasure, doing a little happy dance once more. I can't deny I'm more than a little hesitant but when she looks up at me with those big beautiful expectant eyes, what am I supposed to do?

Taking a bite of the sandwich, dread is heavy in me as the contrasting flavors hit my tongue. I chew for a moment or two before the flavor changes. Both of them morphing into some kind of combination, that I hate to say, works. I continue chewing my bite, swallowing it down before Cassi speaks.

"So, what do you think?"

I look down at the sandwich appraisingly, honestly taken by surprise.

"It's actually not bad," I say as I take another bite.

She practically leaps into the air, pumping her fist in victory.

"I knew it! You love it, right? It's literally the best little late night treat!"

I chuckle at her excitement and realize that in this moment, it could taste like manure and I would agree with her. Anything I need to do to keep that smile on her face, I'd do it. Luckily for me, it really isn't terrible. It's different, but almost in a good way? If I have to eat these damn things every day for the rest of my life to keep her this happy, it would be a sacrifice well made.

"I'm breaking up with Carly," I say virtually out of nowhere.

It forces her celebration to pause, her smile to drop as her eyes watch me carefully.

Real, fucking smooth, Nico.

"When she gets back. I actually was planning to do so when we got back to Boston but then she took that cruise and..." I trail off for a moment and swallow as I look down at Cassi.

She doesn't speak for several moments, though it looks like her breathing has become more ragged. I can practically see the millions of thoughts racing through her mind as she just stares at me.

"You two have broken up before, lots of times."

I nod. "Which is why it needs to be done. It should have been the first time."

"Then why wasn't it?" she asks quickly.

I pause for a moment before shaking my head.

"Honestly, I don't know. Loneliness combined with convenience."

She seems to wince at that, like that was the wrong answer, but it's the truth. I shrug as I set down the sandwich in my hand and reach for her. When she doesn't pull away, I know I haven't totally blown things as I continue.

"I know it's not a perfect answer, hell, it's not even a good one. I just thought...I don't know. I thought it would be too hard to find anyone compatible. I thought it was easier to settle with Carly's...

quirks than to face the trial and error of dating in this day and age. Then I met you."

Cassi's face sours as she pulls away from me and shakes her head.

"If you're about to make a speech about how you were going to keep dating my sister but then you met me and now you want to dump her, you should seriously revise that."

"No, no," I quickly say. "It's not that it's just..." I pause, not quite sure how to capture the right words as I sigh.

"Until that night with you, I'd been content with my life. Don't get me wrong, I was so over our relationship. Her meltdown on Jackie was the last straw and a huge eyeopener to what kind of person I was with. Then I met you—"

"And we slept together before you went crawling back to her," Cassi says callously.

I understand her hesitancy and her defensiveness. She has every right to have her guard up, I just hope I can prove to her that my words are genuine.

"And she called me sobbing, begging for me to at least meet your parents and save face. I had intentions on leaving that next morning and then, well, I saw you again. I had convinced myself that it wasn't an accident. That there was something bigger working. Then every moment I spent with you, you were this sassy, infuriating, perplexing wonderful woman. Suddenly, I didn't care about being away from your sister if it meant giving me the opportunity to be closer to you."

Cassi looks at me for a moment like she wants to believe me before shaking her head.

"You do realize how fucked up that sounds, right? Like you hear it too?"

A humorless laugh escapes me as I nod.

"I know, I also know that you're worried about what...this is," I say as I gesture between us. "I want to make myself perfectly clear when I say that this, us, to me, means more than it probably does even to you. That it may not feel like it because of our current situation and so, as soon as I am able, I'm remedying it. For all of our sakes."

"You don't need to give me all these promises, Nico. I—"

"I don't," I say, cutting her off. "But I think you need to hear them. I think you need to hear me when I say that I have never felt a tenth of what I feel with you, with anyone else. Ever. I think you need to fully understand that I am not just lusting after you, I'm not falling for you. I've already fallen, hard. I'm splattered on the side of the goddamn sidewalk. So, I'm giving you a heads up. You need some time to catch up, and that's okay. I have some things to take care of before I can have you the way I want you, and that's okay too. Just so we are clear, though, I'm giving you the notice because I need you to catch up, babygirl. I'm ready and waiting for you to fall too."

Fuck. My heart is racing. When did that start? I couldn't even repeat half of what I just said. I blacked out. My mouth opened and word vomit just poured out, and it didn't stop until every innermost thought I've possessed over the last week was out and in the open. The idea of playing it cool is officially shot to hell, and the only thing I can hope is that I haven't scared the shit out of her and sent her running for higher ground.

"Nico, I—"

I hold her face in my hands, bringing my lips to hers as I stall her words. When I pull back, I whisper against her lips.

"You don't need to say anything. I don't expect anything. I just...I never want you to worry, to doubt yourself or how I feel about you. I wanted my priorities to be clear, that despite literally all reason or logic, you have sky rocketed to the top of that list."

She blinks once, emotion practically drowning her features as she shakes her head.

"You don't need to wait for me to fall, I'm already there."

Chapter Twenty Three

Cassi

CASSI

We didn't have sex last night, which felt kinda off. For half a second, I was insecure that he was already bored of me. When I shoved away that annoying little voice inside of me, though, I understood. He was proving a point, sending home a message that he has been repeating since we got to Boston. He isn't just interested in sex with me, he wants more. He feels more. And I really didn't know how badly I needed him to prove that.

When he carried me to the master bedroom and held me in his arms all night something in me was soothed, calmed. Settled.

This morning we decided to head to a coffee shop that is just down the road from him, and yeah, I even made him use his two perfectly working legs and walk. His hand slipped into mine so effortlessly, like it's a habit we've adopted over decades together as we strolled the sleepy side street this morning.

I can smell the coffee shop before I see it, and when we round the corner, a quaint shop falls into sight. Nico steps in front of me, grabbing the door and holding it open before I step inside.

Instantly, I'm greeted with the smell of freshly roasted coffee, sweet baked goods and something savory that smells entirely too delicious. The little shop is bustling with customers but most seem to be getting theirs to go instead of taking a seat in their cushy assortment of seating scattered around the room.

"One black coffee, please," Nico says as we walk up to the front before he turns to me.

"Two," I chime in. "And one of whatever that amazing smell is!"

The barista nods and smiles as she taps in our order.

"Our bacon and chive croissants are crazy popular. Anything else?"

"Might as well make it two croissants. This big guy is always eating my food," I say with an annoyed eyeroll.

She smiles and rings it up before Nico offers his credit card over. His mouth drops down to my ear as he whispers to me.

"I literally have never stolen your food."

"True, but I'm really hungry and I didn't want to look like a porker for ordering two for myself."

He makes a noise somewhere between a guffaw and a choke before he looks down at me.

"Did you seriously just call yourself a porker?" he asks as the barista hands his card back.

We slide to the side so the person behind us can order as I shake my head.

"Nooo, I said I didn't want to look like one."

Nico rolls his eyes at me as he pockets his card. His hand reaches down to my waist, pinching it pointedly as he speaks.

"Don't ever speak about yourself like that again. You could order fifty of them and you'd still be breathtakingly beautiful. You're human. You're supposed to eat."

Wow. Thirteen year old Cassi struggling with her body and diet would have literally melted to a puddle and sobbed from that alone. Is everything that comes out of his mouth just perfection or do you think he has writers behind the scenes coming up with pure gold for him to pull out whenever is convenient?

Our order is called soon and we make our way to a comfy looking couch with our drinks and food. I sit down first and I expect Nico to sit across from me in the chair but he surprises me by sitting beside me, resting his freehand on my thigh as he sips his coffee. I look up at him and smile.

I couldn't believe him last night. I mean, I had hoped he was feeling at least a little bit of what I was. But for him to just lay it all out on the table like that? For him to silence every fear I've voiced and kept inside? Absolutely annihilating all of my walls and hesitations with one long winded breath. It took everything in me not to make a complete fool out of myself and tell him that I loved him. Which would have been a mistake of massive proportions because love? One week in? And he's not even single. Yeah, even I'm not that dumb.

"You keep looking at me like that and we're going to have to take this coffee to go," Nico smirks.

I perk up at that.

"Don't tempt me with a good time."

He grins, leaning in to kiss me when a cup is placed on the table and the chair across from us is pulled out.

"Hey," a guy in his mid thirties smiles, taking a seat as his eyes bounce between us.

His black hair is so short it's practically buzzed and his brown eyes swing between Nico and I with a curious smile.

"Jake," Nico says stiffly.

His tone is warm, like greeting a friend but the way his body instantly goes rigid tells me something isn't right.

"I thought you were still in Seattle until tomorrow," Jake says to Nico before his eyes swing to me.

He offers his hand to me and smiles.

"Jake Quentin."

"Cassi Fischer," I say as I shake his hand.

Nico tenses when I use my last name at the same moment Jake's eyes sharpen as he swings to Nico.

"Fischer? As in—"

"Carly's younger sister, yes, I'm sure you've worked that much out already," Nico says curtly.

"Hey, I didn't say anything," Jake says, his hands raised in defense. "She certainly looks nothing like Carly. She actually shook a strangers hand which tells me she doesn't act like her either."

"She is also in the room," I say pointedly, earning an amused laugh from Jake.

"You're right, my apologies. I just didn't know that Nico was in town...or that he brought back a souvenir."

I turn my head to the side in surprise.

"That's a really trashy way to describe another human. Tell me, are you reducing me to nothing more than a souvenir based on me being a metaphorical novelty or do you just value women so little that they are nothing but a prize to be shown off?"

Jake blanches, his face going pale as he shakes his head.

"Swear to god, neither. I was trying to be funny, and nosey. I'm sorry. I meant no disrespect. Really."

Nico squeezes my thigh, as if to put me at ease before he jumps in.

"Jake is head of HR at my company, which is why he's ready to throw up at your properly perceived assumption."

I blink at that as I look to Nico.

"Do I have to work at the company to file a complaint?"

Jake blanches even further, as if that were possible. I watch as Nico's mouth twitches in amusement, though he doesn't give it away as he moves his head from side to side in thought.

"Good question. I can file the complaint on behalf of you,

though the only person above Jake is me so, consider the complaint filed."

"Dude, what the fuck?" Jake says as he looks between us before my serious face drops and a laugh escapes me.

Nico breaks character too and Jake has some coloring returning to his face as he shakes his head.

"You guys are kinda assholes, you know that?"

I shrug, not the least bit sorry.

"Don't be a misogynistic asshole. Excuse me," I say as I stand up and head for the bathroom in the corner.

I round the corner and can't help but pause when I notice that I can hear them perfectly. It's not eavesdropping if it's an accident, right?

"Nico, what the fuck?" Jake whispers.

"What?"

Jake sputters. "Wha...what do you mean what? You leave town with Carly to meet her family and you come home cozied up with her little sister? How old is she? Can she even drink?"

"Yes," Nico snaps defensively. "Her age is none of your business, honestly, neither is anything about her."

"Dude, you know I'd never judge you. I'm just surprised as all. It's one thing to cheat on your girl but to do it with her sister in broad daylight—"

"I'm not cheating on Carly. We're breaking up. She took a spur of moment vacation and we haven't been able to talk but I'm ending it, for good."

"Again, not judging. I'm processing," Jake says.

I hear Nico sigh and I can practically see him shake his head.

"It's a long story but...there is way more to it than you're thinking."

"I'm sure there is. This is so far out of character for you. I... okay, I'm judging a little. Only because I know how much you resented your dad for what he put you and your mom through when he had a mistress."

There is a heavy pause between them before Nico's voice lowers and his tone sharpens.

"This is not that, Jake."

Another pause passes between them before Jake speaks.

"I believe you, sorry I insinuated. I'll tell you, though, you sure know how to pick them. She's a fucking spit fire."

A laugh escapes Nico, one that is practically oozing pride.

"Yeah, she really is."

I don't know why, but that makes me smile. Not really his words but how he says it. I step away from the wall and move to the bathroom grinning the entire way.

When I come back out, Jake is gone and Nico smiles softly at me as I sit down.

"Where did the world's worst HR manager go?"

Nico laughs at that. "Oh I'm absolutely getting him a mug that says that. He had to get going, he told me to tell you goodbye."

I nod. "After he ruthlessly judged us orrrr?" I fish.

"Not us, me. There is a major difference."

"I mean, I am the one sleeping with my sister's boyfriend. Sure, you're cheating on your girl but I'm breaking girl code and sister code. Pretty sure I'm the fucking worst."

Nico shakes his head, pressing a kiss to my temple.

"Don't. You know you're the furthest thing from the worst."

I shrug and Nico grabs my chin, pinching it between his fingers.

"You're a great fucking person, okay? Running into Jake on this side of town was unexpected but he was the best person it could have happened with."

"Why is that?"

"Because besides being my employee, he's also my childhood best friend."

"Really?" I ask.

Nico nods. "We grew up down the road together. Our parents were best friends, we have been attached at the hip since birth."

"So he must know Carly pretty well then."

Nico flattens his mouth and nods. "He's not a fan."

"Hey, me either," I joke in attempt to diffuse the tension. Though to be fair, I think I'm the tension instigator in this moment.

Nico huffs in what I think is amusement before he nudges towards my croissants.

"Eat."

After the whole coffee shop run in, I think we both wordlessly agreed it would be best to stay inside for the remainder of the trip. I mean, if I asked Nico to go out, I'm sure he wouldn't be opposed but now more than ever I feel the need to stay away from others. Nico needs to break things off with Carly before anymore people know about us. If she found out that I was sleeping with her boyfriend, I'm not joking when I say I think she would literally murder me. And then how am I supposed to have hot sex with Nico if I'm dead?

Okay, bad joke, but you get my point.

We wasted away the rest of the day eating, sleeping and fucking each other's brains out. A day well spent if you ask me. Nico is currently taking a shower and I slipped one of his button downs on as I made my way downstairs to whip up some sustenance when my phone began to ring. It's a facetime call from Naomi.

I answer it, propping the phone up as I continue layering the nachos.

"Hey, what's up?" I ask.

"Nothing, just needed a distraction. What are you up to?" she says.

"Making lunch. You?"

"Starving. What are you making? I can be over in five," Naomi laughs.

I tense at that as I attempt to laugh with her.

"No way, moocher."

Naomi's laughter softens as her brows pull together.

"Wait, where are you? That doesn't look like your kitchen. Oh my god. Are you at Alec's house?"

Picking up my phone, I quickly step out of the kitchen and out to the outdoor patio as I nervously laugh.

"Uhm, nooo."

Naomi waits for an explanation but when I don't give her one, she speaks again.

"Cass, where are you?"

"I'm, uh, in Boston."

"Boston? Since when?"

I look around like I'm expecting someone to be listening, even though it would be literally impossible. Still, I turn down my volume slightly so her voice doesn't carry as far.

"I got here yesterday."

When I don't expand, I can see the wheels in Naomi's head begin to turn. She always was the smartest one of our group. I literally see the moment it all clicks for her. Her eyes widen, her mouth drops and her hand raises to cover it.

"Cass...no."

Tucking a piece of hair behind my ear, I run my hands through my hair nervously.

"Yeah, I mean, it just kinda happened."

"What do you mean?" she gasps. "What just happened? You sleeping with your sister's boyfriend or you jumping on a plane so that you have easier access to do so?"

I'm taken back at her accusation and the aggression in her tone. "I—"

"Honestly, I'm really disappointed in you, Cass. I mean, this isn't you. I know you and Carly don't get along but to help her boyfriend cheat? The club was an accident, but this," she says as she gestures to me, pointing to the button down that I now realize is in perfect view.

Feeling completely naked, I hold the shirt together some like that will help as I raise the view of the camera. I feel tears begin to prick behind my eyes at her anger. I don't know why her judgment is bothering me so much but I feel like I'm gonna crack in two. Maybe it's because she's the quiet one of the bunch, the soft one. So if she is this disgusted in me I can't imagine what Ari will have to say about me.

I wasn't going to tell them. I literally just said this to myself. That was when I thought this was just a fling. This...it doesn't feel like that anymore. It feels real, permanent. I fucking hate myself for thinking this way, but it feels like forever as dumb as that sounds.

"You don't get it," I say, shaking my head at Naomi as she interrupts me once more.

"No, I don't. At all. This isn't you. You're worth more. You're not a side piece, you don't deserve your sister's sloppy seconds. You deserve someone like Alec that will make you their entire life. You should be number one, always."

"Would you believe me if I told you that Nico makes me feel that way?" I ask.

"Not if he's still dating your sister," she says flatly.

Ouch.

"It's complicated, Nay," I defend.

She lets out a bitter laugh as she shakes her head.

"It's more than complicated, Cass. It's wrong."

I don't know why but instead of sadness and shame, anger takes the forefront of my emotions.

"I get that you don't have all of the facts and you're drawing conclusions based off the information you have, but respectfully, you don't know what the fuck you're talking about."

Naomi laughs bitterly, a sound I honestly don't think I've ever heard come from her as she shakes her head.

"Okay, Cass. Play the victim. I'm the bad guy, Carly is the bad guy. Not you and Nico, though, right? You guys are just two innocents caught up? Like it's that fucking easy. Society has rules, standards, and you're breaking them!"

Her outrage seems way misplaced and I don't know what the hell to do with it, so instead, I do something I instantly regret.

"Honestly, why am I getting lectured by a jealous virgin? Maybe if you stuffed more than vibrators in your cunt, you'd chill the fuck out and realize life isn't so black and white! It's messy, and I thought my best friend would get that. Apparently not. Do the world a favor and get laid already, you're acting like a miserable bitch."

With that, I hang up the phone, my anger easing for a moment as I realize how far over the line I just went. Fuck.

Chapter Twenty Four
Nico

Cassi told me that she facetimed with one of her friends while she was in Boston. Apparently, Cassi she told her that she was here with me and her friend did not react well. At all. Nothing I could do or say could pull her out of her mood, and that was okay. I just wanted to make things better. It drives me fucking nuts when there is a problem I can't solve. She assured me that she'd be okay and we spent the rest of the night wrapped up together in bed.

When Sunday morning came, she had to go, and I fucking hated every second of saying goodbye. It bothered me a lot more than it should have and she wasn't on my plane for five minutes before I was texting her a plan to bring her back in a few days.

I couldn't put off my board meeting any further and I had a few client meetings lined up that I couldn't miss, but I wanted her back as soon as I could have her. In my city, in my home, in my arms.

Carly told me that she wouldn't be back until next Monday, which meant I had one more weekend that I could spend with Cassi before she got back and then I had that whole mess to deal with. It's going to work out well for Casi too because her classes don't start back up until next week. Still, it's only Wednesday and I don't see how I'm going to make it almost two more days without her. When I said I was addicted to her before, I wasn't lying because this, right now? I am going through a full blown addiction withdrawal.

The time difference is only three hours but those three hours mean that while I'm just getting into the office to start my day, she's still rolling around in bed. A fact that she is making painfully obvious as she sends me a good morning selfie of her black lace panties.

Goddamnit.

Standing up, I shut my office door before walking back to my desk. I hit the call button and prop up my phone as it rings and rings. Finally, she answers, that sweet sleepy smile greeting me as she bats her eyes innocently.

"Good morning."

"Cut the shit, little bunny. Just because I can't tie you up from three thousand miles away doesn't mean I can't screw you into submission. Grab your dildo."

Her eyes widen in surprise as she shakes her head.

"I don't have a—"

"Yes, you do. Don't lie to me. I saw it when I was in your room."

"Wait, really? You snooped through my drawers?"

"No, but I know you well enough to know you've probably got a whole drawer of things to play with, right?"

A mischievous smile spreads across her face as the camera shakes while she rifles around her bedside table before pulling out a dildo.

"Will this one do?"

I nod my head and she smiles as I speak.

"Set your phone up. I want the perfect view for the show you're going to put on."

"I'm putting on a show?" she asks dubiously.

"Yes, now do as I say or I promise you won't like the consequences."

"Okay, okay. Don't get your panties in a twist."

The camera moves for a moment as Cassi sets it onto her bedside table before turning on the lamp for better lighting. She smiles and does a cute little wave that has my heart skipping a beat before she wiggles herself onto the bed and puts her legs up. Slowly, she lets them fall apart, showing me an up close picture of those panties.

My cock twitches at the sight and I palm it through my slacks as I speak through clenched teeth.

"Take them off."

"Hm?" she asks as she sits up to look at the camera.

"Stay there, and take your panties off."

"Say please," she teases.

I stare at her flatly, not amused with her playful nature this morning. It's nine in the fucking morning and I'm as hard as a goddamn steel pipe, and it's all her fault.

She doesn't push me further, instead she wiggles off her panties and sets them to the side.

"Now what?" she asks.

"Now you're going to line up that tip and drag it through your pussy a few times. Pretend it's me playing with you, teasing you."

Her eyes flutter close as she does as I say, dragging the dildo through her exactly as I would. A content little sigh escapes her as I groan, squeezing my cock like it'll stop it from being hard at such an inconvenient fucking time.

"Now push it inside, slowly."

Cassi begins moving it inside her, inch by inch as she moans.

"Quiet, your parents are going to hear you," I growl as I unzip my pants and begin stroking my cock.

I own the company. This is my office. I'll jerk off if I want to.

"I'm trying," she pants as she pushes it inside her deeper, attempting to cover her mouth with her free hand.

Once the dildo is fully seated inside her, she begins fucking herself.

"Stop, grab your panties."

She looks to me with confusion as I nod in encouragement, stroking my cock faster at the sight of her pretty little pussy stuffed full.

Cassi grabs them, dangling them in front of the camera as I nod again.

"Now shove them into your mouth."

Her brows furrow.

"Do it, keep that sweet mouth quiet for me."

"But they're wet," she argues.

I lift a challenging brow. "You've never shied away from sucking your taste off my fingers or my cock."

"That's different...it's...you," she says almost bashfully.

The little blush that tinges her cheeks has my cock jerking in my hand. Christ. She has no goddamn right to be this perfect. This sexy. The girl is twelve fucking years younger than me, too damn young if I'm honest with myself. It doesn't stop me from wanting her any less, though.

"Do it for me, babygirl," I say.

She lets out a little sigh before nodding, pushing her panties into her mouth. The sight has a bead of pre-cum leaking from my tip, and I use it to help stroke my cock better.

"That's my good girl. Now start fucking yourself."

Her hand begins moving the dildo in and out of her, her moans now muffled by the fabric as her hips gyrate on the dildo. My hand moves faster as she fucks herself deeper and deeper until...

My door swings open and Jake strolls inside casually.

"Jesus FUCK!" I shout as I push out of my seat and turn

around, shoving my cock back into my pants as fast as I can. "You don't fucking knock?" I snarl.

Unfortunately, there isn't anytime to end the call and Cassi was too close. She's coming. Moaning and groaning through her panties as she comes all over her dildo. Jake's eyebrows raise in surprise as he looks to me.

"Please tell me you are not watching porn in your unlocked office."

A pause of silence occurs before Cassi clears her voice.

"Definitely not porn."

My eyes close in irritation. Fuck.

Jake's shock dissipates and an amused smile takes over his face.

"Hey, Cassi," he says to the back of my phone.

"Jake, right?" she asks.

"The one and only."

An awkward silence passes between the three of us before Cassi speaks again.

"Well, this is fucking weird. Hope you enjoyed the show, I'm gonna go drive off a bridge now."

Sighing, I shake my head as I reach for my phone.

"I'll call you later, babygirl. Have a good day."

"You too," she says before I hang up.

Jake looks at me in surprise, his mouth opening and shutting like a guppy.

"Not a fucking word," I practically growl.

His mouth slams shut before it opens again and shuts. Over and over until I groan.

"Fuck, fine, what?"

"Babygirl?" he practically spits out. "We're to the level of pet names, Nico?"

"We aren't to the level of anything. You need to mind your business and stay out of my relationship."

He laughs. "Relationship? Bro, you're still technically dating her sister."

I shake my head. "I haven't even spoken to Carly since I left Seattle."

Jake shrugs. "Doesn't make it any less true. You're moving at mock 1 speed with this girl. If you're not careful, you're gonna be on one knee with a diamond ring before you've even properly broken up with Carly."

"So?" I snap.

Shock splashes across Jake's face.

"Dude, I was joking. Okay, all kidding aside, as your best friend I'm obligated to tell you when you're being a goddamn idiot...you're being a goddamn idiot."

"Spare me the lecture, what do you want?"

"I'd love if my rational no-nonsense friend could rejoin us in reality?" Jake tosses out.

"Business, Jake. Work. What do you want?"

He sighs, shaking his head as he sets down a piece of paper.

"Just wanted to remind you of the onboarding we will be doing for the new recruits in two weeks."

I glance down at the paper and furrow my brows.

"I see Alec Thompson is on the list. I thought his start date was pending."

"Yeah, he called and said that things with his grandma are deteriorating and...wait, I didn't tell you about him. How do you know?"

My jaw tightens as I look to the side.

"He's Cassi's ex."

Jake's eyes practically bug out of his head.

"You're shitting me."

"Yeah, small fucking world. The guy is a grade a fucking asshole. If he slips up one goddamn time then I'm gonna—"

276

"Do nothing because we can't fire someone on the grounds that they dated your mistress."

"Don't call her that," I snap.

Jake puts his hands up as he shakes his head.

"Don't tell the head of HR you're planning to execute an unethical firing."

"I wasn't going to," I snarl, even though I absolutely was. "I'm just saying. I don't like him. He's not going to fit in here."

Jake watches me for a moment like he doesn't believe me before he slowly nods.

"Whatever you say, man."

"Anything else?" I grouch.

Jake opens his mouth to say something before he shakes his head.

"Good, get out."

Slowly, he backs away, stepping out of my door before I hit the call button for my secretary.

"Yes?" Virginia answers.

"Can you order me a handle with a lock for my office?"

I let go of the button before I add on.

"And can you send over someone from Tiffany's? I want to buy a piece but I don't have time to leave the office today."

"You want to talk to a rep or?" she hedges.

"I want to buy a piece, a necklace maybe. Tell them to bring options."

"Yes, Mr. Sanders," she says.

It only takes two hours for a rep from Tiffany & Co to come knocking on my door. Since the custodian on staff installed my new locked doorknob, I unlock it as I place my call on mute and invite them in.

A blonde woman in a too tight dress comes swaggering in like she just got off the runway. I'm not the least bit interested as I gesture for her to open the case she's carrying. She frowns slightly before opening it up as one of my clients asks me a question.

"Yeah, Charles, I'm listening."

He begins to rattle on about this new company he wants to invest in, despite me telling him a thousand times that it's a bad fucking buy.

Looking over the necklaces she displays I shake my head at each before pausing on one. I tap on it as I put the call on hold once more.

"I want the diamonds bigger."

She turns her head to the side in curiosity.

"We don't really do customizations for this style. We can help your draw up a new one if that is what you'd prefer," she says, resting a hand on my desk, practically forcing her tits to spill free from her top.

My eyes don't move from hers for a second as I look at her flatly.

"Is that what I asked for?"

She purses her lips in disappointment as she stands.

"I can call the office and see what we can do."

"Do that," I say as I hand her my card.

She looks down at the black piece of plastic before her eyes come to me once more.

"I don't have a price at the moment."

"Do I look like I care? Get me that necklace with bigger diamonds by this weekend and you've got a sale for whatever goddamn price you want."

I can practically see the dollar signs flashing in her head as she nods and pulls out her phone.

"One moment."

It's a simple circle design on a white gold chain. It looks like something Cassi would wear and she will be able to wear it with everything. It's beautiful as is but she needs something with a little more...oomph. I don't want her to just like it, I want her to love it. I want her to wrap it around her neck every morning thinking of me.

The saleswoman slips back inside and nods as she hands me back my card.

"The jeweler said they can have it done by Sunday at the latest."

I frown at that before nodding.

"We can have it delivered here or?"

"I'll pick it up."

"Okay, well, do you need a receipt or...anything else?" she says, really seeming to give it one last shot as she shoots me a seductive smile.

I allow my eyes to roam over her in disinterest before I wave my hand away.

"You can go."

Her face turns sour as I take myself off mute.

"Look, Charles, I hear you, but like we discussed, the ROI is just not there. I can send you over a few portfolios that I think would be a better route."

Chapter Twenty Five
Cassi

E xcitement rushes through me at the fact that I'm literally leaving work right now to head to the airport. I had to come in for a shift today and though I wasn't planning to work Saturday, with classes starting up I'm not saying no to the extra money.

Nico was more than a little irritated that I couldn't come Friday like planned but honestly, teasing him is one of my favorite past times and just like I told him, one more day won't kill him. Though, if I'm being honest. It might kill me.

I don't know how to describe it. Just three weeks ago, I didn't even hardly know the guy existed. I knew a guy was dating my sister. I knew a name and a occupation. That was it. It's insane how quickly someone can become the center of your every day. I go to sleep thinking of him, I dream of him, and then the moment my eyes open, I'm reaching for my phone to text him. It doesn't compare to being with him in person but the whole long distant thing kinda puts a damper on it. Oh, and the sneaking around affair part.

I try not to think of it like an affair because it's not like they are

Katelyn Taylor

happy. It's not like he doesn't want to get away from her. They are completely wrong for each other; he knows it and so do I.

Jesus. Would you listen to me? I sound like every mistress cliché there ever was. It's true, though. What we have, it's different. Special. And people can judge me all they want. That fact isn't changing.

I wave goodbye to Maddie and head for the front door when it's grabbed from me, a body stepping into the doorway before he stops. A smile takes over his face as his eyes lock onto mine.

"Good timing," Alec smiles.

"Alec!" I say, doing my best to mask my surprise. "Uhm, what are you doing here?"

He shrugs. "You've been avoiding me, so I figured it was time I came and saw you."

I smile, but I can feel that it doesn't quite reach my eyes. There is something almost menacing about his tone that puts me on edge.

"Sorry. I've been busy. Picking up extra shifts, classes are starting back up on Monday. Just been busy."

Alec nods like he believes me but there feels like some underlying tone of...something.

"I just...you don't answer my calls or texts anymore. We don't hang out. Did I do something?"

I shake my head as I cross my arms over my chest.

"Not at all. Really, Alec. You're wonderful. I've just been busy."

He nods like he can accept that as his eyes move down to his feet.

"My grandma is nearing the end. The doctors don't expect her to make it to next week."

My heart hurts for him and I reach out, rubbing his arm sympathetically.

"Alec...I'm so sorry. Is there anything I can do?"

284

"No, I've known it's been coming for a while. I already told Sanders & Son that I'll be good to start onboarding in a few weeks. It's time I get back to my life, you know?"

I wince at that and nod in agreement.

"I wouldn't say no to some company tonight, though," he laughs dryly. "I'll take you anywhere you want to go."

I hesitate for a moment before I let out a heavy sigh.

"I'm sorry. You're gonna hate me. I actually have to get going."

His brows furrow as he looks down at the backpack by my feet. Now I'm really regretting bringing it inside the office. I should have just left it in the car.

"Vacation?" he guesses.

"Just a quick trip," I say, hoping he will leave it at that.

Of course, he doesn't.

"Where to?"

I do my best to maintain my composure as I give him an easy smile.

"Boston."

Alec looks at me with suspicion in a way that sets me on edge before it slips away in the next moment.

"Visiting your sister?"

"Yeah, exactly," I agree way too quickly.

He nods. "I gotta be honest. I'm kinda surprised. You guys never seemed like the type of siblings that were...close."

I laugh at that because oh how right he is.

"We weren't...Aren't...We're trying," I say with a shrug as I lie through my fucking teeth.

"Well, can I give you a ride to the airport then?" he asks.

He could, in theory. I could leave my car here like I did last weekend, and it would be totally fine. For some reason, I don't want to, though. Something in me is telling me not to. Maybe he's just too observant and it's putting me on edge. Maybe it's because I don't want to feel like I'm leading him on any more than I already have. Or maybe it's because since Nico has been back in Boston, his jealousy has cranked up a thousand degrees, mostly in the hot way.

"You're so sweet. That's okay, though. I like having my car at the airport for when I come back. You know, delays and all."

Alec's eyes narrow slightly before he nods.

"I get that. Okay, well, safe trip. Text me when you can, yeah?"

"Absolutely," I nod, forcing a smile as much as I can.

He pulls me in for a hug and I wrap my arms around him as I feel him squeeze me. It's tighter than a normal hug and when he pulls away, he turns sharply and practically stomps off to his bike, firing it up before peeling out of the parking lot. The entire encounter has me feeling more than a little unsettled, and I'm half tempted to tell Nico about it. I think better of it, though. He'd only freak out.

Once I get to the airport, I find myself wandering around for a hot minute until I find where I'm boarding the jet, Nico's jet. I can't believe that I'm dating someone who has their own freaking jet. Okay, dating is a loose term. Then again, is it? Fucking doesn't seem right. Maybe seeing? Yeah, I'm seeing him. Either way, how on earth is this my life?

Easy, you swiped it out from under your sister.

Internally rolling my eyes at my inner voice, I do my best to shove that bitch back where she belongs because honestly, I don't have time for her shit.

Once it's time to board the jet, Jackie greets me at the top of the stairs with a smile.

"Welcome back, Miss Fischer. It's wonderful to see you."

I return her smile with a nod.

"You too, Jackie."

A look of surprise passes across her face that has my eyes shifting from side to side.

"What's wrong?"

She shakes her head. "Nothing, nothing. I just didn't realize that you remembered my name. Caught me by surprise."

I shrug simply. "You took really good care of us last flight and you seem really kind."

Jackie's smile softens but it doesn't lose its authenticity. If anything, it increases.

"Thank you...others haven't been as...warm as you," she says carefully.

I give her a flat look.

"You mean my sister, say what you mean. She's a vile bitch. I heard how she treated you when you accidently stumbled."

Jackie cringes at the reminder, shaking her head.

"All I can say is that I'm more than relieved Mr. Sanders has chosen to spend his time with you over her."

"Something we agree on," I laugh.

She does her best to hold back her chuckle, her professional demeanor slipping as she shakes her head.

"Anything I can get you before we take off?"

"Not at all. Please, sit back and relax. I won't be a bother, I promise."

Jackie waves me off and rolls her eyes.

"Please, you're one of the only clients I actually enjoy serving."

"Don't worry, I won't tell Nico I'm your favorite," I say with a smirk before moving to a recliner seat.

Jackie smiles and laughs as she heads to the cockpit, presumably letting them know we are ready to take off whenever. Pulling out my phone, I scroll for a minute when I see a funny meme. Out of instinct, I almost send it to the group chat before I pause. I haven't spoken to Naomi since our call last weekend. It's not like she's going to reach out and honestly, why the fuck would I? She was horrible to me for absolutely no reason.

No, if she wants to apologize, she knows where I'll be. It's not like I'm screwing her boyfriend. She doesn't even have a sister. She has two brothers, that's it. She's trying to pretend that she understands my sister's and my relationship, or her relationship with Nico or my relationship with Nico. She doesn't know shit and when she realizes that she was being a massive cunt, I'm willing to listen to her beg for my forgiveness. Until then, fuck her.

We take off in no time and about an hour into the flight, I decide to take a nap. It's been almost a week since I've seen Nico and if he's aching to be with me the way I am, something tells me I'll be getting zero rest tonight. Better get it while I can.

I wake to the feeling of lips on mine. They are gentle at first, patient. Then when my mind fully wraps itself around the idea, my eyes fly open and I smack the face away from me. My hand lands on the stubbled cheek with a sharp crack before a chuckle rumbles from his chest.

"Jesus, Cass. Good to know you can defend yourself," Nico says as he cradles his reddening cheek. "I was beginning to worry with how pliable that kiss was."

Wiping the sleep from my eyes, I blink a few times before I look around. We've landed, obviously, and I don't see a crew member in sight. Glancing down at my phone I see it's about thirty minutes past when we were supposed to arrive.

"Hi," I say softly.

"Hi," he grins as he looks down at me.

Nico stands to his full height, holding his arms out for me before I jump into them. He catches me easily, pinning me to him as he spins me around before my head pulls back to meet him. Nico kisses me for so long, you'd think he just got back from war, not a board meeting. I can already tell you after six days of being apart, I don't know how the hell we are going to manage things from here on out because any longer than six days and I think we will both tear our fucking hair out.

When we break apart, Nico looks at me like he hasn't seen me in years before he shakes his head reverently and smiles.

"I have a surprise for you."

"Hopefully a dirty one that involves you and me naked behind a locked door?" I ask as he pulls out a blindfold from his back pocket.

Nico smirks.

"The best kind there is."

The drive takes longer than I remember. For a moment, I wonder if we're going somewhere I haven't been before. But when the car stops and Nico guides me up a set of stairs, I smell the Brownstone before I could even see it. The old worn wooden floors hold a scent uniquely their own, paired with whatever kind of scent his cleaning service uses to keep the place smelling amazing.

Slowly, Nico guides me up the stairs and though I can't see, I know we are heading straight for the bedroom. Perfect.

When we step inside, he stops me, before slowly stripping me down piece by piece until I'm standing in front of him naked and blindfolded. Excitement is practically buzzing inside me as he lays me down onto the bed and takes my left arm, wrapping rope around my wrist before tying it to the headboard. He gives a similar treatment to my other wrist before he grabs my leg.

"Let's see how flexible you can be, bunny," he says before tying a knot around my ankle and pulling my leg up towards the headboard.

I feel a deep burn in the back of my leg but I do my best to breathe through it as Nico ties up my other leg. Sucking in a deep breath, I let out another shuttering one as he speaks.

"Fuck, Cass. You look so beautiful like this. So perfect."

"It's intense," I say tightly.

"I know, and you're doing so fucking good for me. C'mere, let me see those eyes," he says as he removes the blindfold.

My eyes blink several times, as if they forgot how to see before I look at him. He is naked too and he's kneeling in front of me. My eyes roam over his muscular arms, down to his chest and abs before pausing on his cock. Fuck. That thing is work of art. A sculpture of it should be placed in every museum so that it can stand the test of time. Then again, I don't want anyone else in the world to know about it because then they'll want a shot at his perfect cock too and I'm a selfish bitch.

Nico's hands run up and down the bottom of my thighs, slowly pushing down to stretch me deeper. I wince as heat envelops me and he shushes me softly.

"Good girl, just like that. Keep breathing. Fuck do you know how perfect you are?"

"No, but I'll never turn down a compliment," I say through clenched teeth.

A chuckle echoes through his chest as he shakes his head, his hand gliding down my thigh before resting on my ass cheek before he smacks it hard. I try to buck from the impact but I am rendered virtually immobile.

"You're so perfect, Cassi. You're beautiful, and smart. You've got the best fucking sense of humor," he says as he smacks me again.

I cry out in pain as pleasure quickly follows suit.

"Please," I beg.

"Please what?" he asks.

"Please just fuck me already."

A short chuckle leaves him as he scoots closer, lining his cock up to me.

"If I hadn't been fucking aching for you, I'd edge you. Make you wait. Bring you to the edge over and over again until you were a dripping quivering mess for me."

I practically shake at the horror of his words. I can't handle that. Not right now, not like this.

"Fortunately for you, I'm about as desperate as you are."

With no further warning, he pushes into me, deepening the stretch of my legs further as he practically lays his body on top of mine. I cry out as my legs are given no choice but to obey, the sturdy hold of the rope beginning to feel more like a lifeboat than a restriction. It's providing me stability, safety. Or maybe that's how I like to justify why I enjoy being tied up and used for a man's pleasure so goddamn much.

"Christ, babygirl. I've missed you," Nico pants.

"Me too," I nod.

"Being without you, I fucking hate it," he snarls as his hips snap forward viciously, like he's taking out his frustration on me.

"I hate that you're not beside me when I wake up or fall asleep. I hate that you live your life on the other side of the goddamn country. I hate that I haven't made you mine in all the ways humanely possible."

The pleasure and pain are melding together into such an intoxicating combination, I'm practically floating. So much so, that I almost miss his words. Almost.

"What's stopping you?" I ask, breathlessly as he pushes into me deeper than before.

"Time, because it's only a matter of time. You look like mine, you *feel* like mine," he says, emphasizing his words with each thrust. "So, tell me, Cassi. Are you?"

My eyes move back and forth between his, so much emotion in them. At first, all I see is primal need and desire. Then, slowly, it recedes, a hint of nervousness and uncertainty lays at the base of it all.

"I'm yours if you're mine," I say softly.

Nico's eyes close, something passing across his face before he opens them once more and nods.

"I've been yours since you stepped into that room in the club."

Euphoria washes over me. Not just from the way Nico is literally fucking me raw. Not from the way his fingers move against my clit like it's a fucking musical instrument and he's the world class player. A rush of warmth spreads from my chest to every inch of my body, the simple act of us together running so much deeper as we confirm what we both have already known. This is not just lust. This is not just passion. This...us...this is fate, and neither of us are willing to let it go for anything.

Our orgasms collide simultaneously. No words egging us on. No final moment that seals it both for us. It's as if our bodies are in sync and they have no control over it, no other choice but to fall apart together.

Nico leans down gently, placing a kiss to my forehead before he leans up and begins quickly untying me. A wave of pleasure in the form of relief rushes through me as each limb is untangled until I'm laying on the bed limp and exhausted.

Carefully, Nico scoops me into his arms as he carries me to the bathroom where the tub is running. When did he even get up to turn it on? My head is in a daze as he slowly steps into the jacuzzi tub, lowering us until we are submerged by the warm water. I sigh softly as I relax into it while Nico begins gently massaging every inch of my body.

I'm like dough in his hands as I melt into his touch. We sit there for so long that we end up draining the water when it goes cold before filling it back up.

I'm currently hanging halfway out of the tub as Nico rubs my back as I speak.

"You know, it sounds silly, but when I got here, to this house...it felt like...I don't know. Like coming home."

His movements pause and I close my eyes and internally curse at myself. Great job. You freaked him out.

Slowly, I turn to see how bad the damage is when I find him watching me with a steady gaze.

"Yeah?" he asks.

I cringe at my stupidity.

"Sorry. Forget I said anything. I think I'm still orgasm drunk," I laugh before facing the wall once more.

Nico resumes his work, rubbing my lower back as he speaks.

"It could be, if you want it."

"Hm?" I ask.

"Your home. Here, with me. If you wanted it to be."

I give him a sympathetic smile as I turn to face him. I appreciate him trying to make me feel better for sticking my fat foot in my mouth but he doesn't have to placate me.

"I appreciate you saying that but isn't that putting the cart before the horse?"

He shakes his head simply. "Not at all."

I frown for a moment before a laugh escapes me.

"Nico, you're not even single. You're dating my sister, and you're offering your home to me. Offering to share it, share a life. Don't you think that's jumping the gun a little?"

His hands stop moving as his eyes burrow into mine. For some reason, I don't want to look at him. I don't know why, exactly. Maybe I'm just embarrassed I brought this topic up to begin with. Maybe I don't want to hear his response, especially involving Carly. Maybe I'm just a little chicken shit.

"This place was just a property I owned until you stepped inside. You made it feel like a home. It's not just you that feels that way, Cass. I didn't even go back to my penthouse after you left. I've been living here because I haven't felt this...good in so fucking long."

I'm surprised by his words, but of course he doesn't stop there.

"As far as I'm concerned, Carly and I are through. We have been for a long time. Of course, we have to have a conversation, but I'm not focused on that. Not when I literally have my future in the palm of my hands," he says as he grips my sides pointedly.

I shake my head.

"Let's pretend she will take the breakup well, which prepare yourself, she won't. What? Are you going to show up for Christmas on my arm? That will be a little awkward don't you think?" I laugh sarcastically.

"Absolutely," he agrees. "But you're worth all of the awkward holidays, the misplaced judgment and any goddamn whisper in the world. I'm not going to toss aside our chance to be happy because the way we met was..."

"Unconventional?" I supply.

A rough laugh escapes his as he nods.

"To say the least."

I smile at that as his hand begins tangling through my hair.

"At the risk of scaring you off, I'm here to stay, Cassi. I'm not afraid to skip a thousand steps with you because here," he says, resting a hand on his chest, "I'm already there. I've been here for some long it actually scares the shit out of me because how is it possible that I literally fell in love with someone at first sight?"

The breath is stolen from my lungs as he shakes his head.

"Don't act surprised. I fought it for as long as I could, and failed miserably, but the truth has always been there. I haven't even known you for a fucking calendar month and I don't care. I love you, and I want you with me always. No matter what that means or looks like."

"Nico," I whisper hoarsely as emotion overwhelms me.

"You don't need to say it back, in fact, please don't. I don't need it. I just need you to know that I'm here, and you will always have a home with me. Always."

I practically slam myself against him. We're inches apart but it's too far. My lips press against his as he holds me in place. Holy fuck this is crazy. It's insane, honestly. Love? Impossible. This fast? Under these circumstances? The more I sit with it, though, the better it feels. Don't get me wrong, I can still completely recognize that this whole thing is absolutely batshit. I just really don't have it in me to care.

Chapter Twenty Six

Nico

I'm fucking pissed. I was guaranteed that I would have the necklace by Sunday, and now here I am Sunday morning, dropping Cassi off at the airport, sans necklace. I slipped off this morning before she woke up to grab it, and when I arrived, they told me that their courier had been delayed. I was unreasonably pissed off and stormed out of there in a fucking foul mood. A mood that seemed to practically melt away the instant I stepped into the brownstone and smelled Cassi's perfume in the air.

"I'm sorry again about your surprise being delayed," I say as I hold her hand in mine in the back of the car.

She looks to me with a sweet smile as she shakes her head.

"And I told you, you don't need to get me anything. I also wouldn't have even known there was a surprise to be had if you hadn't told me, so all of this weird misplaced guilt is on you."

I let out a sharp laugh at that and kiss the side of her head. True.

"I'll have it for you the next time I see you. Maybe I can come to Seattle?"

"You do have a fancy jet at your disposal," she smiles.

"I'll talk to Virginia and see what she can do about my schedule this week, after I deal with Carly."

Cassi's nose wrinkles at that as she looks out the window. Yeah, my sentiments as well. See, it's not as easy as us just breaking up. We live together, have for a few years now. Our lives are intertwined and just because I don't want to be with her anymore doesn't mean I want to leave her out in the cold.

I've thought over what I'm going to say and how I'm going to handle things a million times over, but like Cassi said, this will not be going well. At all.

Chapter Twenty Seven
Cassi

I hated leaving Boston. I swear, each time that I came back to Seattle made me hate it more and more. I felt more displaced, more alone, and no, it's not just because I haven't had a full conversation with one of my best friend's in over two weeks and haven't spoken to the other since our blow out.

Pulling the hood of my jacket up, I rush towards the building for shelter because of course it's raining. It's spring in Seattle, that's all it does is rain. When I step inside my first class of the day, I find that I'm one of the first people here. Of course, I didn't beat Naomi. She's always early to everything. No matter what.

For a moment, I debate on sitting away from her. I mean, we haven't talked. We haven't hashed things out. We are most certainly not good. When her eyes meet mine, and she offers me a timid wave, I decide to extend an olive branch.

Hiking my backpack up on my shoulder further, I move through the class before taking a seat beside Nay, leaving an empty seat between us for Ari. I'm extending an olive branch, not lending a whole goddamn tree.

"Hey," she says first.

"Hey," I greet before looking down at the paper laid in front of me.

Advanced Photography. Who said this was going to be an easy a? Arianna swears that we did but honestly, I remember her begging and pleading us to take it so we could all have at least one class together. The fact of the matter is, I'm not a fan of photography. That's Ari's thing. Naomi is pre-med and me...I'm...me. I'm the drifter of the group, the one that doesn't know what she wants to have for breakfast let alone what to do with the rest of my life. I started college because it was what I thought was expected me, but now I'm a junior with no declared major and no fucking clue.

Wow, that was a little morose for a Monday morning.

"How was your break?" Naomi asks.

"Fine," I say as I turn to her. "You?"

"It was...interesting."

I lift a questioning eyebrow at that and wait for her to explain but she doesn't.

"Are you still..."

"Sleeping with my sister's boyfriend? Yeah, I am," I snap. "That's what you really wanted to know, right? You want to bitch me out? Tell me what a horrible person I am some more? Go ahead, I'm ready for it," I say as I turn to her, spreading my arms out as if to welcome her shit attitude.

She shakes her head and sighs as she focuses on filling out the syllabus agreement. I scoff and roll my eyes as the professor asks everyone to take their seats. I didn't even realize everyone was filing in while Naomi and I were talking, if you can even call it that.

One person is noticeably absent, and that person suddenly appears at the door, earning a scowl from the professor as she rushes inside. Naomi and I wave to Ari and she runs a hand through her black hair before taking the seat between us. Good.

"Dude, you live right across the street. How can you be the last person here?

I huff under my breath.

Ari looks around nervously as she keeps her voice low.

"Uhm, yeah. So, I'm kind of not living there anymore."

"What do you mean?" Naomi whispers.

Arianna licks her lips nervously as her eyes move from mine to Nay's.

"I moved."

"Where?" I ask.

"Now that everyone has finally joined us, we can get started," the professor says, shooting a pointed look to Arianna.

Asshole.

He practically bores me to tears with his lecture. All about expectation and seizing the moment when it comes to your art. Blah, blah, blah. I'm eager to take my mind off the dramatic chaos of my life over the last few weeks so when we are dismissed, I pick up right where we left off.

"Where did you move? When did you move?" I ask Arianna.

"We could have helped you!" Naomi adds in.

Oh, look who is pretending to be a good friend all of the sudden.

"So, uhm, remember your birthday?" Arianna asks me.

For some reason, I tense. Did Naomi tell Arianna? I mean, it doesn't matter if she did. It's not like I'm keeping it a secret from Ari. Or at least, I wasn't planning to. Okay I was for a little but whatever. Things have changed and I'm not planning on doing so anymore.

"Well," Arianna continues. "I hooked up with someone."

"We know, and then you went back the next week, right?" Naomi chimes in.

"Yes, exactly. Well, someone turned out not to be just anyone. He was...Logan."

"Logan?" I frown, trying to place the name.

Do we know any Logan's? The guilty look on Arianna's face

tells me that's a bad thing for some reason, but I'm struggling to understand why.

"Cunninham," Arianna adds in.

The name clicks into place and both Naomi and me stand there in shock. Our jaws are literally unhinged before I shriek.

"You fucked your stepdad?!"

Okay, honestly I don't feel so bad about sleeping with my sister's boyfriend anymore.

Arianna shoots me an irritated look as we grab our bags and stand, rushing out of the class before we are out in the quad.

From there, Ari dives into an extremely detailed retelling of the last two weeks of her life. Finding out she slept with her *ex*-stepdad, she emphasized the ex part a lot, to hooking up with his brother, then with him, and then the fall out of her mom finding out.

"So...you moved in with him?" Naomi asks.

I wait for her to go on the attack with Ari like she did with me, but for some reason, she doesn't. What the hell? Is she reserving her bitchiness just for me or what?

"Yeah, yesterday," Arianna says.

I can't help but let a laugh bubble out of me.

"Are you crazy?"

"I think so," Ari says with a sigh.

Naomi smiles and rubs her arm lovingly.

"Does he treat you well?"

Arianna nods.

"Then we're happy for you," I say, glancing to Naomi to check that she's actually happy for her.

Naomi casts me a look like she is, but I still see the hint of judgement playing in her eyes. Honestly, what is her deal?

"Thanks," Arianna says, looking too us with suspicion before she asks, "What ever happened with you two that night?"

"Hm?" I ask.

"I know you both hooked up, we've all never shared details,

though, which isn't like us. Now you know why I didn't share mine because, I mean, I wasn't exactly proud. Your turn bitches, spill."

As if saved by the bell was a real thing, Naomi's phone rings and she feigns frustration.

"Oh, got to take this. See you guys later!" she says as she runs off.

Honestly, that's a good fucking question Ari. What did Naomi get up to? She claims she's still a virgin after that night at the club, but I haven't asked her if she's still clutching that card since. Is that why she's being so crazy? Did she finally get fucked and feel guilty or some shit? Or maybe it was who she fucked?

Arianna looks to me expectantly and I decide, what the hell.

"Okay, but you can't tell anyone."

She scoffs. "Like I ever would."

I nod at that. "Okay."

I dive headfirst in telling her everything. Thank god we both don't have a class for an hour because there is more to go over than I expected. I catch her up on Alec and Nico and how we fell for each other and didn't mean to. I also fill her in on how Nico is breaking up with Carly tonight and we're going to be together.

Arianna doesn't give me the same judgment that Naomi did, but she does watch me hesitantly.

"Babe...are you sure he's going to break up with her? Not that I don't believe you, I just don't believe men. Most of the time. Almost never, really. You know how it is, when a man is taken and swears they are going to leave their partner, they almost never do."

I don't know why I feel betrayed by her doubt. It's dumb and misplaced and I recognize that, but it still hurts all the same.

"He's going to, and then...I don't know. We haven't figured out the details of the long distance thing. Him being stupid rich has its advantages though," I laugh dryly.

Arianna nods and tells me that if I'm happy, she's happy. I can't tell if she means it or is just regurgitating what I said. Either way, it doesn't really matter. She didn't react like Nay did and for that, I'm grateful. I also didn't tell Arianna that Nay and I aren't really talking. I don't want our weird stuff to affect their relationship.

Throughout the day, I check my phone incessantly. Mainly because I haven't heard from Nico which is a rarity. I got the usual good morning text, we chatted back and forth for maybe five minutes before he went silent. I assume he's busy with work, or maybe with Carly. He told me that she wanted the jet to come pick her up last night but obviously it couldn't because it was too busy taking me home. Am I bitch if I admit that I kinda got a kick out of that?

Nico said that she should be home tonight and that's when he's going to do it. Rip off the band aid. I told him he should have 911 pre-dialed because she is going to go certifiable on his ass when he breaks things off. Not because I think she loves him or anything, but she has certainly become accustomed to the lifestyle he affords her, and she won't be letting that go easily.

Chapter Twenty Eight
Carly

I swear to god if I didn't have one of Nicholas's credit cards on me, I would have had a full on meltdown. I called him Sunday night to tell him that I was ready for the jet to come pick me up in Miami. Can you believe that asshole said that the plane was in route on the west coast and I'd have to fly commercial? Commercial.

It was bad enough I had to fly down to Miami commercial, at least I was with my friends, though. Now having to do it a second time? And he didn't even sound sorry.

I don't know what is his deal. Ever since we had that fight in Seattle, he's been so distant. We fight literally all the time. We break up a few times a year at least before he comes to his senses and comes crawling back. This time, though, things feel...off. I can't explain it.

The kid behind me kicks my seat, again, and I've had e-fucking-nough. Hitting my call button, the stewardess comes over to me as I lean forward to speak with her. She greets me with a smile, her teeth smudged with her ninety nine cent lipstick as her coffee breath has me practically gagging.

"What can I help you with?" she asks.

"Yeah, you can help me by getting that little crotch goblin's feet out of my back!" I snap.

The stewardesses eyes go wide as she glances behind me before looking back to me.

"Seriously, isn't there like an age minimum for flying first class? We all pay a lot of money for some peace and quiet and I don't need my flight ruined by some little shit."

"I'm sorry, are you talking about my son?" A man leans forward from the row behind me.

I turn to him with a sneer but drop it quickly when I take a look at him. Obviously tall, well built, an Armani tailored suit and a watch on his wrist that easily costs a quarter of a million. My eyes flick down to his hand to see a golden band across his finger. Like that's ever stopped me.

Jasper or Jack or whatever his name was had a ring on too. We chatted at the cruise bar for approximately two minutes before he was chucking that thing into the ocean, though. I don't know why but married guys are always the best fucks. Maybe it's because they have something to prove. Or maybe it's because they have all of this pent up energy from their hag of a wife not giving it up. Either way, lucky me.

The cruise was a nice little distraction from reality. Don't get me wrong, I love Nico and all but when he's being an ass, he doesn't put out and I have needs just like anyone. Especially with his little attitude he's been having, I knew he wasn't going to be up to taking care of me which is why I practically jumped at the opportunity to take a little cruise. Suffice it to say, I'm coming home more than satisfied and ready to kiss the ground Nico walks on for a while until he softens up again. That's usually all it takes to make him realize he's desperate for me.

I haven't had a full on affair in over six months when Sean and his wife decided to give things a go again and he actually meant it.

Gag. Usually, I just have a few one night stands when Nico is traveling or working late. Though, Mr. Armani looks like he could be my next contender.

"I'm sorry," I say, giving him my best doe eyes. "I'm so exhausted. I don't even know what I'm saying. I've just been having the hardest time since my husband cheated on me," I overshare.

That card usually goes one or two ways. Men either turn away from it, fearful of the messiness and drama of getting involved with a taken woman, or they flock to it. They want the excitement, the rush, and the guarantee of an emotion free fuckfest.

As I guessed, Mr. Armani changes his attitude quickly, leaning forward further as he speaks to me.

"I'm so sorry to hear that. We all have hard times, I understand."

"You do?" I ask with faux relief.

He gives me an understanding smile and I arch my back slightly, allowing my cleavage to spill forward. Predictably so, his eyes greedily take in the sight as I smile at him from beneath my eyelashes.

"You're so sweet."

"I'm Kevin," he says with a grin that tells me I've snagged him.

"Carly," I smile.

I'll be honest, I didn't know that airports had daycares for kids. Or maybe they don't and he just paid a stranger off to watch his kid. Either way, it doesn't matter. Kevin quickly dropped off his son into some play area and fucked me like he had one day to live in the airport bathroom. Not the sexiest place I've done it but the rush was enough to have me coming all over his cock.

After we exchanged numbers and he paid for a town car to take me anywhere I wanted to go, I pull up to my apartment complex.

The driver grabs out all of my bags and the bellman is quick to grab a cart.

"Welcome back, Miss. Fischer," he says.

I wave him off as I saunter through the main lobby and move to the elevator, pressing the penthouse button followed by a scan of my keycard. I'm whirred up to the top before stepping out of the elevator and into our apartment.

"Helllllo? I'm back," I call out, finding the place strangely empty.

Glancing down at my phone I look at the time. Nicholas should be home from work by now, it's a Monday. Shrugging my shoulders, I drop my purse onto the counter as I make my way into the bedroom. I need a shower and a fucking drink.

I begin getting undressed when I notice Nicholas's side drawer is cracked open. Curiosity has me moving towards it as I peek inside. There, I find a blue Tiffany box, a rush of excitement filling me as I open it.

A gorgeous circle pendant diamond necklace is laid against the fabric, shimmering even in the dark bedroom. Wow, I guess he's not as mad at me as I thought. I was convinced he was going to break up with me, again, before I left for my cruise. What can I say, clearly he can't get enough of me.

Honestly, I can't imagine ever not being with Nicholas. We've been through so much together. He's my forever end game, or at least until he gets too old or dies or something. The fact is, no man has ever tried to love me the way Nicholas has, besides my dad but like obviously he doesn't count.

He's rich, handsome, and can eat pussy better than any man I've found to this date. He's a keeper, if he would just pull that stick out of his ass from time to time. I'm glad that he understands just as much as I do that we're meant to be. We can fight and bicker all we want but in the end, it will always be us. I'll make sure of it.

Running my fingers across the necklace, I'm tempted to put it on now and surprise him. I think I'll let him give it to me, though. Preserve his male ego and all that. It really is a beautiful piece. God. I so deserve this.

Chapter Twenty Nine

Nico

I can tell she's here the instant I step foot through the door. It's like a veil of negative energy I step through, and sure enough, when the elevator doors open, I see her on the couch scrolling on her phone with some trash TV show on.

She glances over to me before looking down at her phone.

"You're home late. I'm starving so please tell me you have some kinda of food."

Here we go.

Slipping off my suit jacket, I set it on the back of the chair as I begin rolling up the sleeves of my dress shirt. I cross the room until I'm in front of her before I take a seat on the coffee table. Carly side eyes me over her phone as she shakes her head.

"What?"

"I want to end this."

Boom. Done. Band aid ripped off.

"End this?" she asks, like she's never heard those words in her life.

Like I haven't personally said them to her over a dozen times. This time is different, though. This time, it's over.

"Us. This hasn't worked in a long time and I know neither of us are happy. It's time to part ways."

Carly sits up, tossing her phone to the side as she turns her head to the side.

"Where is this coming from? Is this because I went on that girls trip?"

"No, it's not. It's been coming for a long time. Remember how we agreed I'd meet your parents in Seattle and then we would go from there? This is where I want to go.

She scoffs and tosses her hand out by her side.

"Well, yeah. That was before you wanted to stay even longer. I figured we were fine after that. We laughed, had sex, you bonded with my parents. This is honestly so shocking, Nicholas."

"It's Nico, it's fucking Nico! Everyone on this goddamn planet calls me Nico except you. Everyone knows I can't stand the name Nicholas except you! You're a spoiled, entitled, brat and I don't want to be with you anymore! I don't want to live with you, I don't want to be near you. I want to get the fuck away from you!" I snap as I jump to my feet, clapping my hands together with each word to emphasize my point.

She looks shell shocked at my explosion, and for a moment, I feel guilty. Tears begin to gather in her eyes but she doesn't let it show, quickly swiping them away as they fall.

"Wow, I'm...I'm sorry. I didn't know you were so unhappy. I—"

Her voice chokes, cutting her words off as she looks down at her hands.

"I know I haven't been the best partner, and I'm sorry. Really. I...I guess I don't have an excuse," she says with a shrug of her shoulders.

I feel myself softening with empathy, but I don't allow it. She plays these games every time we break up. This time is different, this time is final.

"I know that this will be adjustment for you. I took the liberty of securing you a few interviews for firms around the city. I submitted glowing letters of recommendations and I've secured you an apartment a few blocks away. I've paid the rent through the year so you can get back on your feet gradually."

She looks shocked by this, and it's as if she's just now fully understanding how serious I am.

"Uhm, thank you. I...that's very generous of you."

I nod my head, waiting for her to say more. Instead, she just looks at me with big sad doe eyes, that unfortunately for her, don't really do much for me.

"I have movers that are coming tomorrow morning to move all of your things to your new apartment. They'll handle everything. I've cancelled your line of credit and will be changing the locks starting tomorrow afternoon."

I knew that one was going to a shocker for her. Her face is stunned that I've moved so quickly, when really, I've been planning all of this from the moment Cassi and I gave in to one another back in Seattle.

Swallowing roughly, Carly nods.

"I understand. I...I'm sorry, Nichol—" she cuts herself off, shaking her head. "Nico. I'm sorry this didn't work out. I'm sorry I couldn't be better."

Again, typical manipulation shit that I won't be playing into. I shrug my shoulders callously and awkwardly, Carly stands.

"I uhm, I'll get as packed as I can before the movers come tomorrow. I..." she pauses, her eyes searching my own. "I wish you a lifetime of happiness, you deserve it."

I nod, not able to return the sentiment in this moment. She winces like my silence hurts most of all before she walks down the hall, shutting the bedroom door behind her. Her soft sobs echo through the apartment and I blow out a heavy breath before heading out the door.

The tight ball of anxiety that has been twisting in my chest all day eases when I step into he elevator and hit the lobby button. That went a hell of a lot better than I thought it would. Instead of anger she just seemed sad. I really do hope she finds happiness elsewhere, though. For a while I convinced myself we could make each other happy enough, that what we shared was enough. Now that I've gotten a glimpse at what real love feels like, real connection, the imitation just won't do.

My fingers are flying across my phone as I send a text that I've been dying to all day.

Me: It's done. We're free, babygirl.

I stayed at the brownstone last night and stayed on the phone with Cassi until she fell asleep. She couldn't believe how well Carly took it and honestly, I'm still in shock myself. Maybe I built it up too much in my head or maybe deep down, she has known it was coming for a while. Either way, I'm officially a free man, which means that I can pursue and be with the woman I'm completely fucking gone for guilt free. Finally.

I'm fucking pissed I couldn't take off the next few days. All I can think about is getting to Cassi. Unfortunately for me, I've taken off way too much time lately, honestly more time than I've taken off in the last ten years, and I have obligations that can't wait. First up is a meeting with one of my biggest clients, Arnold Maywhether. A rich as sin mine tycoon. He owns over fifty gold mines and a handful of others, and we manage all of his portfolios.

He only likes to meet with me and for the price of the retainer we charge him, he can have whatever he wants. I've been putting off this meeting with him for weeks and this morning was the last chance to see him before he goes on vacation with his wife. I've met her a few times and she's actually quite lovely. They've been together for over forty years and seem like one of those true couples. The ones that stand the test of time.

That's how we scored his business in the first place, that was my parents. Or at least, to the public eye. They were married for forty six years before my dad passed away. My mother never remarried and passed ten years later. On the outside, my family looks like the perfect picture of a wholesome family business. Beneath the smoke and mirrors, my dad was like any other rich asshat distracted by the dollar signs in his bank account than his family and the tight ass assistants over his wife. My mother pretended not to notice, but she knew. She always knew.

When Jake tried to compare me to him, it cut deeper than I would like to admit. I'm nothing like him, and I'd rather die than ever be assimilated to a man like him.

Stepping out of the elevator and into the entry way of Sanders & Son, I smile to Margie, our receptionist as I walk back to my office. Glancing at Virginia's desk, I notice it's empty. She must be grabbing coffee.

As I open my door and step into my office, I notice it's not empty. There, Carly is sitting in my chair, swiveling around as she faces me.

"Hello handsome."

What the fuck? Gone is the morose look of rejection and sorrow. She's dressed to the nines in attire that can barely pass for business casual as she stands and sashays her way to greet me.

"What the hell are you doing here?"

"Sanders, is that anyway to speak to your fiancée?" Arnold scolds from the corner of the room.

Fuck. I didn't see him.

"Sorry, Arnold. I didn't see you there. I...wait, fiancée?"

"Yes," he smiles, crossing the room to shake my hand. "Congratulations, son. She just told me all about the engagement. I can't believe you proposed to her at Mariano's just like I did to my Mary."

My head whips back and forth between Carly and Arnold in confusion because what the fuck is going on?

"Arnold, there is some kind of miscommunication here. I—"

"You know I hate doing business with those playboy types. No one cares about the family these days. It's good to see you finally making an honest woman out of this gem."

"Oh Arnold, stop. I'm an engaged woman now," Carly says with a blush as she shoos him away.

A huge diamond ring catches my attention on her left hand, and I snatch it midair to examine it. She smiles at me happily as I glare at her.

"What the fuck is going on?"

"Nico," Arnold chastises as Carly smiles.

"It's fine. We had a bit of a late night," she winks.

Arnold laughs like he's in on a dirty joke before nodding.

"I'm going to use the restroom, I'll give you two some privacy. Congratulations again."

"Thank you so much!" Carly smiles as she rests her hand onto my chest.

As soon as Arnold is out of the room, I toss her hand off of me and take several steps back.

"What the fuck do you think you're doing?"

Her blissful smile drops as she gives me a flat look.

"Jesus, you very well may be the worst actor I've ever met in my life. I'm securing you another fat investment from that rich son of a bitch. You're welcome."

"Why the fuck did you tell him we're engaged?" I snap.

"Oh, because we are, baby. See, you even bought me this gorgeous six carat ring," she says as she wiggles her ring in my face.

"I didn't buy you anything," I scoff.

She shrugs as she paces through my office, taking a seat once again in my chair.

"Well, it was your credit card that made the purchase, ergo, you bought it for me. How could I say no?" she smiles, lifting her shoulders up as she admires the ring.

Running a hand through my hair I shake my head.

"I don't have it in me to keep up with whatever stupid fucking game you're trying to play, Carly."

"Baby, this is not a game. This is real. Did you honestly think I was going to let the best thing that ever happened to me walk out the door and I wasn't going to fight for it?"

"Fight for what? We're over, Carly."

"We're over, when I say we're over."

She slaps down a magazine onto my desk and my face pales as I look at it. An impressively well photoshopped picture of me on one knee proposing to her is on the front page with the words "Billionaire CEO Nicholas Sanders proposes to longtime girlfriend.".

"What?" I snarl as I clutch the paper in my hands.

"Five other online media outlets have published their coverage on it and our engagement party has been all planned. Invites have already been sent out."

"What engagement party? We're not fucking engaged!" I shout, because my god, it's like talking to a fucking wall.

She fakes shock as she covers her hand over her heart.

"Are you saying you want to break off the engagement? I don't think that will look too good to your clients, your investors, the board."

I stare at Carly in disbelief as she shrugs her shoulders.

"The choice is yours, I guess, I know you'll make the right one, though. The party is next weekend. My family is thrilled and I told them you'd send the jet for them. Make sure you wear that black suit I love," she says before pressing a kiss to my cheek before sauntering out of my office.

What the actual fuck just happened? Did I just get forced into an engagement? Does she really think me breaking off an engagement would hurt my reputation that bad? So, what? I lose a few clients? I doubt I'll lose anything once I tell people she's a fucking psycho who made it all up. I want to know how she moved so quick with everything. I mean, she had to of been...wait.

Her family?

She talked to them already?

Oh fuck.

Chapter Thirty
Cassi

I stare at my phone for longer than I'd care to. Longer than I realize. I don't know how to do anything else, though. I'm numb, confused and fucking pissed.

You are cordially invited to the celebration of Carly Fischer and Nicholas Sanders' engagement.

Below is an address and a date as well as a gift registry link.

Engagement? They are engaged? Since when?

It feels like my heart has plummeted to the ground, like my stomach has been twisted into a thousand knots and the only thing I can do is...stare.

"Hello? Earth to Cassi?" Arianna says, waving a hand in front of my face.

I look up from my phone as my eyes meet hers across the table. She must see the shock on my face because her teasing smile vanishes as she slowly lowers her pizza.

"What is it, Cass?"

I try to speak, but my throat is too tight. That feeling that you get right before you're about to burst into tears? Yeah, amplify that tenfold at least.

"I...I..." Shaking my head, I slide the phone over to Arianna.

She takes it curiously, looking around the school's cafeteria as if someone was going to read over her shoulder before her eyes move across the screen. Her face morphs from curiosity to shock to anger as she looks up at me.

Yeah, my sentiments exactly.

"What the actual FUCK is this all about?" she practically snarls.

"What is what about?" Naomi asks as she comes to sit down beside Arianna.

"This," she snaps as she slides my phone over for Naomi to read.

I wait for the snide comment. The I told you so or...something. I practically wince in preparation for it but when her eyes meet mine, they shimmer with heartbreak and empathy.

"Babe," she whispers with a shake of her head as she reaches out and touches my arm.

I don't pull away, but I don't say anything either.

"Did he tell you?" Naomi asks.

"No," I finally rasp. "He...we had plans for..."

Shaking my head, I let out a shuttering breath.

"He's a fucking asshole who deserves his dick chopped off. I'll do it, too," Arianna practically seethes.

Naomi shakes her head in disappointment as she squeezes my arm.

"He is a son of a bitch, and you deserve so much better. You get that, right? You understand that his shitty behavior is not a reflection on you or your worth?"

I'd love to agree, but unfortunately I fear I have turned into that woman that is so dependent on the man I thought I loved affection and actions, I don't know what to think. It's cliché to think that I'm the problem, that I must have done something. That I wasn't enough in some aspects. I just...I can't believe he'd do this. He didn't even have the decency to end things with me before the goddamn engagement party invitations were being sent out?

"Guess you were, right, Nay. We should have never gone there in the first place," I say with a bitter scoff.

"No," Naomi says urgently before muttering under her breath. "I'm sorry, Cass. I was out of line. Our phone call and every moment after. I...I've been struggling and that's not on you, nor was it fair for me to put it onto you. I'm so sorry. If I could take it all back I would in a heartbeat. I didn't mean any of it. Truly."

Her blue eyes are watering like she's about to burst into tears. She's such a goddamn empath, always has been. When someone is hurting, she just about keels over in pain at just the sight of it. It's one of the many things I love about her. Even if her words and, honestly, actions leading after hurt, I don't have it in me to hate my best friend. Especially not when everything else is fucking crumbling around me.

"You were trying to look out for me, Nay. I get it. We're okay," I say before pausing. "And I'm sorry for blowing up on you. I never should have thrown your virginity in your face like that. I was out of line."

As if we've summoned him, my phone rings, buzzing against the table as all of our eyes swing to his contact name. His picture is one I took of him when we were in bed together a few days ago.

A few days ago.

How can we go from that moment, wrapped up in the sheets, him promising me forever, that he loved me, that he wanted me...to this? In just a few days?

Naomi reaches for the phone, declining the call. I nod in thanks before the phone starts up again. This time I decline the call and we all sit in anticipation. Within seconds, the phone rings again and again. No matter how many times I decline the call, he calls right back.

He's no doubt calling to cover his ass. Make up some bullshit excuse. It doesn't matter, though. I don't want to hear from him. I don't want anything to fucking do with him.

"Are you okay?" Naomi asks softly.

"No," I answer quickly.

The girls nod before Arianna pipes in.

"Want me to cut his dick off? Would that make you feel better?"

I look to my friend before shrugging.

"Couldn't hurt."

I picked up a shift after my classes were done for the day. Really, it's just to help out with the after school rush because oddly enough that is a thing. Parents don't want to take the time off work or pull their kids out of school so our office stays open until eight at night on the weekdays.

After we get the lobby cleared, it's looking like we will be able to actually leave early. Glancing to my side, I see Rebecca, the full time receptionist playing a game on her phone when the door opens. She sinks a little lower, as if to say 'this one is all you' and I do my best to hide my sigh of irritation.

"Hi, how can I help yo—"

My words stop immediately as I stare at the man in the doorway. Nico looks to me with frantic eyes as he quickly crosses the room.

"Cassi, I need to talk to you," he says breathlessly, as if he ran all the way here from Boston.

"I'm working," I practically spit.

He winces at the ferocity in my tone, but I don't give a fuck. I don't want to see his face. I don't want him near me. I don't want anything to do with the lying fucker before me.

"Please, Cass. I need to explain. It's not what you're thinking."

"You need to leave. Now," I say stoically, earning the attention of Rebecca who puts her phone down to watch us curiously.

Nico sighs in frustration as he shakes his head.

"No! I'm not going anywhere. Please, just give me five minutes," he says, his voice rising as Maddie walks in from the back.

"What is going on in here?" she asks before her eyes land on Nico, her gaze turning poisonous.

She found me crying in the bathroom before I started work and I spilled everything to her in one embarrassing run on sentence.

"What the hell do you want?" she asks as her eyes look him up and down.

Nico sighs as he looks to her.

"I just wanted to talk to Cassi."

"Well, she's working, and she has asked you to leave. So unless you want a cleaning, I suggest you turn around and march your ass out of here," she says.

Nico frowns for a moment before nodding.

"I would."

"Would?" Maddie asks.

"Like a cleaning, please. If Cassi can hear me out while I do it."

I narrow my eyes at him as I shake my head because, is he dumb?

"You won't be able to talk while you're getting your teeth cleaned," I say flatly.

"Let me try, and if you still don't want to talk to me after, I'll leave."

Sighing, I run a hand through my hair, knowing this will probably be his one and only offer to leave me the hell alone.

"Fine, whatever."

Maddie looks to me as if making sure I mean it before she shrugs.

"Alright, second door on your left, don't worry, Cass. I'll make it hurt."

Nico gives her a look as he walks past her.

"You know I can hear you, right?"

"I'm aware," she says simply before she follows him down the hall.

I turn to face Rebecca as I shake my head.

"You good to cover the desk for a bit?"

She shoos me away.

"I'm fine, and if I had a man that looked like that begging for my attention, I definitely wouldn't be frowning like you are."

I don't hold back my scoff as I stand to my feet. If you only knew.

When I come back to the room Nico is in, he's already laying on the chair and Maddie is getting him ready. She begins scaling his teeth, scraping and stabbing his gums more than a few times, causing him to yelp in pain.

"Ow!"

Maddie rolls her eyes. "Don't be such a bitch. You're fine."

Nico grumbles, or at least tries to with his mouth open as I stand there with my arms crossed.

"Talk," I say.

"Cassi," he says. "It not what you fink," he says, Maddie's entire fist pushing into his mouth, I honestly think just to fuck with him.

"I nin't ruhose," he continues.

"What?" I ask.

"I didn't ruhose," he continues.

Poke. Another stab from Maddie has him squirming in the chair.

"She shet it uh," Nico says slowly, trying to emphasize each word, but I have no idea what he's saying.

I am enjoying watching him squirm, though.

Maddie looks to me and I wave her off.

"Looks like you got lucky today. I was just getting started," she says as she offers him the bowl to spit in.

He spits a large amount of blood as he scowls at her before looking to me.

"Cass, Carly set it all up. I broke up with her last night, she was really calm, like I told you. Then I came into the office and she was in there with one of my biggest clients. She told him we got engaged and photoshopped a picture and everything! Got it printed in a magazine and blasted online."

"She also sent out invitations for your engagement party," I fill in flatly.

Nico shakes his head in frustration as he stands from the chair. He tries to reach for me but I pull away. Hurt splashes across his face but he quickly buries it as he speaks.

"I promise, Cassi. I would never. I broke up with her, we were done and she just...didn't accept it?" he laughs bitterly.

My arms are still folded over my chest as I shrug my shoulders.

"How am I supposed to believe you, I mean, that's a pretty unbelievable perspective, Nico. And what's the outcome? She forced you into an engagement so you're gonna go through with it orrrr?"

"No, fuck no!" he practically snarls. "Of course not. She's already invited all of my major clients. Half the fucking city. I can't cancel it."

"Why not? Just tell them she's fucking crazy, which she is, and that you don't want to marry her."

"It's not that simple, Cassi. Most of my clients care about reputation, about who they are associated with. If this isn't handled right, my entire company could fold. Hundreds of people out of work. I have to play this carefully."

I just stare at him for several seconds before I shake my head.

"Well, good luck with that."

He frowns. "What do you mean?"

"I mean, that sounds like a whole lot of nothing. If your business means more to you than being with me, that's fine. If you think I'm going to sit back while you play fiancé to my sister, though, you're out of your goddamn mind."

Nico shakes his head as he reaches for me once more. This time, I allow him as his eyes are pleading with me.

"I'd never. She's just...cunning. She knew this would tie my hands which is why she's lining everything up like this. I promise, this will end soon. It just can't end in a scandal."

"Like the entire city of Boston finding out that you're not actually engaged to your long term girlfriend, but fucking her younger sister instead?" I offer.

Nico grimaces but nods. My irritation tempers slightly because saying it out loud, I hear it. Sort of. I mean, it doesn't paint either of us in a good light. I understand his industry has a great deal to do with reputation, image. I mean, if I was going to invest millions of dollars with a company, it probably wouldn't be with the one whose owner's sexual exploits are on the front page of the news. Which is what would happen, Carly would make sure of it.

"Just give me a little time to fix this mess. I'll negotiate with Carly. Give her some kind of offering so she drops this ruse. I don't know, but I'll fix it. Please, believe me."

I'm hesitant to. Maybe that makes me a bad person, but I see no good coming from this. No good coming from playing into her hand. It's what she wants. To buy some time, to convince him to fall for her once more. Does it make me horribly insecure if I'm fearful that she may convince him?

"Nico, I don't have time for this kind of drama. I shouldn't have to put up with it. This...us...we were never supposed to be together. For reasons just like this."

"Don't say that, don't diminish what we have, Cassi. Please. I know it's fucked, but I promise, it will be fixed and we will get our chance, babygirl."

I hate myself for weakening for him. I'm probably stupid as hell for it too. I can physically feel the ice that has been layering around my heart all day cracking, though. It's thawing from his pretty promises and sweet declarations. I believe he wants to be with me and I know, he will do anything in his power to achieve that. I just... maybe I'm a pessimist but I do not see a way out of this mess without one or both of us getting hurt.

Chapter Thirty One
Nico

S he doesn't believe me. I can feel it. I can see it in her eyes, and it fucking kills me. I don't blame her, though. If the roles were reversed, I'm not sure I'd believe me either. As soon as Carly left my office I fucking ran to Jake. We called in our PR company and I explained everything, even divulging my current relationship with Carly's sister, though of course, Carly doesn't know that detail.

Our PR manager, Brittany, was particularly nervous, which didn't leave Jake or I feeling good about the situation. Her first concern was bad press falling back on the company. I mean, the fact that news outlets were already involved in mine and Carly's 'relationship' meant that for their own interest, they would be following us very closely. Me spontaneously breaking off our engagement or me going to the press and dismissing her claims of a proposal would only result in a 'he said she said' that Brittany informed me we would not win.

I told Brittany I didn't care the fall out, I would not be marrying Carly for publicity. She assured me that I wouldn't need to let it go that far, but it would help tremendously to allow a little time before quietly breaking off the 'engagement'. Her logic is that new drama is always circulating and the best thing for us is to wait until something new takes everyone's focus, and then Carly and I will quietly separate. It's like she doesn't have a clue who we are dealing with.

Still, there may be some kind of option I can offer. A chunk of money, a house, a fucking yacht. I don't give a shit. I just want the psycho out of my life. Or at least as far removed from me as possible since there is a very high chance that there will be a Sanders and Fischer wedding. It just won't be to Carly. If Cassi will wait for me through this shit storm.

I jumped on a plane as soon as I finished the meeting with Brittany and headed straight for Seattle. Cassi wasn't answering my calls, understandably so, and I had to see her. I had to talk to her. I couldn't go another second with her assuming the worst. The devastation in her eyes when she looked to me was everything I expected and more, and it nearly cracked my heart in two.

After my gums finally stopped bleeding, I sat in the waiting room until Cassi was done with work and now here we are, in her car sitting at the airport. I have moves to make in Boston that unfortunately can't be made here. I asked if she wanted to come back with me for a few days, but I already knew the answer.

"I have classes and work and you have...a lot of shit to deal with," she says with a shake of her head.

I nod my understanding.

"I'll be contacting my lawyer in the morning. See what we can do in cases of defamation for myself and the company."

Cassi lets out a short laugh and shakes her head.

"If you think Carly will let this go for anything less than... everything? You're completely mistaken."

Sighing, I run a hand through my hair as I nod.

"I know, one way or another we will make it out the other side. Together," I say, as if it were a certainty.

I take Cassi's hand in mine before pressing a kiss to the back of it. She gives me a tight lipped smile, like she wants to be happy but she doesn't know how to.

"I'll see you soon, okay?"

Cassi nods. "See you at your engagement party," she says on a bitter laugh.

Reach out for her face, my thumb grazes against her cheek gently.

"Hopefully things will be resolved by then. Don't give up on us, please."

She swallows roughly and nods as I press my lips to hers. When we pull apart, she looks a little more at ease.

"It'll be over soon," she says.

"So soon," I agree.

It was in fact, not over so soon. I had spoken to lawyer after lawyer, all confirming that there was really nothing concrete that I could do about Carly's stunt. Not preventatively. I'd have to sit back and wait for shit to hit the fan before we could go after her, which really fucking sucked.

The engagement party is tomorrow, and though I have every advisor under the sun, including Jake, urging me that attending is a good idea, I can't fight the urge to say fuck it all to hell and drop a tell all myself. I've typed one up half a dozen times and have been tempted to send it to the media outlets so that the narrative can be flipped for fucking once. But I haven't, and I hate it.

Cassi and I have spoken every day, but there is hesitancy between us. A wall, and though she has every right to have it there, I want it ripped the fuck down. I'm finishing getting ready in the bathroom of my penthouse when I step into the bedroom and find Carly sprawled naked on my bed.

"Jesus Christ. Put some fucking clothes on," I snarl as I look away, tossing the nearest item of clothing towards her.

"Oh please, you can't even look at me?" she scoffs.

"I'd prefer not to, no," I say as I head for the door, stepping out into the kitchen. "How the fuck did you even get in? I change the locks?"

She trails after me, deciding not to put on the shirt I threw at her.

"I called a locksmith," she says with a shrug of her shoulders.

I turn to look her in the eye, derision heavy in my gaze as I shake my head.

"You're fucking psychotic."

"You're my fiancé, Nicholas. We haven't slept together in weeks and you won't even let me stay at my own apartment."

"This isn't your apartment!" I snarl as I clench the side of the kitchen island. "I bought you an apartment, got you all set up when I dumped your fucking ass and you responded by telling the whole goddamn world that we are engaged."

She doesn't respond, just stares at me like she's waiting for me to get to a point. My eyes practically bug out of my head as I point at her.

"Do you not see a problem with that? You're essentially black-mailing me into marrying you, is that what you want?"

Carly rolls her eyes like I'm being dramatic as she shakes her head.

"I don't see why you're fighting us so hard. We have been happy for three years, it was time to take a next step, and I'm not going to apologize for fighting for us."

A humorless laugh escapes me as I shake my head.

"You're not fighting for us, there is no us, Carly."

"Then why are you even coming tonight, hm? Why did you send the jet to pick up my family?" she taunts.

Because I'm trying to find a way to get the hell away from you with as minimal damage to my reputation and company you crazy bitch.

Of course, I don't say that. Just as I've been advised, I'm keeping my mouth shut and moving forward while the suits do all the work. They better hurry up before I blow everything to hell, though.

Carly rounds the island towards me as her hand reaches out to touch my shoulder.

"Nicholas, c'mon. Stop thinking about this so hard and—"

I rip away from her before she can even touch me, shaking my head with disgust.

"Do not touch me. Get the fuck out of my apartment before I call the cops," I say as I grab my keys and wallet and head for the door.

"You're seriously not even going to fuck me!" she shouts in outrage.

Yeah, I'd rather my fucking dick fall off than stick it in her.

I'm not heading to the office today, I'd be fucking useless even if I did go in. Instead, I'm swinging by the Brownstone, putting the finishing touches on a few things before Cassi and her parents land. I told her they could stay in a hotel or the Brownstone, whatever was more comfortable for her. It made me happy to hear she wanted to stay there instead of a hotel. It gave me a glimpse of hope.

I've been planning these changes over the last week or so but finally, it's all finished and now I can make sure it's perfect before she gets here.

Chapter Thirty Two
Cassi

"I just can't believe Nico flew us on his jet! Can you even believe that thing, Henry?" my mom gushes.

"It was quite something. What about you, Cass? You seemed awful quiet?" my dad asks, nudging my shoulder as we make our way out of the plane and onto the tarmac.

"Hm? Oh yeah. It was really cool!" I say, doing my best to feign excitement.

I've been on the jet several times now and don't get me wrong, it hasn't lost it's novelty by any means, I think I'm just desensitized to this trip in general. Mainly because I'm here for the engagement party of my sister and kinda but not really boyfriend. How fucked up is that?

I send a check in text to Ari and Nay. After the shit that Ari went through last week, I don't expect her to touch base anytime soon but surprisingly, she's the first one to send a gif of a person drowning before pulling themselves up onto a dock. Smirking at my phone, I shake my head before pausing.

I can feel Nico's eyes on me before I even see him. When I look up, he's standing there in front of a limo. God, he can be so ostentatious sometimes. I think he enjoys spoiling my parents, though.

His eyes never leave mine, to the point that my mom turns around to look at me, as if she were verifying that is where his attention lies. Her brows furrow for a moment before she smiles and turns to face him.

"So good to see you, future son!" she laughs.

My parents were shocked when Carly called them and told them that they were getting married. Though my mom hinted at it when they were both in Seattle, none of us actually thought it would happen. Most of all me.

They don't know that Carly is basically trapping him into this, and Nico asked me to keep it to myself. At first, I didn't like the idea of that, and that negative voice inside of me convinced myself it's because she wasn't trapping him. When he explained that he needs to operate as normally as possible until he can develop a safe exit strategy, it made sense. Still pissed me off, though.

Nico smiles, hugging my mom before shaking my dad's hand.

"Thanks for the flight, that was something," dad says with a shake of his head.

I watch as Nico nods and smiles.

"My pleasure, I hope they treated you well."

"Psh, we were like royalty," my mom smiles.

Nico smiles like he's pleased with that before his gaze returns to me.

"Good to see you, Cassi."

"You too," I say, unable to stop my heart from flip flopping in my chest.

It takes everything in me not to run into his arms. To let him catch me and never let go. I didn't realize just how much I missed him until...well, now. Though we texted and facetimed every day since he came to Seattle, it's not enough. It's not like the real thing.

Now that he's in front of me all of my fears and hesitations...it's like they are melting away by the second, until all that remains is...him.

Nico hesitates for a moment before taking a step forward, pulling me into a hug that is far too brief. When he releases me, I can feel myself practically aching, and the look in his eyes tells me he feels it too. Clearing his throat, he gestures for the limo behind him.

"Shall we?"

My mom and dad hurry into the limo, not able to contain their excitement. It makes a small smile touch my face as I watch them and I look up at Nico, speaking softly so it's just the two of us.

"Thank you, this is all very sweet."

He shakes his head as the back of his hand brushes against mine.

"It's literally nothing, Cass."

Just that small touch has my stomach slipping and my pulse racing as I nod and slip into the car. Nico is quick to follow behind me, shutting the door as he slips inside. My parents cozy up in the back and I sit on the side as Nico takes a seat across from me before the driver takes off. We all make idle chit chat as Nico's foot slowly moves into the middle of the car, brushing against mine. It's an innocent move, barely even noticeable. But I see it for what it is. A touch, a desperation to be near, a silent message of 'I can't wait to hold you'.

Once we get to the Brownstone, a wave of comfort washes over me. Like coming home. I felt stupid when I told Nico that this place felt like home, but god it's true. I've never felt like I belonged anywhere so much as when I'm here.

Nico shows my parents around, giving them a short guide before he throws a look to me and opens up the back patio. I look at him confused for a moment before I step through the threshold and my mouth hits the ground.

Lights are strung like a canopy above the space, a beautiful firepit is sitting in the middle of the patio with seating around it. Brand new furniture and plants are perfectly scattered around and the brick flooring looks like it's been stained with a warm brownish red color. It's...

"Perfect," I whisper under my breath.

My parents are looking around with smiles, admiring the space but it means so much more to me. My eyes move to Nico's who is watching me with a careful look.

"Do you like it?" he asks me.

I nod. "It's beautiful."

He smiles at that. "It used to be kinda run down. I got some amazing tips on how to revamp it and it was a no brainer."

My heart squeczes inside my chest as I look at him. I'd give anything to be alone right now. I want nothing more than to jump in his arms and never let go, but unfortunately, all I can offer is a smile and a nod. There was a certain allure to the forbidden nature of our relationship before, but is it silly to say that I'm over that? That I'm craving more, I'm craving something real. Where Nico and I can walk out in public hand in hand and not try to explain ourselves or worry that someone who shouldn't see, will? Is it so wrong that I don't want to be the hidden away sister forever. That I want people to one day hear about my wedding to Nico and fly all the way across the country just to celebrate?

Whoa. Did I seriously just say that so casually? Like Nico and I marrying is an inevitable. I'll be honest, since high school, I haven't thought about marriage at all. I had the teenage puppy love that I thought was forever with Alec. After him, I didn't even have that. I was accepting of the idea that maybe the whole marriage and 2.4 kids with a house on the hill maybe wasn't for me. Which, I know, sounds ridiculous considering I literally just turned 21. I guess I'm an all or nothing kind of girl.

"Cassi, you okay?" Nico says, almost like he's asked several times.

Fuck, how long have I been rambling inside my own head?

"Yeah, great. Can I jump into the shower? I always feel gross after a plane ride, even in one as nice as yours."

Nico watches me carefully, like he knows that's not true. Still, he gestures for me to step inside as he gives me directions to the upstairs master with the shower. I nod in thanks and make my way inside as I hear my mom chattering his ear off about wedding dates, location and all of the other things that the bride's family should be thinking about. Not how bad she wants to climb the groom like a tree. The slutty sister badge is reserved specially for me.

Grabbing my suitcase from the foyer where I left it, I carry it up the stairs and push my way into the master as I look at the bed. It's made perfectly, like it always is.

Unless Nico and I are tangled up in it, our bodies practically attached to one another from dawn until dusk.

Shaking my head and those thoughts away, I begin slowly unpacking my things. Normally, I don't bother, but we're here until Sunday evening and...I don't know. It just feels good. Like I'm tricking myself into believing that I'll be here longer. That I won't get on a plane in two days while Nico and my sister stay in Boston and...I don't even want to finish the rest of that sentence.

Once I'm unpacked, I start up the shower before stripping down. I step into the shower, which really just means stepping around the glass shower wall. It's one of those fancy stone floored showers with several rain showerheads on the ceiling. The walls are covered in mosaic tiling and the water is kept inside by glass wall pathway of sorts.

As I step into the shower, the warm water runs from my head to my toes. It feels actually amazing and I practically sink into the feeling when I hear a soft snick like a closing of a door, followed by the metal ting of a lock. Looking up, I see Nico stepping up to the shower, looking at me through the glass wall. His eyes run over me reverently as he shakes his head.

"You're so fucking beautiful, babygirl."

"Are you crazy?" I whisper. "My parents are literally downstairs."

He shakes his head again. "They went out for lunch."

I pause for a moment before my eyes widen with understanding, a small smile crossing my face.

"Well, what are you waiting for?" I tease.

Nico grins, surprising the hell out of me when he doesn't even bother to take off his clothes. Instead, he walks straight into the water, fully clothed and not a regret in sight as he cups my face into his hands and presses his mouth against mine. I sink into his touch, sighing as I attempt to meet his every move. The kiss is full of passion, desire, and more than a little desperation.

Our tongues battle for dominance as we trade off nipping and sucking on each other's lips. The entire thing is like a needy pleasure driven mess and I fucking love every second of it.

Without missing a beat, Nico releases my face with one of his hands as he begins undoing his belt. It isn't long before he is rubbing his tip through my pussy, pausing on my clit before swirling it several times. I shutter in response, as he does it again and again before his hands drop.

I'm about to voice my protest when I feel his arms scoop beneath my thighs, lifting me into the air before pinning me to the wall. My legs wrap around his absolutely drenched waist as my eyes flare with excitement and he gives me a half lifted grin before he's pushing his cock inside me. My back bows off the wall for a moment and I let out a moan as he withdraws before pushing back into me. Over and over again, our bodies work together like they are desperate for one another. It's because they are, we are.

These last two weeks have been fucking hell, and I'm ashamed to say I've questioned if this is worth it more than a few times, if we are worth it. Right in this moment, though, there is not a doubt in my mind. Not just because the sex is good, which trust me, it always is. I have no doubt because something inside of me feels safest when I'm with him, happiest. Something inside of me intrinsically tells me this is where I belong. So, through all the bullshit, we will make it out the other side. One way or another. Together.

"I love you," I say, the words just tumbling out of my mouth before I can even attempt to stop them.

My face staunches in shock as I shake my head, Nico continuing to thrust in and out of me as surprise fills his eyes. I let out a surprised laugh as I shake my head.

"Oh my god, I don't know where that came from, but I do. I-I love you. I love everything about you, the way you make me feel, your heart, your brain, your asshole sense of humor."

Nico lets out a rough chuckle at that as he smiles, encouraging me to continue, like each word is giving him a new sense of life.

"Most of all, I love the way you love me. The way you care for me. I'm sorry it's taken me a while to say it. I've felt it for so long but—"

He cuts me off with his mouth on mine, one of his hands moving up to hold the back of my head as he pushes my body further against the wall. When we break apart, he rests his forehead against mine and sighs.

"Don't ever apologize. I'm happy that you love me even a little, but I'm even happier you waited to tell me until you were ready. The truth is, I can love enough for the both of us in this relationship. Whatever you need, I can do it, Cassi."

"Relationship?" I tease as my hips rise, meeting his as he pushes against my g-spot.

Nico rolls his eyes as he shakes his head.

"Don't even play coy, babygirl. You're mine, and I'm yours. We've been over this."

"We haven't labeled it," I say, I mean, for good reason. Honestly, I'm just trying to mess with him.

His movements pause for a moment, his eyes roaming over my face quickly as he shakes his head.

"How can we label something so certain? So permanent? You're not a girlfriend; you're not a partner. You're...forever."

My heart trips over itself at that and I wrap my arm around his neck, dragging his head against mine as I grind against him. With his clothes on, our bodies don't make much noise together. I mean, I guess my mouth is on my body and that little fucker is making a lot of noise right now.

I whimper and moan into Nico's mouth when the door handle to the bathroom jiggles, startling us both. We freeze as Carly's voice sounds through the door.

"Hellllo, Cassi, are you in there?"

Nico looks to me, nodding in encouragement.

"Yeah," I say. "What's up?"

"Mom and dad were supposed to meet me here but I guess they went to lunch? And where the fuck is Nico? They said he stayed behind at the house."

My heart is beating out of my chest as I attempt to steady my voice.

"Carly, I don't know where your fucking fiancé went. Can I take a goddamn shower in peace?"

The insanity of me saying that sentence while her fiancé is firmly buried inside of my pussy is definitely not lost on me.

Carly scoffs through the door. "You're such a fucking bitch, you should have just stayed in Seattle."

"If mom and dad would have let me, you bet your ass I would have!" I throw back.

I hear her mutter to herself before loudly shrieking Nico's name. When the front door slams shut, Nico picks up right where we left off. I look at him like he's half crazy, honestly, how did he stay hard when we almost got caught?

"Come for me, little bunny."

I open my mouth to refuse him, when he wiggles his hips just right, pushing deeper than before and sending a moan tumbling from my mouth.

Fuck it.

Chapter Thirty Three
Cassi

When we get out of the shower, Nico and I dry off and get dressed. Thankfully for him, he has plenty of spare clothes here and is back to looking ever put together in minutes. I however, am rifling through my clothes, trying to figure out what to wear. I know that Carly and my parents had plans to do some sight-seeing. Huge surprise, I'm not interested in participating. So I think I'll just hang back here, watch some TV. Catch up on some assignments, pluck my eyes out with some tweezers. You know, just a short list of the things I'd rather do than spend a day with Carly.

I'm digging through the dresser wearing only a towel when Nico comes up behind me, kissing up and down the side of my neck. I smile at the touch and turn my head to look at him.

"I have something for you," he says.

"Yeah? Is it your hard on? Because, spoiler, you already gave it to me and I loved it."

He narrows his eyes with a smile and swats my ass.

"Don't be such a smart ass," he says as he pulls a light blue jewelry box out of his pocket.

It's dry, so I can only imagine it wasn't on his person when we had our little shower together. As if he can read my mind he shakes his head.

"I've had it here for a week or so. I wanted it here, in our home, ready for you."

How dumb am I for practically swooning at the words 'our home'? We are sickening, I swear, but I love it.

Slowly, I lift the lid of the box, revealing a glittering diamond necklace. It has a circle pendant, again, absolutely drenched in diamonds. The entire box is practically shimmering as he takes the necklace from the box and lifts it into the air.

"Turn around," he says.

I do as he says, facing the full length mirror as I watch him place it around my neck. This is really a good look for me. Wet hair, white towel, stupidly expensive necklace.

Once Nico has fastened the clasp, I touch it gently, looking down at it before back into the mirror.

"Nico it's...perfect. I mean, it's beyond perfect. I can't wear this."

He frowns. "Why not?"

I turn to look at him as I smile and shake my head.

"Everyone is going to think I robbed a bank, or maybe just a jewelry store," I laugh." Girls like me don't wear things like this. We can't even afford to look at it."

"You can now. It's yours, I had it made just for you. I'll have a thousand more made if that's what it takes for you to start to understand how fucking precious you are," he says as his thumb brushes against my cheek.

I can't help but ruin the moment a little as I shake my head.

"A thousand more? How fucking rich are you? I want a number."

Nico lets out a rough laugh as he smiles.

"Rich enough to buy you anything your heart desires, though I may need to sell a few summer homes to keep the funds liquid," he smirks.

"Summer homes? Where are we talking?"

He shrugs. "The usual places. London, Paris, Tuscany, Maldives."

My eyes bug out of my head. "The usual...sir, I want to go to the Maldives stat. Make that happen, will you?"

Nico grins and nods, wrapping his arms around my waist as he drags me into him.

"Deal."

"Fuck, that was easy, deal," I smile before leaning up and pressing a kiss to his lips.

Nico also tried to get out of sightseeing with my family but of course, my parents weren't having it. They insisted they spend time together. Luckily I was spared. No one asked about the necklace because I decided to put on a sweatshirt. Though I know you're supposed to take nice jewelry like that off when you sleep, I absolutely slept with it all night, and have zero regrets doing so.

Now it's the night of the engagement party, and the happy light feelings I was experiencing yesterday with Nico have essentially shriveled up and died. Especially when we arrived at some ballroom and I saw a large sign welcoming us to the engagement of the future Mr. & Mrs. Sanders. I wanted to puke right then and there. Hopefully onto the sign.

As we step inside, I'm overwhelmed with how many people are there. At least two hundred people fill this ballroom, glittering gowns, black tie suits and waiters dressed to the nines serving passed hors d'oeuvres. I look down at my simple black cocktail dress and suddenly feel so small in this world. I look to my parents who are sharing similar looks of uncomfortability among one another.

My dad is wearing the best suit that he owns, though it really doesn't hold a candle compared to the rest of the men in the room. My mom opted for a nice lavender dress with a lace shawl. Though looking around, she looks more ready for afternoon tea than a lavish gala like the one we have somehow found ourselves in.

Disdain filled looks and noses in the air are the only things we see until a warm face pops up through the crowd, hurrying his way towards us. Oh my god. Nico looks like...heaven? His suit practically wraps around his body like a second skin. His hair is perfectly styled and in place and oddly enough, I think my favorite part is the bow tie. Why is he so cute in a bow tie? That's it. He's wearing bow ties for everything from now on. I don't care if he will look like an eighty year old man at work, he'll be my eighty year old man.

Nico heads straight for me, his smile growing and growing until he hesitates, his eyes darting to my parents as he quickly changes directory. I'm disappointed, but relieved. My mom has been keeping an extremely close eye on me since we came to Boston. It feels like she knows something is up, which I know is my own paranoia but still.

"You both look fantastic," Nico says as he presses a kiss to my mom's cheek before shaking my dad's hand.

"Quite the fancy set up you guys got here," my dad says as he looks up at the six chandeliers that are as big as my car.

Nico nods, giving the room a passing glance and a shrug. To him, this place is a dime a dozen. Just another Saturday night. To us...it's unimaginable. I can't believe this has been Carly's life for the last three years. No wonder she never came home much.

"Cassi," Nico says, "You look...stunning," he says with a shake of his head.

I feel my smile grow wider than it should, but I can't stop it.

"Thank you, I like your bow tie."

He smiles like that was funny compliment, but he enjoys it all the same before nodding his head.

"That necklace is stunning."

"Isn't it?" my mom chimes in. "I asked her where she got it and she won't tell us!"

I roll my eyes like I'm irritated as I look at my mom.

"I told you. I got it online. Super good deal on used website. I'm pretty sure it's cubic zirconia," I say with a shrug.

Nico chokes on his champagne that he's sipping before he breathes through it.

"Yeah, I don't think so. They look real to me."

I look down at the necklace and nod.

"Maybe so. The guy I got it from seemed like a cheapskate, though, so who's to say?"

Nico pins me with a look that is part amused, part irritated. He shakes his head as he takes another sip of his champagne, keeping his eyes on me like I'll be punished for that later.

Can't wait.

In the next moment, Carly struts on stage in a wedding gown. I shit you not, a full blown wedding gown. My god she is just embarrassing.

"Hello everyone! Thank you so much for coming! If you could all clear the dance floor, Nicholas and I would like to share our first dance as an engaged couple."

"Is that a thing?" I scoff, earning my mom's elbow to my side as Nico sighs, placing his empty glass onto a circulating tray.

"Guess so, excuse me," he says as he meets Carly in the middle of the room.

They come together, Carly's hands on his shoulder and in his hand while he holds her waist with the free one. She smiles up at him like she has never been so in love. You have to pay extra close attention to notice that she is scanning the crowd just as much as she's looking at Nico, though. Her head is on a swivel, ensuring all attention is on her. She's so insufferable.

"She just loves the spotlight, doesn't she?" a man muses beside me.

I look up to see Jake, Nico's best friend.

"Hey Jake," I smile.

He makes a little face that has me tilting my head in curiosity. Shaking his head, he takes a sip of his drink and laughs.

"Sorry, it's nothing. I just...you're nothing like her, are you?"

My brows furrow as I look at him.

"What do you mean?"

He smirks. "It took ten introductions with your sister before she remembered my name."

I roll my eyes. "That doesn't surprise me. She's been with Nico for three years and can't remember that he hates being called Nicholas."

"Yeah," Jake says with a softer smile, like he's understanding something clearly. "Want to ruin her fun and join in?" he says as he offers me his hand to dance.

I grin at that. "I thought you'd never ask."

Jake lets out a laugh as he escorts me to the dance floor before we begin dancing a few feet away. Carly shoots a venomous look to us before gesturing for us to get off the dance floor. It's too late, though. Behind us five other couples quickly join in. Then a few more, and a few more until I can't even see them anymore.

As we sway to the music, Jake keeps an appropriate amount of distance between us before he whispers into my ear.

"How are you holding up?"

"What do you mean?" I ask as I keep myself facing his shoulder.

"You're at your boyfriend's engagement party to your sister. It would be understandable if you were freaking the fuck out. Though, I gotta say, from the outside, you're playing it off well."

I lean away from him a moment, watching him assessingly.

"You don't like me," I state.

It's not a question, not a probing curiosity. Just a fact.

He shakes his head as he gently turns us with each sway.

"On the contrary, I actually do a lot. You seem good for him. I've never seen him this way about anyone, ever."

"But?" I hedge.

His eyes come down to mine as he speaks.

"He's the best man I know, he'd walk through fire for the ones he loves and something tells me you've earned your way to the top of that list extremely fast. You have the power in your pinky to destroy him. Please don't."

I frown at his words as he swings me out for a spin before returning me back to his arms.

"I wouldn't. I couldn't. I...he's the one that holds the power to destroy, believe me."

His mouth twitches like he wants to smile at that as he nods.

"For what it's worth, I'm rooting for the two of you."

"Thanks, Jake."

Jake nods as his eyes go over my head before mischief fills his features.

"Want to fuck with him a bit?"

"Hm?" I ask.

"Don't hit me," he says before leaning down and placing a lingering kiss to my cheek.

Within seconds, a body comes diving between us, shoving us apart. A few heads turn but it's nothing too obvious as Nico grips Jake's suit tightly, snarling through clenched teeth.

"What the fuck do you think you're doing?"

Jake laughs and shakes his head.

"Just dancing with a pretty girl."

Carly comes over quickly, tugging on Nico's arm.

"What the hell, Nicholas! You can't just leave me to rough

house with your friend. You're embarrassing me!" she practically shrieks.

Every head that wasn't turned in our direction certainly is now. The second hand embarrassment is so fucking strong.

"Hey, lower your voice there, sweetheart," my dad says as he dances with my mom beside us.

"Daddy, not now!" she seethes.

"Yeah, dad. We have to let her throw a full tantrum or she has to start all over," I snark.

Her eyes come to me, vicious intent before her gaze falters, flicking down to my neck as a steeliness enters her gaze.

"What is that?" she asks as she points to my neck.

For a moment, my pulse races before I force it to settle.

"A necklace?" I say like she's an idiot.

Her eyes narrow like sharpened knives.

"Where did you get it?"

"I got it online, where did you get your botched lip filler?" I throw back, attempting to get her off the fucking subject.

Damnit, I should have never worn this thing. It brings too much attention.

"C'mon," Nico says as he attempts to pull Carly back onto the dance floor.

She shrugs him away, though, stepping closer to me as she stares at the necklace for a little longer. Then, everything happens in slow motion. Her eyes slowly rise to mine, her head moving to look to Nico, then to me, back to Nico and finishing on me before what I can only describe as fire sparks in her eyes.

"YOU FUCKING BITCHHHH!"

Her scream is deafening, immediately drowning out the music as she tackles me to the ground. I attempt to push her off of me as she begins smacking and clawing the fuck out of me. For a skinny bitch who doesn't eat anything, she's surprisingly strong and with every hit, I see stars. Nico and several others attempt to grab her off of me and I take that advantage to crawl out of her reach.

Jake is the one to wrap her up but he makes the mistake of leaving his foot in front of her and she stomps on it with her heel before punching him in the balls. Jake goes down like a sack of potatoes, writhing on the floor in pain as Carly jumps on my back and begins choking me with necklace.

"You stupid cunt! This was supposed to be mine! This is mine!" she screeches, smashing my face into the marble floors over and over again.

Blood is pouring down my face, my nose no doubt broken into fucking pieces as her body is finally hauled away. I look up to see my dad locking her into place as Nico pulls me further from her. My mother also kneels down beside me, taking a napkin to my nose as horrified looks stare down at me.

"Babygirl, are you okay?" Nico asks in panic, looking over me.

My mom stiffens at his words as collective gasps sound out.

"Ha!" Carly screams like a mad woman. "I knew it! Oh you son of a bitch! You've been fucking my sister behind my back!"

"We broke up," Nico says as he stands between Carly and I. "I dumped you as soon as you came to back to Boston but you went psycho and concocted this entire fucking fake engagement! I went along with it to protect my company but fuck that and fuck you! This crazy bitch is nothing but an unhinged ex-girlfriend," he says, turning to face the room.

Turning around, he kneels to face me before lacing his fingers through mine. My mom has taken several steps away from me, looking between me and Carly in shock.

"And I'm in love with Cassi," he says.

More gasps ring through the room and though I'm still dazed from Carly's attack, I can't miss the white hot rage that slashes across her face. With my dad still holding her in place, she lets out a scream that has nearly everyone covering their ears.

Before anything more can be said, security move through, snatching Carly from my dad and placing her in handcuffs.

"Everyone, please clear the way."

"Wait! Stop! She's the fucking thief! She stole my fiancé!" Carly screams as the cops begin reading her rights.

I see Jake limping, walking with them as he shakes his head as my dad runs a hand through his hair. He looks to me and Nico before sighing and facing my mom.

"I'm gonna follow them, see where they are taking Carly."

A police officer comes through the door in the next moment and makes their way towards us.

"Do you need an ambulance?"

"Yes," Nico answers before I can refuse.

He nods and radios in one before leading us out of the ballroom. Nico keeps our hands together before helping me to my feet. The world spins and I have to blink several times to keep myself steady. Nico takes notice immediately and bends down, scooping me into his arms as the crowd slowly separates for us. I see an older looking man shake his head in disappointment as Nico walks by, but if he notices, he doesn't react. Instead, he keeps his head held high like his only objective is getting me to the ambulance.

My mom walks behind us quietly, not saying a word as we meet an ambulance out front. As paramedics jog towards us, I see Carly being put into a squad car. Well, put in is a relative term. She has her legs spread on the car, preventing her from going through the door. She looks like a nightmare, white wedding gown stained with blood, a face full of anger and vengeance as she screams and shouts into the night.

My father is being held back by a police officer as he shouts at Carly to comply. Of course she doesn't, though, bucking and screaming as she completely falls apart into chaos. Her head rears back and cracks the police officer holding her in the face, forcing him to drop her to the ground. She screams in pain as he holds his nose, cursing through his hands.

"She broke my goddamn nose!"

Hey, me too. Twinsies.

The paramedics get me assessed in the ambulance before looking to my mom and Nico.

"Who is going with?"

They exchange a look before she gives me a tight grimace.

"He can. I'll meet you guys there."

Nico falters for a moment but my mom is already walking away towards my dad. I don't know why her disappointment hurts so much, but it really fucking does. Nico climbs into the ambulance and sits beside me, holding my hand as we take off to the hospital.

Not how I thought my day would be ending.

Chapter Thirty Four
Nico

Cassi's nose is broken and she has a concussion and I'm on a goddamn warpath. The police followed us to the hospital where an officer questioned me and then Cassi for over an hour before finally leaving. When he asked Cassi if she wanted to press charges, she said no, and it took everything in me not to climb the fucking walls.

According to Mary, Carly is currently being processed in jail. It doesn't matter that Cassi doesn't want to press charges, she assaulted a police office, resisted arrest and I guess Jake is pressing charges, so in shorthand, she's fucked.

Henry is currently down there, trying to figure out bail, but it's a Saturday night and she won't be able to see a judge until Monday at the earliest. Good. Let her fucking rot in there for all I give a shit.

They won't let Cassi sleep because of her concussion and they want to keep her overnight for observation due to the severity of the trauma. Her entire forehead has swelled up and is turning black and blue and her nose is currently in a splint and will take weeks to heal. I'm fucking sick over it. I'm sick that I couldn't get to her sooner, I should have. I let her down and she got hurt, and I have no one to blame but myself.

What I can't figure out is how Carly knew the necklace was from me. Did she see it before I moved it to the brownstone? Did someone say something? I don't know who would. It's my fault nonetheless. I shouldn't have given it to her during this...tense time. I wanted to do something special, just for us. I wanted Cassi to know that even if we were going through our own version of hell, she was on my mind, she was my priority. And it fucking ruined everything.

I've had no less than a dozen missed phone calls from Brittany, all have been sent to voicemail. I don't have anything to say to her. That plan we had? To keep things quiet, to break apart behind the scenes and spin the story before it hit the streets. Yeah, I blew that to all hell, and honestly, it's the least of my concern. My entire company could go bankrupt, my accounts could drain in a second and I wouldn't even bat an eye.

My only concern and focus is the woman in the bed before me, staring at her hands as her mother berates her.

"I honestly just can't believe this. How could you do this, Cassi? I know that you and Carly have your issues, but to go after her boyfriend? Or fiancé? Whatever. It's just...it's not like you. Like her, maybe, but not you. You're my good girl, my sweet girl. I just..." Mary shakes her head in frustration and I stand up, having quite enough of it.

"I'm sorry, Mary. I mean absolutely no disrespect when I say this, but if you don't start treating your daughter with the respect she deserves, I will have you removed from the hospital."

Mary stares at me in shock as I shake my head.

"C'mon, this is Cassi we are talking about. You are going to sit here and shame her for falling in love when your other daughter attacked her? You want to play like Carly is the victim? My mother was cheated on her entire marriage to my father. Believe me, no one knows the psychological damage it does to loved ones better than me.

"We weren't together out of some ploy to get back at Carly. We didn't do it because we didn't care about the consequences. We fell in love. We met while Carly and I were on a break, and we tried to push our feelings aside. Clearly, it didn't work, and I am sorry that things got so out of hand, but this is your daughter. Your child is hurt and humiliated, and you need to start acting like the mother I know you are."

Cassi is staring up at me wide eyed while Mary's mouth is parted like she's never been more offended in her life. Let her be, I didn't say anything that wasn't the truth.

"I just...this is all very shocking. I knew you liked him, Cass, but I had no idea that feelings ran so deep...on both sides. I, just, I need to process."

"Then please, go process away from here because she is hurt and needs to heal, more than just physically," I say.

Mary stares at me like she doesn't know who the hell I am, but I really don't care. I stand my ground because she is more than welcome to be here, but not to guilt or abuse Cassi. Gathering up her things, she quietly steps out of the room and moves down the hall.

I turn to look down at Cassi, running a gentle hand through her hair.

"Are you okay?"

"Define okay?" she laughs bitterly, her voice slightly off from the injury to her nose.

"I'm so sorry, Cass. I'm so sorry everything blew up and that you were hurt. I just—"

"Nico, stop. You didn't do this. She did. I just...I want to go home."

I nod, though hurt stabs inside me at the thought of her leaving.

"I'll have the jet ready for you when you get discharged."

She frowns, tilting her head to the side.

"No, dummy. I mean, I'm ready to go home to...our home," she says, her words softening slightly as if she was vulnerable.

A rush of euphoria washes over me as I take her hand in mine, pressing a kiss to the back of it as I nod.

"I'll take you home, babygirl."

Chapter Thirty Five
Cassi

I t's been a week since Carly was arrested. I've barely spoken to my parents since, but my dad did tell me that he posted bail for her. She's not allowed to leave the city of Boston until her trial which won't be for a month or so. The police reached out to me again and asked once more if I wanted to press charges. Honestly, they more so encouraged it. With the cop she assaulted and Jake already doing the same, my testimony would only further drive a nail into her coffin. I refused, though. I'm not going to let anyone paint me out like I'm the reason for her situation. At least, no more than they already have.

I was honestly shocked that my parents were so...is disappointed the right word? I mean, I guess I never really factored their reaction into things. I was too worried about Carly blowing the fuck up on me, which she did, and my friends judging me, which they kinda did but dropped the judgment quickly.

Due to the state of my face and my mental health literally being a dumpster fire, Nico and I both agreed that I should at least take the week off classes and work and stay in Boston. Though, with that week coming to an end, I think I'll be stretching it to two. I'll probably lose my job at this rate and who knows what will happen with school, but is it bad that I no longer care?

The splint for my nose came off yesterday so I am starting to look a little less like I got into a nasty bar fight and lost.

It was a fight with my sister in a ballroom, and I never stood a chance with the rage she was wielding.

I'm currently on facetime with Naomi and Arianna as they ask me for the hundredth time when I'll be coming back.

"I don't know," I sigh.

"What do you mean, you don't know?" Arianna asks. "I mean, Cass, your whole life is here. You can't just leave."

I shrug my shoulders.

"I'm happy here, I feel like I finally...fit. If I was in your guys' position, I'd be saying the same but can you just pretend to be happy for me?"

Ari puts her hands up in defeat as she shakes her head.

"You know what, done. Life is too short to not be with your person. Trust me," she scoffs bitterly, shaking her head.

"Seriously, with all these hospital visits, I think we should wrap Nay in bubble wrap and keep her safe," I say on a laugh.

"Something tells me our little Nay bay has someone overseeing all of those details," Ari says.

I frown. "Why do you say that?"

"Because I don't recognize that bedroom and she isn't even paying attention to what we're saying as she talks to someone out of camera."

I look down at Naomi's screen before my eyes widen. Ari is not wrong. Her lavender colored walls are not in sight and she has herself on mute as her mouth is moving quickly before she glances down at us and takes herself off mute.

"Sorry guys."

We both stare at her and she looks from side to side.

"What?"

I shake my head. "We were just waiting to see if you were going to tell us a bullshit lie about whose bed you're in or if you were going to play it off like you don't know what we're talking about."

Guilt immediately etches across her face as she looks around nervously.

"What do you mean? I...I'm home."

"The answer was B, Cass. Did anyone have B?" Arianna asks.

I smile as Naomi shakes her head, running her fingers through her hair.

"We're just fucking with you. I mean, we're curious what's been going on with our virgin bestie, but you don't have to tell us if you don't want to."

She opens her mouth like she wants to speak before putting herself on mute for another moment. Her mouth moves for a second before she looks to the camera.

"I gotta go. Talk soon."

With that, her face disappears and I look to Arianna with furrowed brows.

"Okay, that was really weird, right?" I ask.

She nods. "Super weird. Let's give her some space, but send the calvary if we don't hear from her in forty eight hours?"

"Twenty four," I counter.

She nods her head. "Deal. Love ya."

"Love you too," I say before we end the call.

Nico pokes his head into the bedroom with a shy smile like he's been waiting to come in but didn't want to interrupt.

"Sorry to bother you. I need to run into the office and wanted to know if you wanted to stay here or come with."

I pause for a moment before sliding out of bed.

"I've only been to the doctor and here since the party. I'd love to get some fresh air...if you think it would be a good idea?"

I know that he's lost some clients since the whole...incident. Huge ones. I overheard him on the phone and honestly, it didn't even sound like he was trying to save the relationship. He basically told them to go to hell in business talk.

"It's fine. You're always welcome there. I can show you around a bit, show you off," he says with a wink.

"Yeah, with my bruised up face and swollen nose, I'm sure to win the hearts of every man, woman and child," I snark with a laugh.

He shakes his head at me like I'm ridiculous before wrapping his arms around me and placing a kiss to my forehead.

"You're perfect, as always."

I can't help but smile before he gives me a quick wink and laces our hands together, pulling me towards the door.

When we get to Nico's office, all eyes are on us immediately. Being the literal boss that he is, he makes eye contact with most, smiling and nodding in greeting as he holds his head high and moves to the back of the office. I try to do the same, but I notice the curious stares to be drawn to me more than him...by a lot.

Uncomfortability creeps in as Nico gives me a short tour of everything. He introduces me to his CFO, a few of his senior executives before we pop our heads into HR where Jake is smiling.

"Hey you two. What brings you to my neck of the woods?"

"I have a meeting with Hamfield that I've been putting off. Can you keep Cassi company?"

"No problem, Cass and I are fast friends, right?" Jake smiles as he loops his arm through mine.

"The fastest," I agree, matching his excitement.

Nico looks between us before letting out a laugh as he shakes his head. He leans forward, pressing a soft kiss to my cheek as his eyes come to me.

"I'll just be in my office. If you need anything, have Virginia get me."

I nod and smile as Nico walks away, looking over his shoulder to me a few times before he disappears around the corner.

"He's worried about letting you out of his sight," Jake says from behind me.

I turn and nod. "He's always worried about something."

Jake smiles in a way that I can't quite decipher as he shakes his head.

"Not usually, just when it comes to you."

I like that for some reason. I do my best to hide my grin at his words but it's practically impossible.

"Want to grab a coffee or something?" Jake asks.

"Sure," I say as I follow his lead.

He smiles and waves to a few people before we stop at the breakroom. Before us are three fancy espresso machines as well as a machine that will pre-make almost any coffee you ask for. We chat about where I grew up and where Nico and Jake grew up when a girl pops her head into the breakroom.

"Sorry to interrupt, Jake, can I borrow you really quick for this job posting?"

"Sure," he says as he leans away from the counter. "Want to come with or chill in here?"

I tilt my head to the side, gesturing towards the boxes and boxes of donuts.

"I'll hang with the snacks."

He laughs and nods as he walks away with the girl. I lift the lid of one of the boxes, struggling to choose between a maple bar or a jelly filled donut before I go for the maple bar. A low chuckle sounds from a few feet away that startles me.

"Man, I was so sure you were going to go for the jelly filled. They were always your favorite," Alec says as he begins sauntering towards me.

"Alec!" I say in surprise. "What are you doing here?"

"I work here now, started a bit ago now. Not like you'd know since you ghosted me."

His tone is accusing and cold, but his face still has on that perfect smile. It unnerves me as he continues moving towards me, only stopping when we are literally toe to toe. Alec looks down at me, his head tilting like he's waiting for me to disagree. Shit, this conversation is long overdue.

"Alec...I'm sorry. There isn't much else I can say other than I am, truly."

Alec's eyes narrow slightly as if he were waiting for more before he lets out a bitter laugh.

"That's all I get? Seriously? One lousy apology? I loved you for *years*. I thought we were going to have another *chance*! I made plans with *you* in mind."

His tone grows more menacing with each word and by the end, his pleasant smile is gone, rage being the only thing left in sight.

"I'm sorry," I say again, taking a step away from him.

He meets me, closing the distance once more. I back up again and again until my ass hits the counter. Shit.

"Sorry? For what, exactly? For leading me on? Or for being a fucking disappointing version of the girl I once knew?"

His words stab hurt inside me as he continues, resting his hands on either side of me against the counter.

"My grandma died, in case you were curious. Again, not like you were around for that. You're never around for anything, now that I think about it. You'd float in and out of my life whenever it suited you."

"Alec, I..."

My words trail off as his eyes widen with rage and his nostrils flare.

"You what? Can you just accept any kind of responsibility for what a shitty person you've been? Or are you hell bent on being the victim? I mean, look at what you did to your fucking sister!" he shouts.

I still as another humorless laugh rips through him as he lower his face to mine.

"You think I haven't heard? The entire east coast heard about her meltdown to your affair. Tell me, were you fucking us both at the same time, or did I at least get to hit before he had his turn?"

My eyes dart around for an exit, but Alec just leans in further. I try to lean away but I'm trapped and he practically lays his chest against mine as he snarls into my face.

"You're not even worth a second of the time I wasted on you. You're selfish, cold and the only good thing about you is this," he says as he roughly cups my pussy.

I shove him away roughly, hoping that will give me enough of an opening. He's like a brick wall, though. I push him again and again, smacking his arm before I finally smack his face.

"Get OFF of me!" I shout.

His head whips to the side with a crack of my hand before he turns back, a crazed look in his eyes as he rears his hand back and delivers a smack that has me seeing stars. I cry out in pain as the sting burns my cheek before his hand buries into my hair, yanking roughly.

"I fucking hate you! You are hell! You're the worst thing that ever fucking happened to me. Why did so many good people around me die when you are sitting. RIGHT. HERE." He shouts, shaking me with each word.

Another slap comes across my cheek as he screams into my face.

"ANSWER ME!"

In the next moment, a force hits us. Alec is being ripped away from me as I look and see him pinned on the ground beneath Nico. I watch as Nico's arm winds back before punching Alec in the face. Over and over again he delivers blow after blow as a crowd quickly rushes into the breakroom. A woman comes to me, asking me if I'm okay but I can't answer. All I can focus on is Nico beating Alec to a pulp while Alec laughs almost maniacally.

Jake pushes into the room through the crowd, shouting at everyone to get back before he hauls Nico up and away from Alec. No one really goes to check on Alec for a solid thirty seconds before a guy reluctantly kicks his shoe and asks if he'll live. Based on the looks he's receiving, I take it more than a few people were listening to our...argument. Awesome.

Jake has Nico in a hold, his arms pinned back behind him as he rages like a bull. His breathing is rough and ragged, his face beet red with anger as he stares as he keeps trying to lunge for Alec like he's not nearly finished with him yet. I don't know how he could do more damage, though. Alec is a bleeding mess on the floor as he cups his nose, attempting to open his rapidly swelling eyes.

"Calm the fuck down! Now! Focus on her, look at your girl. She's okay, she's okay," Jake says into Nico's ear.

Reluctantly, his eyes move to mine, his anger easing for a moment. Nico's gaze runs over me from top to bottom before he shrugs Jake away. Jake lets him go, standing back a few feet as he keeps an eye on both guys before clearing out the break room.

Nico's hands gently cup my face as his eyes frantically search mine.

"Are you okay?"

I didn't realize it until now, but I'm shaking, like uncontrollably shaking. I think Alec shook me up more than I wanted to admit and now I'm sitting here shaking like a fucking leaf.

"C-can we go?" I ask.

Nico nods, pushing his way through the few remaining people as we head for the door. He shouts at someone behind him to have his schedule cleared for the day before we are to the elevator and stepping inside. Jake has been following us and stops as he looks to us from the door. Nico tucks me into his chest, wrapping his arms around me protectively as he looks at Jake.

"That little fuck is fired! Call the police because we will be pressing charges."

"Get the police involved and he could press charges against you," Jake points out.

Nico lets out a hollow laugh as he shakes his head.

"I wish he fucking would."

Jake raises his hands in defense before looking to me. He mouths 'call me if you need me' and I nod in thanks as the elevator doors close. It's not like I have Jake's number, nor have I ever reached out to him for anything, but I think he means in case Nico needs help. I'm not sure many others could reign him in like that. Not when he was so far...removed from his own body it seemed.

Pulling back, I look at Nico's hands, several of his knuckles are split open and bleeding. I frown as I inspect them carefully.

"We need to get you cleaned up."

He shakes his head, smoothing out my hair as he presses a kiss to my temple.

"I'm fine, babygirl. If you're safe, I'm fine."

Chapter Thirty Six
Cassi

Nico is meeting with the board today. After the incident with Alec, we waited in the parking garage for the police where they took my statement. Ironically enough, it was the officer who got their nose broken by my sister. As soon as he saw us, he shook his head and cursed under his breath saying, "I would love to stop seeing you two."

He took down my statement as well as pulled the surveillance cameras the company has in the break room which confirmed the altercation and led to...well, Nico's altercation. Just as Jake predicted, as soon as Nico had me press charges, Alec pressed them against Nico. Everything has gone to shit lately and though I know I should feel regret, that I should look at the common denominator of the chaos in my life, ie, my relationship with Nico and run fast and far. I don't want to. I don't want to because in the midst of all of this, he's remained by my side, steadfast and unyielding.

Does that make me dumb? Probably. Does it make me happy? Absolutely. Do I still hope to god that this is the end of the fights and police reports and fucking drama? God help me, I fucking NEED it to be.

Legal matters aside, Nico is under review from the board because it doesn't matter if you own the company, people don't really like a boss that beats the shit out of their employees. Even if said employee deserved it. The meeting today will determine whether he is taking a leave of absence or...god I don't really know what all can come from this, honestly.

I'm still in shock that it happened at all. My sister freaking out, that was expected. Alec, though, he was a wild card I never saw coming, which is dumb of me because he was always insanely jealous. I was in the wrong, too. I led him on, I played on his feeling because it was a suitable distraction and then I just...disappeared. He was right to be pissed with me.

I know that Alec has a lot of trauma around death and loss and abandonment. His grandma going had to of triggered more than a little something inside of him and I have no doubt he feels survivor's guilt for his parents' accident. Still, I can't believe he would do that. That he would scream, that he would hit me. He's never hurt a fly the entire time I've known him. I know it was the grief talking and acting, the betrayal but fuck. I'm not afraid to admit that I was absolutely terrified of him in that moment. That he morphed into someone who I didn't even recognize, one that I had no clue what they were capable of.

Shaking my head, I focus on the walk ahead of me. I'm bored to death in the house all alone and I need to get out and do...something. So, I decided to walk down to the cute coffee shop Nico first took me to. I don't expect to find a familiar brunette standing before me, timidly looking to me.

"Hey, Cass," Carly says quietly.

I'm on edge immediately, but I try not to let it show.

"What do you want?"

She looks down at her feet for a moment before looking up at me.

"I wanted to apologize."

I raise a disbelieving eyebrow to her as she continues.

"Mom and dad said you were staying in Boston and I know how much Nico liked this place," she says as she looks up at the building.

"I'm not interested in anything you have to say, Carly."

She nods her head like she understands, and that has my brows furrowing because since when has Carly been able to put herself in anyone's shoes? Since when has she apologized or tried to atone for her words or actions?

"I just...I'm really sorry. I wanted to talk and I...I realize how dumb that sounds," she says, her voice tight and choppy as a tear falls down her face.

Goddamnit. I hate myself. I hate myself so fucking much. I hate that I can't flip her off and walk in the other direction without losing a wink of sleep. The truth is, though, despite all of the fighting and bullshit that's gone on...well, forever, between the two of us, she's my sister.

"Five minutes," I grit through clenched teeth.

Carly looks up at me with surprise before nodding quickly.

"Yes, yeah. Thank you. Do you want to talk inside or?"

"I'm going to the coffee shop down the road, c'mon," I say as I move past her and head down the road.

She tries to keep up with me but my legs are much longer and therefor, keep me firmly ahead. When we step through the door, comfort from the familiar smell fills me before I see Tammy. She was the barista that helped Nico and I the first time we came in here, and our schedules seem to line up perfectly because she is here literally every time I come in.

"Good morning, Tammy," I smile.

"Hey! What can I get you?"

"Let me get it," Carly says, wedging herself between me and the counter.

I lift my hands up and shake my head.

"Can I get a vanilla latte?"

Tammy nods as Carly wrinkles her nose in disgust.

"I haven't had one of those in a while. Does this place make a decent one?" she asks with a wrinkle of her nose as she inspects the coffee shop with contempt.

Doing my best to suppress an eyeroll, I nod my head.

"What the hell, we'll see if they can handle it. Make it two, soy for mine, Carly," she says in a way like she should know who my sister is or something ridiculous.

Tammy looks to me as if to ask if she is fucking kidding, but I don't have any type of comfort to offer her. Believe it or not, that is Carly being pleasant. I blink slowly before looking away. I was beginning to not recognize my sister.

There she is, found her.

Carly hands her card over as Tammy shakes her head before beginning to ring us up.

"I'm gonna grab a table," I say as Carly nods.

Fucking hell. What have I gotten myself into.

Carly stands to the side and watches Tammy make the drink like a hawk. When Tammy finishes up, Carly scoots the cups towards her, without saying thank you of course, before she opens the lids and inspects the collars with our names written on them. She stands there for a solid fifteen seconds messing with them before I'm fed up.

"Carly, what are you doing?" I say.

She turns to me and rolls her eyes.

"I'm making sure they are properly labeled!'

"Who cares? They are the same drink."

"I do!" If they didn't label them properly I might drink your nasty dairy milk," she says before turning back to our drinks.

"Here is yours! Have a good day," Tammy says as she hands Carly's to her before handing her mine as well.

Carly looks her up and down before shrugging her shoulders and sashaying towards me.

"Thank you for letting me apologize. I just...I feel awful honestly. The way I acted was...insane."

I watch her carefully because again, who is this self-aware version of my sister? I don't recognize her.

"To apologies," she says, holding her cup up for a cheers.

I shrug my shoulders and cheers her cup before taking a small sip while she does the same.

Carly makes a face like she's not impressed before taking another sip.

"You have four minutes," I say flatly.

She gives me a flat look before shaking her head.

"Anyways, I'm sorry. I freaked out because you know, you kinda stole the love of my life," she laughs bitterly.

"Carly, I didn't steal h—"

"Regardless," she says holding her hand up in the air. "It's been over between Nicholas and I for a long time and I needed to accept it. It was just hard and then to see that not only had he given up on me but moved on with you...I lost it."

"What about the necklace made you realize it?" I ask, a burning question both Nico and I have wondered.

She looks down at her lap before back at me, her breathing coming a little heavier than before.

"I saw it in his bedside table when I got back from my cruise. I thought it was for me. Then when he didn't give it to me, I kinda forgot about it...until I saw it around your neck."

Ah.

Makes sense.

"For what it's worth, I am sorry, Carly. Neither of us meant for it to happen. It got really complicated really fast but neither of us ever wanted to hurt you."

She lets out a short breath in what sounds like a silent chuckle before she does it again and again, opening her mouth to take a breath. Her eyes look to me in confusion as her hand goes to her chest.

"What the fuck?" she pants as she picks up her cup, her eyes widening before he looks up at me and clutches her chest. In the next moment, she's slumping out of her chair and falling to the floor.

"Oh my god! Carly!" I gasp as I drop down beside her.

My eyes run over her, as if I could find something physically wrong with her as she stares up at me.

"Fuck...you....F-fuck," she stutters before her eyes roll into the back of her head and her body sinks into the floor further.

What the hell?!

"Someone call 911!" I say as I check her neck for a pulse.

I'm not a fucking doctor or anything but I can't feel anything. Oh my god. Oh my god. I try to line up where I think her heart is and begin pushing on her chest. I'm not CPR trained or anything but I've seen it done on TV enough times and know that if she goes without a heartbeat for too long, she's done for.

An ambulance arrives surprisingly fast and they rush in before taking over for me.

"What happened?" they ask me.

"I-I don't know. She was talking and then she couldn't breathe or something and just collapsed. It didn't feel like she had a pulse."

The paramedics lift her onto a gurney and begin carrying her out to the ambulance when something falls out of her pocket. A tiny clear baggie with some kind of powder in it. I bend down to pick it up, looking at it for any kind of markings or indication as to what it is.

"Is that coke?" the paramedic asks.

I've never seen a pale green cocaine before, and trust me I've... never done cocaine in my life. Nope. Not me.

"I'll take it to the hospital, see if they can figure out what she od'd on."

I hand the baggie over to the paramedic as I step into the ambulance with them. First, I send a text to my parents telling them that Carly is being rushed to the hospital. Then, I send one to Nico.

Chapter Thirty Seven

Nico

"We understand where you're coming from, Nico, but you can't punch out an employee just because he grabbed your girlfriend," Lionel, one of the board members of Sanders & Son says.

I lean forward in my chair as I rest my forearms onto the table.

"He didn't grab her, her hit her. Repeatedly. For all anyone knew he was going to beat the shit out of her or fucking rape her right then and there. I protected not only my girlfriend but a woman from one of our employees. My character should not be called into question for this."

A few of the members nod their heads in agreement while Lionel and a few of his buddies give me sour looks. I don't give a fuck what any of them say. If they try to put me on a leave of absence or force me to give up my company, I'll take their asses to court. End of discussion.

My phone buzzes in my pocket and for some reason, I take this extremely inappropriate time to check it. Cassi is home by herself and though it's probably some junk email or something, I have to make sure.

"Are you seriously checking your phone, right now? We are discussing the future of this company and whether your presence will be apart of that?" Lionel snaps.

My eyes move across the screen, my gut twisting as I stand. I move towards the door without another word when Lionel calls out to me again.

"Nicholas! Nico! If you walk out that door, you are fired, do you hear me?"

I pause for a moment, looking back to him as I level him with a steady glare.

"I will make your life fucking hell. Go ahead, I dare you."

With that, I step out of the conference room before I take off running to the elevator, Cassi's text playing on a loop in my mind.

Cassi: I had coffee with Carly and she collapsed. Nico...I think she's dead.

I raced to the hospital as fast as I could. When I got there, I found Cassi speaking with a few police officers. Jogging up to her, I step in between her and the officers as I cup her face.

"Babygirl, what happened?"

She looks up at me with red rimmed eyes as she shakes her head.

"I-I don't know. One moment, Carly and I were talking and then she just...dropped. She clutched her chest and passed out. The doctors haven't told me anything yet. I...I don't know what happened to her, Nico. I don—"

Cassi devolves into a fit of sobs as she curls into my arms.

"Sir, what's your name?" one of the officers says.

"Nico Sanders," I respond.

One nods before pausing. "I know that name."

Fuck. I know this is going to look awful.

"I currently have some restraining orders in place...one of them being against Carly."

Cassi turns to look at me in surprise. I didn't tell her I filed a restraining order against Carly and Alec. I also haven't told her I filed them for her too. A little forged signature in the name of keeping her safe? I feel no regrets.

Both of the officers share a look before their eyes move to me.

"And now she's in the hospital, and you're sitting here comforting your ex's sister?"

Yep. I knew as soon as I said anything that they'd be looking at me like that. Before I can respond, a doctor comes into the waiting area and sees Cassi. He heads straight for her and a wave of nausea overtakes me when I see the look on his face.

Cassi tightens in my arms as she slowly pulls away, like she's trying to be brave and face what I know he's about to say. She knows it too, I'm just not sure she's fully ready to hear it.

"Family of Carly Fischer?" he verifies.

She nods before taking my hand into hers, squeezing tightly.

"How is she? What happened?"

I feel the officers behind us creep forward slightly to listen in.

The doctor keeps a straight face but there is a hollowed tone to his words as he speaks.

"She came in with what appeared to be sudden cardiac arrest. Despite multiple attempts at resuscitation, we were not able to revive her. She died as eleven thirty five. I am so sorry for your loss."

I expect Cassi to sob. To breakdown and fall apart. Instead, she turns to stone. Unmoving, no reaction, no words. She just...stares. The doctor seems to shift on his feet like he's unsure how to move forward when a police officer steps forward and intervenes.

"Were the drugs found on her person the cause? Was it an over-dose or something more?"

"We can't say for certain just yet. The lab is still testing the substance and we will inform you of what we find as soon as possible."

His eyes move to Cassi's once more.

"Is there someone we can call for you? Parents or?"

"They are on their way from Seattle," Cassi rasps.

The doctor continues trying to talk to her but I can tell she's tuning everything out. She's practically slipped off into another world as the doctors and police officers speak to one another before looking to me.

"I know it's not the best time, but we need to ask a few more questions down at the station."

My eyes practically bug out of my head.

"Are you fucking kidding me? Her sister just died."

"While she was with her," the other office fills in. "Until we know the true cause of death, this is an open investigation and I'm looking at the two main subjects. I'm sorry, it's protocol."

"To hell with protocol! We will answer your questions here but we're not going anywhere until...until she's able to see her parents. Until they can grieve together."

The cops share an irritated look before one of them nods.

"Lets step somewhere a little more quiet."

Chapter Thirty Eight
Cassi

"Were you upset with your sister? I reviewed the notes from last week. Looks like she roughed you up pretty good."

I look up at him in surprise as I shake my head.

"Do you seriously have no tact or are you a fucking idiot?" I ask.

Nico squeezes my leg in warning as his lawyer leans forward.

"Please rephrase your questions to be a little more empathetic given the current situation, or this interrogation is over."

I'm amazed at how quickly he was able to get here. Nico called him and literally less than seven minutes he was strolling into the room, demanding all of this information and making the cops both sigh in defeat.

"Fine," the older cop says. "You guys clearly had your differences. Did her reaction to your relationship make you angry?"

"No," I say firmly.

He turns his head to the side in curiosity. "Really? See, if I had a sibling who disapproved of a relationship of mine, I'd feel frustrated. Upset. Maybe even a little pissed off."

"Well, I sucked her boyfriend's cock clean before I rode it until he blew a load in me, so I can't exactly blame her," I snap.

Nico squeezes my thigh in warning again, but I ignore him. Fuck these guys. They are seriously trying to say, what, that I killed my sister? How is that even possible? What on earth could I have done to make her heart stop?

I feel numb but also...odd. I don't know how to explain it, I mean, she's my sister. I should be curled up into a ball in the corner right now. She's gone. I'll never see her again. A really fucking terrible part of me feels a small amount of peace at that thought, and I fucking hate myself for it.

My lack of emotions I know is not helping my innocence in this moment, but on the other hand, I've done absolutely nothing wrong, so I don't really give a shit. Though, that may be a wrong approach and possibly how I end up wrongfully in jail if I don't cool my temper.

There is a knock at the door before one of the police officers steps outside of the little room they shuffled us into. He's only out there for a minute or so before he's sitting back down and crossing his hands onto the table.

"Do you know what foxglove is, Cassi?"

I furrow my brows before slowly nodding.

"It's a plant," the cop says. "It grows all over the place, pretty, but when ingested can be extremely poisonous."

"What does that have to do with this interrogation?" Nico's lawyer interrupts.

The cop doesn't take his eyes off me, instead, watching me like a hawk as if he were waiting for a reaction, a movement, anything he can run with.

"The powder found on Carly's person was powdered foxglove. It's estimated several grams were slipped into her coffee which caused her death."

"She was poisoned?" I say with confusion.

"It appears so," he says as he leans back into his chair casually. "You two went to coffee to talk things out after a physical altercation, and she was poisoned. Do you see where I'm going with this?"

"I didn't kill my sister!" I hiss as Nico's lawyer gestures for me to stay silent.

"Do you have any evidence my client even touched the deceased's cup before it was consumed? They were not in a home, they were in an establishment. What proof do you have that my client had any part to do with it?"

The cop cuts a sideways look to him as he sneers.

"Let's call it a gut thing."

He turns back to me before he shakes his head.

"I can't help you until you start telling the truth, Cassi. Did you slip foxglove in your sister's drink and then maybe plant it on her?"

"Don't answer that," Nico's lawyer whispered.

Fuck that, I'm absolutely answering, because it's ridiculous.

"No!"

The cop scoffs as he shakes his head.

"Looks like we very well may need to take this conversation to the station."

"Not so fast, you are going to need to provide us with more evidence before my client is going anywhere with you."

The other cop glares at him before pulling out his phone, he makes a quick call before speaking into the phone.

"Hey, Jimmy. Can you pull the cameras from the coffee shop? I want to see the coffee the girl was served being made and if anyone touched it before she drank it."

A pause occurs before he nods his head and hangs up the phone.

"One concrete piece of evidence coming right up, sir. If you'll excuse us," he says before they both push to stand, stepping outside.

As soon as the door shuts, Nico's lawyer turns to me sharply.

"Tell me right fucking now, did you do it?"

"Bill," Nico intervenes.

He ignores him, keeping his eyes on me.

"Did. You. Do. It?" he questions pointedly.

"No! Of course not."

"Are you sure? Because if you had anything to do with it and they can prove it, we need to pivot our strategy and quick."

I look to Nico for help and he wraps his arm around me as he shakes his head.

"She didn't do it, Bill."

He huffs out a breath before looking to Nico.

"Did you?"

Nico gives him a flat look as he shakes his head.

"Well, those cops are like two dogs with a bone. If there is anything off, they will hang you out to dry, innocent or not."

"And I pay you to ensure that doesn't happen," Nico snaps.

Bill mutters to himself as he begins sifting through some papers in his folder while my stomach turns in knots.

The officers came back into the room about twenty minutes later.

"Looks like you're both free to go."

"What?" I ask.

The older cop nods as the younger one folds his arms almost petulantly, like he's pissed we are getting off...for something we didn't fucking do. Make that make sense.

"What did you find?" Bill asks.

"Looks like Carly pulled the foxglove powder out of her pocket and slipped it into the drink she thought was yours," the older cop says.

"Mine?" I echo.

"Camera footage shows her fiddling with the cups with the baggie in her hand and when she looked away, the barista switched cups."

"She did?"

I can't form much more eloquent questions than that as my mind is currently being overwhelmed.

He nods. "She confessed to the whole thing when questioned. She stated she had no idea what the powder was, but she could tell there was ill intention and so she switched it. She's being booked for manslaughter."

Tammy? Oh my god, no.

"Why is she in trouble when Carly was the one who was trying to kill her sister?" Nico guffaws.

"Because that's how manslaughter fucking works," the younger cop seethes.

We all lean back at that, like he's about to jump over the table and the beat the shit out of all of us.

Holy fuck. Carly tried to kill me? She tried to poison me? Tammy, although not ultimately knowing what she was doing, saved me?

"If I had drank that coffee...if she had drugged the right cup... I'd be dead?" I question softly.

The older cop nods. "It looks that way. With that high of a dose, it only took seconds for the effects to overwhelm her, one of those being heart palpitations that lead to cardiac arrest."

"Where did she get it from? I mean, I know my sister. She wouldn't have found it, grounded it to a fine powder like that...she was...not the most resourceful woman there ever was."

"We went through her phone and found a text message strain with someone she's been in contact with for years. Chances are, this wasn't the first time she's obtained this substance, whether for someone else's use or not."

A strange look passes over Nico's face as he listens to the detectives speak, leaning forward as they continue before he cuts them off.

"What could happen if it was a lesser dose? How long would the effects take?"

The cop shrugs.

"Depends according to the lab. They said from minutes to hours, sometimes even days if it's a small enough dose."

Nico's eyes widen as he slumps back into his chair.

"Oh my god."

"What?" I ask as I look to him, his face now completely pale and lifeless.

Slowly, his eyes come to me, a hollow horror filled look as he shakes his head.

"I...I think Carly killed my mother."

Epilogue
Cassi

The bomb of Carly killing Nico's mother shocked us all, and when someone at the department leaked the story, the news outlets had a field day with it. When Nico had explained his mother's disapproval of Carly, their constant arguments over Carly's true intentions and the out of the blue cardiac arrest on an otherwise relatively healthy woman, it was like puzzle pieces clicking together.

The police immediately re-opened the case and though the foxglove didn't appear in her toxicology report, the case was closed, listing it a homicide. The betrayal nearly tore Nico in two. He's been in therapy every day since then. I have too, because I'm equally not okay.

When my parents arrived in Boston, they called me frantically with an update and I couldn't hold the truth from them. The cry my mother let out is one that will haunt me for years to come.

I met my parents at the hospital, but I didn't recognize them. They looked like a shell of themselves, numbly going through the motions as they stepped through those doors. When the doctor informed them of Carly's cause of death, and Nico supplemented that the drink was intended for me, my mother collapsed with grief. She cried out for her baby while simultaneously holding me in what felt like protection.

Since that day, things have felt...off between us. They don't blame me for what happened to Carly, of course. She tried to kill me and ended up killing herself by mistake. That's a situation that carries too many emotions to even begin to name. At least, that's what my therapist tells me.

More tension came between my parents and I when I told them that I would not be returning to Seattle. It's not that they don't approve of Nico, quite the opposite actually. They just never really got time to process the idea of us together. It went from him dating my sister to being fake engaged to her to being outed that we'd been sneaking around to my sister trying to kill me and inadvertently dying.

It's been an emotional and dramatic few weeks to say the least.

My parents had a funeral for Carly in Seattle and I did go with Nico, Arianna and Naomi by my side. It was somber day, filled with complicated feelings. Especially when we added in the piece about Carly also being Nico's mother's murderer, only for the reason that we can assume she was standing in the way of her and Nico's long term relationship. For good reason, I'm sure.

It was an odd feeling, sitting at the funeral of my almost murderer. Even more odd when considering the fact that inside that casket laid my sister's decaying corpse. The sister I grew up with, shared holidays and birthdays and family vacations with. The one that hated me as much as I her...then again, maybe more. Despite our differences, I could have never imagined even wanting to take her life away, let alone doing it. So for her to be so ready to do so to me...I ...I'm not sure I'll ever be able to move past that.

I feel equal parts and angry and relieved that she is out of my life. How terrible am I? My therapist diagnosed me with severe PTSD, anxiety and depression. No surprise there.

When I was in Seattle for the funeral, I quit my job and dropped out of college. Some would say I was making radical changes to capture some sort of control on my life, and maybe they are right. The decisions felt good, though, and I don't regret them for a moment.

Nico arranged everything for me and had all of my things set to the Brownstone where we have begun living full time. During a time that should feel happy and blissful, I hate to admit, those feelings aren't a part of our day to day. You know what ones are, though?

Healing. Safety. Comfort. Warmth.

We give as much as we take from one another, a true partnership in it's most beautiful form and despite the absolute hell we have been through, and continue to live through, we make each other better, happier. One day at a time.

Extended Epilogue
Nico

These last few weeks have been some of the best and worst of my life. Cassi has moved in and every moment spent with her is like a new high of happiness that I never thought would be achievable. In the same breath, there is a heaviness to her eyes, to her smile. One that isn't easily ignored or forgotten. Instead of trying to erase it, all I can do is support her, try to make her have more good days than bad. That's the only thing I have the power to control right now, that's what my therapist yaps on about at least.

Cassi's parents have been disappointingly distant. I will never understand the grief they are facing with the loss of their child, but it is as if they have forgotten they have one other child, who nearly died at the hands of the other. It's easier to toss her to the wayside than face that truth and mar Carly's memory further, I think.

Though, they have reached out recently, apologizing for being so absent, Cassi is not ready to rebuild a relationship. Not like the one they had, at least. Don't get me wrong, I adore Henry and Mary but protecting Cassi and her mental and physical wellbeing will always be my top priority. So, for now, distance is what we all need.

Cassi and I have began a new tradition that every Sunday, we drive to my mother's grave and have lunch with her. I haven't visited her grave since her funeral, the thought of it too painful for me to bear. With Cassi, I found my strength in doing so and in turn, some peace. It felt like a necessary closure discovering the details of Carly's horrors. Though I carry an immense amount of guilt with me, it feels...healing to know exactly what happened to her.

Yet I'll never be able to silence that little voice inside my head that tells me it was all my fault. Had I never pursued Carly, stayed with her, introduced her to my mother....the list goes on, she would more than likely be here. Then again, I might never have met Cassi, and that is something I struggle to wish.

Tammy, the barista that unknowingly saved Cassi's life is facing manslaughter as well as a handful of other bullshit charges. I have Bill working for her and he says he feels optimistic he will be able to get her off with some probation. I hope so, I owe her more than I could ever express and have promised to repay her in any way possible once this mess is behind her.

Arianna and her fiancé have visited us for a weekend, and Naomi has promised to do the same soon. Though I don't know the details, it appears she is neck deep in hot water. From what I gather, Cassi doesn't know much about her situation but whatever she does know, she hasn't spoken a word to me. I see the nervous looks Cassi and Arianna have shared, though. The whispered phone calls Cassi and Naomi have shared. Arianna's fiancé and I have both offered to help in any way we can, but of course we have been turned down. So long as no harm or trouble comes to my love, I will sit on the sidelines and wait.

We're laying in bed tonight, watching one of Cassi's favorite movies that she has seen a million fucking times. She laughs at the same lines during the same scenes every time. And every fucking time it brings smile to my face.

I don't know what the future holds for us for certain, we are in survival mode at the moment. The board moved to not suspend me, but I decided to take a sabbatical instead. I will resume work when I am ready but until then, I'm living my days with the love of my life by my side.

There is a little velvet box in my bedside table drawer, practically begging to be taken out. I know now is not the time, though. I didn't even mean on purchasing it. I was walking down the street one afternoon and I just saw it, glimmering in the window and I knew she had to have it. She's not ready for that at the moment, though, and that's okay. I am, and I'll patiently wait until she is. This thing between us is not just permanent, it's forever.

Pressing a kiss against her head, I lean into her further as I hold her tighter. I can't even believe that all of this has unraveled in such little time. That both of our lives flipped onto their heads from that One Night. One Night of Scandal turned into our start of forever.

Thank You

Guys...that was kinda fucked up. I won't even pretend to be innocent. What the hell is wrong with me? If you haven't ready Arianna and Logan's book yet, you need to get on that asap! If you're ready for more, have no fear, we are going to figure out what on earth has been going on with Naomi and why she was being such a judgy little bitch in this book? You all know the saying tho shalt not cast stones in a glass house? Mhmmmm.

Start reading One Night Section here! (Arianna's story)
Pre-Order One Night Surrender here! (Naomi's story)

If you are looking for your next read, then look no further! Angsty, emotional, forbidden love with a scorching amount of spice is at your service below!

The Gallows Hill Series – A dark academia reverse harem
Deceit – Book 1
Descent – Book 2
Demise – Book 3
Damnation – Prequel (Though I suggest reading after!)

The Alphaletes Series – Interconnected football romance stories
The Loyalties We Break
The Walls We Break
The Hearts We Break

The Rules We Break

Stand Alones –
Deliverance – An FF forbidden romance
Gratify – A forbidden age gap
Graves – An MFM stalker romance
Jagged Harts – An MMA enemies to lovers
Graves & Griggs: A Very Bloody Christmas (Novella crossover of
Gallows Hill Trilogy x Graves)

Acknowledgments

To my Alpha, Sara, thank you for everything you do! This book was a rough one in more ways than I can count haha I so appreciate all of your guidance, dedication and love. I am forever thankful for you!

To my Beta's, Courtney and Thalia, BLESS YOU BOTH! Thank you so much for devouring this one so quickly and providing such amazing insight on how I could make these two shine! Adore you both so so much!

To my editor, Laura and my proofreader, Judy, thank you so much! You both are out here doing the lord's work. Thank you so much for turning my chaotic nonsense of a book into something pretty, polished, and understandable. Thank you for helping me deliver a fine tuned story without ever losing my voice.

To my street team and ARC readers, thank you all for your support! Every page read, every review left, and every post made truly means the world. I'm not even a little shy to admit that I have hands down the best people behind me.

To my readers, whether this is your first book by me, or you've been by my side since day one, thank you. There are millions of authors out there, billions of books and you chose mine. Each one of you pushes me to write when my fingers ache, plot when my brain is mush and keep moving forward when I'm ready to give up. You all are the best readers anyone could ask for and I love each one of you desperately.

www.ingramcontent.com/pod-product-compliance
Lightning Source LLC
Chambersburg PA
CBHW060222030726
47499CB00004B/1150